MW01115461

For Perry

As different as we are, you show me every day what respect and friendship look like

Chapter 1

Erin

Four Years Ago

"Sam, you've got a damn key. Why are you knocking?" I march to the door, thinking she must have an armload of wine and snacks. When I open the door, it's not Sam on the other side. Shit. Shit. Shit. "Oh, Jack, what are you doing here?"

"I came to apologize. I was a dick, and I'm sorry. I've fucked things up and… and I wanted to say that you were right. We've been good friends this past year, and I don't want to lose that."

I'm not sure what to say to him, so I don't say anything. Dammit, Sam. Where are you?

"In case I've messed things up too bad, I've brought your things over." I continue to keep my mouth securely shut, which he interprets as a dismissal. His eyes turn sad, and he says, "Here, I'll just leave them on the porch. You can box mine up and leave them in your office library. I've got to come by to switch out some sample binders next week anyway."

He looks like a puppy that I've just kicked and not at all like the asshat from yesterday. Dammit to hell. "No… Jack, come in. It's fine." I step aside, allowing him to enter, and I close the door telling myself to get this over with and get him out of here. "What things did I leave?"

"Your purple jacket and that basket of Cambria wine you won at their open house."

"Oh, right. I forgot about that." That's my favorite jacket. I'd have been pissed if I didn't get that back.

"Just set them down in the kitchen. I think all you've got here is your Bluetooth speaker. I'll run and get it from the office."

While I'm walking in that direction, he calls out, "You open to having a back-to-friends toast? We were good as friends, and I hope we can go back to that." I grab the speaker and look down at my watch. Where the hell is she? I close my eyes and silently will Sam to walk through the door. She's running late, and I'm way too frazzled for a let's-make-up conversation.

Ok, so what else does he have here? The speaker… and… right, he's got a phone charger in my car.

The garage is off the kitchen, so I move in that direction. When I walk back in the kitchen, he doubles his efforts, "You know we've been wanting to try this ever since we learned a quartz company had their own wine."

That's it…. My sister is fired…. "Just one glass." He smiles the schoolboy smile that has always been so welcoming. "Great. Everything in the same place?"

As I'm walking to the garage, I answer back, "Same place."

I come back with the charger and set it down

beside the bluetooth speaker. He slides a glass over to me as he finishes pouring his own.

Picking the goblet up, I give away my weakness. "I have wanted to try this since the moment the rep told me about it." Jack puts his nose up to his glass and takes a whiff. "I've heard it's very good." He lifts his glass and toasts, "To friends."

"To friends."

This wine is very good, but I need him out of here. It's getting late, and I'm sleepy. Where is Sam?

Jack is talking to me, but it's all wrong. I can't focus and only pick up a few words now and again.

"...loose enough yet? We need to get going pretty..."

I'm not leaving. I need to find Sam.

"...fuck it. I've got time."

My hand grasps something and I throw it... *Please, Sam...*

"...god, Erin... finally... I knew you would feel..."

"...mine now..."

"...never letting you..."

Sam! I hear Sam.

"...THE HELL? ERIN ARE YOU..."

"...business, you stupid..."

"...SAID SHUT UP!"

"...please... I need help...my sister..."

Someone else is here.

"can you open your eyes for..."

"... the needle and bottle... test them at..."

"...is your sister allergic to..."

"...Taylor, please follow behind the ambulance..."

"Don't worry Ms. Westin, we're getting you to..."

"...en route. Twenty-six-year-old female. Drugged with unknown..."

"...need to have a SAFE examiner administer a kit..."

I need to turn off this beeping alarm clock. I reach for my phone on the bedside table, but there's no phone and no table. "Sam?" *What's wrong with my voice?* I sound awful. I reach up to rub my eyes, but... *What the hell? Something's stuck to my arm.*

"Erin! I'm right here. Are you ok? How do you feel?" I look around the dimly lit room as Sam hurries over to me. She looks terrible. Her long blond hair is up in a bun with pieces sticking out all over the place, and her clothes are all wrinkled. Her normally lovely face is puffy and blotchy, and her blue eyes are bloodshot. She's been crying.

What happened?

"Where am I?" Sam takes my hand, "You're

at the hospital. You were…" She doesn't continue. I hear a noise off to my left and turn to see two figures standing near a large door.

"What the hell is going on?"

The two figures approach the bed; a man and a woman I've never met. I can tell right away by their clothes that they don't work for the hospital. They're both sporting serious expressions, and I can see the glint of a… badge inside the man's jacket.

The woman speaks first, "Ms. Westin, I'm Detective Eve Peyton. This is my partner Mike McKenzie. We're with the Homewood Police Department. You've been brought to UAB Hospital because it was suspected that you had been drugged."

Drugged? There's no way. I never accept drinks that aren't handed to me by the bartender, and I never leave a drink unattended. Even when I'm at a table with friends I leave a napkin over my glass. I know how to be safe.

"Where? Who did it?" I look to Sam, but she doesn't utter a word. She just shakes her head, and the detective continues.

"Do you know a Jack Rodgers?"

Wait. What? What does he have to do with anything? Shouldn't they be out checking the security footage of the bar I was in? I look at the woman, then the man. They don't say anything else, and it becomes apparent they expect me to respond. I take a deep breath and exhale. "Yes, I know Jack. He's a product rep that visits area design firms. He was a friend of mine, but I had to quit hanging out with him recently." The detectives exchange a look that I can't interpret.

The man begins again, "Ms. Westin…"

"Please, call me Erin."

"Erin, can you tell us why you felt you needed to cut ties with him?"

"Yeah, um, Jack and I had been friends for about eight months. It was really a group of us; several designers, a couple of architects, and some product reps. We would sometimes get drinks after work, attend continuing education courses together, really, anything industry related. Sometimes, it was most of us, and sometimes, it would be just a few. The "who" would change based on work and travel schedules that were ever-changing. Somewhere during that time, Jack began acting a little different. I couldn't pinpoint when it happened, just that I began to notice."

"Can you explain what you mean by different?"

"Well, it was just little things… like making jokes that were slightly possessive or feigning jealousy over attention from or given to other people. It wasn't anything too serious or threatening. In fact, the first time I missed a get-together to meet a deadline, he came by the office to bring coffee. I thought it was a nice gesture. Then I was promoted, and it started happening more often. After I'd missed three or four get-togethers, he began questioning me about who else was having to stay late…"

I shrug my shoulders and add, "Again, I thought it was out of concern. In this industry, you sometimes hear of people getting promoted just so they'll be more willing or more easily coerced into putting in extra hours. Eventually, he started asking about my daytime site visits. He wanted to know where they were and who I was going with. We weren't dating and certainly hadn't slept together, so it began to feel a little weird at that point. Because of that, I began spending less and less time going out and more time hanging out with Sam. When Jack started complaining about the amount of time I was spending with my sister, I decided it was time to cut it off completely. Most of the group had disbanded to another job or another city anyway, and I realized that he hadn't been paying the same attention to others in the group.

It seemed to me that somewhere along the way, he had gotten the wrong impression about our friendship. So, I asked him to meet me for coffee Thursday after work. My plan was to apologize to him if I had given mixed signals or led him on, but ultimately, to tell him that I was not interested in a romantic relationship.

I figured that we both might suffer a little embarrassment over the situation, but would move on from this just fine. I was wrong. He wasn't embarrassed or dejected, but shocked and angry. He demanded to know who it was that I was fucking behind his back.

I reminded him that we're not dating and that it was none of his business if I was with someone or not. In the middle of this coffee shop, filled with people, he went crazy for a moment; calling me a cock-tease and an ungrateful bitch that needed to learn my place. I was too shocked to respond or even walk away. After his outburst, he quickly calmed down and started being his ultra-charming self again.

He said he understood and apologized for the outburst. He assured me that he was acting like an ass because he realized some time ago that he had fallen in love with me. He asked if we could still be friends and said that if I changed my mind, to give him a call. He gave me a hug and left without any further problem.

"Can you think of any reason you might have let him in your house last night?"

Last night… I press the heels of my hands against my eyes. "I… can't remember what I did last night."

"That's all right. Just tell me under what circumstances you might have let him come over."

"I don't know. After he left the coffee shop, I felt weird, guilty. I was racking my brain to see what I had done to make him think I was into him. I even called Sam and asked her to come over last night and hang out. I had planned to get her take on the whole situation."

But, what does me being in the hospital have to do with Jack? I don't like where this is going, and nobody is telling me anything. "Would somebody please tell me what is going on here?"

The man gestures to the woman, and she nods.

"Your sister arrived at your home shortly after eight pm last night. When she pulled into your driveway, an unfamiliar car was parked in front of the garage. Considering the reason you had asked her to come over, she became concerned about you. She reported to us that when she reached the front steps, she heard some disturbing sounds coming from inside and barged in the front door. You were on the floor of your living room and seemed unresponsive. She drew her weapon and ordered a man away from you and checked on your condition. After discerning that you were impaired, she called 911."

The man takes over at this point, "Your sister held the man, later identified as Jack Rogers, at gunpoint until police arrived. Once our officers arrived at the scene and evaluated the situation, they immediately placed him in custody and called us. By the time we arrived, you were already on your way to the hospital. We took a statement from your sister and determined we had probable cause to search

Rogers' vehicle. When we did, we found tape, rope, drugs, and a bag of cash. It appears as though your sister's intervention prevented Rogers from abducting you."

"Abduction? Gunpoint? Why don't I remember any of this?"

The male detective answers, "Ketamine, the drug we found in Rogers' car, is known to cause memory loss. If that is the drug determined to have been used on you, it is unlikely that you will remember anything that happened in the last twelve hours. Even things that happened before you were drugged." He pauses as if deciding to continue… "This might sound calloused, but the memory loss is probably for the best."

"What do you mean by that?"

Detective Peyton speaks again, "Because Erin, when Sam arrived, Rogers was sexually assaulting you."

Wait a minute… I was… Oh… I don't feel so…

"Damn it! Eve, she's gonna pass out."

…

Someone places a cool cloth to my forehead. I open my eyes and see that Sam and the two detectives are still here. I close my eyes and hope to have it all be gone like the morning after a nightmare. When I open my eyes again, nothing has changed. They're all still there.

"I was… raped?"

"It appears so, yes. To confirm the presence

of and determine the type of drug used, the hospital took a sample of your blood for testing when you were brought in. We'd like your permission to administer a rape kit." I look to Sam, her red-rimmed eyes are filled with regret and spilling over with fresh tears.

She's hurting. I may not be able to remember anything that happened, but she'll never be able to forget. It's too heavy a burden for her to bear, and I'm incensed at what this bastard has done to us. "Yes, do the kit. Nail this bastard."

"Thanks, Ms... um, Erin. We'll be in touch." Detective Peyton hands me her card, and they leave.

Sam takes a seat in the bedside chair and drops her head in her hands. "I'm so sorry, Erin. I should have been there."

I place a reassuring hand on her shoulder. "Sam, this is not your fault. He did this, not you."

She looks up and lashes out, angry at herself. "You don't understand. You asked me to come over. I said I would, but got wrapped up in a project and was late getting to your house. If I had been there, he wouldn't have hurt you."

"Stop blaming yourself. You heard what the detective said. With all that equipment in his car, it's obvious that he was determined to get to me one way or another. If you had been there tonight, he would have just tried another time. Or maybe, he would hurt you for being in his way." Sam shakes her head sadly. There is nothing that I can say that is going to make her stop beating herself up over this. She lays her head on my lap and weeps over her perceived failure to protect me. I stroke her hair and mourn her loss of innocence and security.

Shortly after the detectives leave, my nurse comes in to find Sam asleep in my bed next to me. She grabs an extra blanket and covers her up. Now that she's calmed down and resting, I ask the nurse if I can shower to get this sick feeling off my skin.

"Oh, honey, I wish I could, but if you're going to be examined for evidence, I can't let you do that."

I hope it's soon. The longer I sit here in filth, the more anxious I become. At this point, I don't know if he used a condom or not. Could I be pregnant now? I need to get this over with so I can get out of here and get clean.

Later in the morning, the nurse brings a woman in and introduces her as a S.A.F.E. Examiner. The examiner, named Emily, explains everything she's going to do and evidence she'll collect. I answer all her questions, then allow myself to zone out for everything else.

After the exam is complete and the doctor determines I'm not having any adverse effects from the drug, I'm cleared to go home. Sam drives us to my rented house in Homewood and parks in her usual spot. Since my car is still in the garage, we use her keys to go in the front door.

Detective Peyton told me that she had instructed the crime scene techs to remove any signs of the attack when they collected their evidence. When I open the door, everything looks as it did when I left for work yesterday. Despite knowing what happened here, it doesn't feel any different… at first.

Sam, however, is still standing outside, staring at the floor. No doubt she's visualizing the scene all over again. I feel stupid. I didn't think about the possible effects that being in this room again could have on her. I walk back out the door, close, and lock it, then take her hand and lead her around to the back door.

She seems to be able to handle being in the kitchen. To give her something to focus on, I ask her to make some coffee while I have a shower. She nods, and I walk to my bedroom. It feels clean in here. I can tell that this room was untouched, and I relax a little.

I strip off the borrowed scrubs and step into a scalding hot shower. I scrub and scrub until my skin is raw and red before climbing out to dress. Once I'm dressed, I walk out to join Sam but find myself taking a detour to the front of the house.

Standing in the living room, it angers me that my memory was stolen from me. While I'm glad I don't remember the attack, I hate that I don't even remember the drive home from work. Who did I call while I was driving home? Did I make any stops along the way?

I walk around, trying to conjure something that would tell me why I would allow Jack entry to my home after what happened in the coffee shop. Despite my best efforts to remember, there's just… nothing.

Frustrated, I walk to the sofa and pick up a crooked pillow to straighten it. I pick up another crooked one and freeze. Panties… ripped… the ones I put on after my morning shower yesterday. Since I found them, the detective's team missed them. With a shaking hand, I pull out my phone and send a text to the female detective's number. She can deal with it if it's important.

Coming in here was a mistake. I don't know what I was so determined to find or why I was looking. Now that I have found something, the whole place feels like it's shrouded in filth.

I can't stay here.

Dropping the pillow where I stand, I race back to the kitchen. Sam is pulling something out of the oven when I start dry heaving into the trash can. She wets a dish towel and rushes over, placing the cool cloth on my neck.

As soon as I've recovered, I ask if I can stay with her. Since she's still blaming herself for what happened, she seems relieved and agrees enthusiastically.

It's not her fault. I blame myself. I remind her that I keep my door locked at all times, and there were no signs of a break-in, so that means I let him in. The bitch of it is that I'll never know why. I could have called and begged him to visit, or he could have held a gun to my head, and I wouldn't remember because of the drugs. All I do know is that this place doesn't feel like home anymore.

Fortunately, my lease is up in five weeks. The little house came furnished, so it shouldn't take us long to gather my things. Most of our personal memories are at our shared home, the lake house.

For now, I'll just grab enough for a few days, and we can get out of here. I'll come back to pack up later.

As I throw things into a suitcase, I'm certain this will be a good change. Sam and I are going to need each other to get through what happened.

Suitcase in hand, I walk out the door; finally grateful that I don't remember last night. As I turn the key, I think about the panties and pillow as a cold shiver works its way down my spine.

Chapter 2

Erin

That night, I can't sleep. I still feel as if my skin is crawling. Since finding the ripped panties and despite me having no memory of the attack, I still feel filthy and helpless. Unable to shake the feeling, I get up and take my third shower of the day. It doesn't help. After a long while, sheer exhaustion takes over, and I eventually fall into a restless sleep.

Sometime later, I am awoken by an awful dream. It felt so real that I can't say for sure it was nightmare and not memory. In the dream, I'm being smothered by a dark form. I can't get up, I'm trapped.

I wake tangled in the blankets, covered in sweat. Looking over at the clock, I see that it's only four-thirty. I could continue to lie here, but there's no way I'm going back to sleep now. Guess it's time for coffee.

When I walk into the kitchen, I see that Sam isn't sleeping either. It's a stupid question, I know, but I ask, "Sam, what's wrong?" She looks back with hollow eyes. I want to shake her, to make her let go of the pointless guilt. "Sam, neither one of us bears any blame for what that bastard did. I'm glad I don't remember… and I'm sorry that you'll never forget, but this is not on you, and this is not on me."

There is a tremor in my voice when I add,

"I'm scared, Sam. I'm having memories or nightmares. There are things in my mind, images that might be real, and that might not. A part of me wants to know, but another part is too afraid to find out."

Sam has always been an empathetic person, and this trait overcomes her guilt. She moves quickly to me and wraps me up in a warm hug. Comforted by my sister's love, I let go of trying to be strong and just cry loud, soul-shaking sobs. I cry because I'm afraid and that makes me angry. I don't know what I'm afraid of, but the fear is real.

Sam holds on to me for dear life. She strokes my hair and whispers to me until the sobbing subsides. Coffee forgotten, Sam leads me to her large bed, and she climbs in beside me just like when we were kids afraid of a thunderstorm.

We spend the next day in our pajamas, neither one of us feeling like venturing out. On Sunday afternoon, I get a call from Detective Peyton asking to come over.

She gets to Sam's apartment around four to update us. She looks a lot different than she did in the hospital. Or maybe I can just see her clearly now. She has long red hair pulled up in a practical ponytail. Her make-up is minimal, but that doesn't lessen the intensity or sharpness of her blue eyes and facial features.

She accepts an offer for coffee, and we all sit down in the living room. The sharp-eyed detective doesn't waste any time, "Rogers is going to be arraigned tomorrow morning. His charges will be read, he'll enter a plea, and bail will be set."

Bail! I hadn't thought about that. "What are the chances he'll get out?"

"I wish I could say none, but he's got no prior record, no rich family to sweep him out of the country. If he can make bail, he'll be out tomorrow."

Sam asks, "Is there anything we can do to stop it?"

"The DA will request high bail given that the crime was premeditated, but there's no guarantee it will be granted."

"What if he comes looking for me?"

"Officially, I can tell you to keep your eyes open, don't go anywhere alone, and if he approaches you, call the police. Unofficially, get whatever self-defense weapon you feel comfortable with and keep it with you at all times. Be smart. And, if something doesn't feel right about a situation, get the hell out of it and call someone. Here's my cell number." My face must show the panic I feel. Her eyes and voice soften, and she explains, "Look, these are only precautions. Just be careful, ok?"

The next morning, Sam and I arrive at the courthouse and are joined by detectives Peyton and McKenzie. Besides what she's wearing, Detective Peyton looks just like she did yesterday. Detective McKenzie doesn't look as I remember him from our meeting at the hospital. He has dark hair that is graying slightly at the temples and a permanent "don't fuck with me" expression. And he's big. Not flabby, but tall and muscular. I admit to feeling safer with him here.

Between the four of us, there are no friendly greetings exchanged and no meaningless platitudes offered. We're here for one reason alone; to see if Jack will be released on bond or remanded to jail until the trial.

Sam and I are ushered into the courtroom by the detectives and take our seats. Never a fan of law dramas, I haven't seen enough on TV to know what to expect from these proceedings.

A bailiff opens a door, and Jack is escorted in wearing a prison uniform. His normally perfect sandy blond hair is a mess, and his Abercrombie face is lacking its usual luster. When his brown eyes land on me, he turns fully in my direction. This allows me to see the ugly black eye on his left side and strange patterns of scabbing on his arms

I sit there trying to work out how he turned into such a monster instead of looking away. That turns out to be a bad decision. His attention locks onto me, and he winks. I nearly jump the rail to get at him, but the detectives must have noticed his crude gesture and clamp down on my shoulders from where they're seated behind us.

Lesson learned, I turn my face forward and determine not to move them from the judge's bench.

Once the judge enters and the proceedings begin, for the most part, I'm lost as to what's taking place. The only part of the entire thing that makes sense to me turns out to be the worst possible outcome.

Five thousand dollars bond. I don't believe it. I was raped and almost kidnapped to who-knows-what end, and bond is set at five fucking thousand dollars? Incensed, I jump out of my seat and yell at the judge, "Five thousand, is that all my life is worth to you?" He bangs his gavel and shouts as I feel myself being dragged from the room. In his eyes, I see pity or disgust. I'm not sure which.

Detective McKenzie has me by the arm, pulling me through the heavy wooden doors as he whisper-yells, "Erin, calm the hell down!" As soon as we clear the opening, I shrug out of his grip and storm down the massive hallway. I've seen enough of this shit-show. Sam catches up to me and doesn't say a word. She knows that when I'm this angry, I cry, and I'll be damned if I'm going to do that in full view of all these assholes.

Our plan was to go to lunch after leaving the courthouse and before heading to my house to pick up the rest of my things. No longer in the mood, and wanting to avoid people, we stop by

Nabeel's, and Sam runs in to pick up some chicken salad and pita chips instead.

When we get to my place, I grab the bags of food and head for the door. On my porch, is a small pot of the cutest bluish-purple flowers. I look for a card but don't find one. The petite blooms remind me of my elderly neighbor next door, Mrs. Waverly. They must be from her. She's a sweet lady that I've become quite fond of. I visit her on most Saturdays, and we have tea together.

She detests coffee. "Erin, coffee has never done anyone a favor. It stains your teeth and permeates your clothes and your breath. Teas are soothing and can help you wake, sleep, and be healthy."

She pulls out a delicate tea set and her hands with their crepey, translucent skin, perform a proper tea service. After that, we just sit and talk for a while.

I should go thank her for the sweet gesture. "I'll be right back, Sam. I want to go say thank you to Mrs. Waverly". I give Sam the bags, and she takes the food in. I pick up the pot and walk over to the cottage style home next door. When she answers the door, she greets me with a cheery, "Erin, dear, what are you doing here on a Monday?"

"I just wanted to say thank you for the adorable flowers." I hold up the pot and her eyes light up before her brow furrows.

"Those are quite beautiful, dear, but I didn't send them."

"Oh... They could have come from my boss. Do you know what they are?"

"Those are Forget-Me-Nots." My smile fades, and my hands develop a slight tremor.

"Are you all right, dear?"

"Ah, yes, ma'am… would you mind keeping these for me? I'm afraid I would only kill them."

"They are quite lovely. Are you sure you don't mind?"

"No. Of course not. Please, enjoy them. Have a nice day, Mrs. Waverly." I turn and walk woodenly back to my door.

As I'm walking into the kitchen, I hear Sam say, "I've got everything set… Erin, what's wrong? Where are your flowers?"

"The flowers didn't come from my neighbor. Did you know they were Forget-Me-Nots?"

"No, I… You don't think…? Do you want to call Detective Peyton?"

"And tell her, what? That I'm afraid of flowers? No. I'm not crying wolf until I see fur. If I freak out about every little noise, they won't believe me if or when he actually does try something."

We sit at the table, and I pick at my food for a while before giving up and gathering what remains of my belongings. Once everything is packed into our cars, I make one last walk-through and stand in the living room. Sam is already outside, still refusing to walk through this room.

As I look around, I'm hit with... I don't know. It feels like I've been struck by lightning or I'm having a panic attack of some sort, and I hear this guttural, rhythmic grunting in my head.

I run for the door and slam it without looking back. I don't ever want to see this place again.

The next morning, I'm tempted to call in sick to work, but since I've never done it before, it would bring that much more attention to me when I did finally go in. So, I force myself to get up, shower, and change into and out of every piece of clothing that I brought. Everything gets rejected because it makes me look feminine and weak or slutty. Not that I ever felt that way in them before, but everything's changed now. I end up selecting a black suit with simple black heels. To me, it feels like the closest thing to a suit of armor except for the camisoles I usually wear underneath. They show an acceptable amount of cleavage, but today, make me feel too exposed. Angry at Jack and myself for making this so difficult, I yank off my suit jacket and pin up the straps of my cami to raise the neckline.

Finally ready to go, I practice pasting a smile on my made-up face and walk out the door.

I get to the office early to meet up with my boss before anyone else arrives. Fortunately, my case didn't receive news coverage. The only people that know what happened are my boss, Lee Donaldson, and work-friend Sherry Stanson. Lee and I have been together in some capacity or another for over ten years and have become quite close. He started out as one of my college professors, then we were colleagues, and somewhere along the way, best friend. We make an odd pair. He's the age my father would be if he were still here, has beautiful white hair, sparkling eyes, and a wonderfully snarky personality.

As soon as I walk in, Lee greets me with a giant hug. "Erin, what are you doing here? You should be at home resting or plotting a revenge murder." I bark out an inelegant laugh and wipe a stray tear.

"I don't want people to get curious and if I'm a no-show, they certainly will." Sensing that my explanation will not be enough to allay his concern, I add, "I'm really not sure how to explain it, but because I was drugged, I'll never remember what happened. There's no PTSD because my conscious mind didn't experience any trauma. The only emotion I feel is anger. And, as you know, anger focuses me. I need the job to keep me going. I can draw and do specifications, but it might be best if Sherry is the one in client meetings for a while."

"But, Erin, you said he's out on bond. Aren't you afraid..."

"I will not hole myself up. This building has great security, and Frank, the guard, always walks us to our cars if we're alone. It'll be fine."

Lee hugs me again and says, "I'm glad you're…ok."

"I'm not yet, but I will be."

The workday passes like any other, which is reassuring. The rest of the week is also wonderfully normal; go to work, return to Sam's, rinse, and repeat.

When Saturday rolls around, I take Sam to visit Mrs. Waverly. She would be worried if I didn't show and I would be afraid that she might fall if she went to my house looking for me.

When we arrive, she gushes over Sam. "My, my. You're just as pretty as your sister. Opposite in every way, but just as lovely."

I try to look at Sam through her eyes. She really is beautiful, and most of her features are the opposite of mine except for the nose. Where I'm petite, she's nearly six-feet tall. I have long brown hair and green eyes. Hers are blond and blue.

The physiology is easy to explain since we're half-sisters. But, since I was only a two when she was born, we never knew the difference. My father remarried after my mom left us, then when Sam was eight years old, her mom died in a car accident. Having no other family, dad raised us on his own. It was just the three of us until we lost him six years ago to cancer.

Mrs. Waverly ushers us in and seems excited to have another guest. I make a grand effort to mask the hurricane blowing inside. She doesn't ask, which means I'm doing a good job.

Sam is quickly falling for the older lady; even smiling and enjoying the tea lecture. I think she also sees in her the grandmother that we never had. That's why I hate to tell her I'm moving. Mrs. Waverly is genuinely disappointed, "Please take care of yourself, dear. I'm no fool; I can tell you're keeping something from me." I give her a teary hug and promise to keep in touch; then we leave.

The following Monday, I'm working on a space plan for an office remodel when the front desk calls me to pick up a delivery. It's probably those Mannington samples I've been waiting on. When I reach the front desk, Frank points to a small arrangement of Forget-Me-Nots.

I school my features, so no one sees the panic welling up inside. I smile at Frank and grab the flowers. On the way back to my desk, I remove a small envelope tucked in the top and toss the flowers in the breakroom trash.

In the relative privacy of my workstation, I open the envelope with shaking hands. In it, is a single white card with a message written in elegant script.

"I miss you."

I pick up my phone and dial a number I

haven't had to use before. "Peyton here."

Six Months Later

"Eve, what just happened?" The detective looks at me, eyes full of regret. "The DA got him to plead to a lesser charge."

"But… Why? How? A syringe was found with traces of Ketamine inside with my blood on the needle. One of the wine glasses tested positive for Rohypnol."

"The defense attorney claims that the drugs were part of your collective plans that night. Rogers claims you both wanted to experiment with the drugs."

"That's bullshit! What about the rope, tape, and stuff in his car?"

"Rogers says you had a penchant for kinky sex."

"But we never had sex before!"

"I know that, but impossible to prove."

"What about the stalking? The flowers, notes, pictures?"

"I'm sorry, Erin, but with no prints or any other evidence, we couldn't tie any of that to Rogers."

"If they're so confident that they can explain all this away, why plea at all then?"

"The defense is worried about Sam's testimony. She'll testify that you were upset with him and you were the only one impaired that night. And, she's very credible as a witness.

That's why the DA agreed to drop the conspiracy to kidnap and move with a lesser charge of rape – second degree and possession of a controlled substance."

"So, what does this mean?"

"He'll get five years max and could be out in three."

I sink down to the chair in Eve's office, unable to hold myself up any longer.

"Look, Erin. You don't have to be afraid, and you don't have to be helpless. Take some defense classes, get a gun, learn to shoot, do whatever you need to do. Too many times, our hands are tied until the victim is beyond help. Don't let yourself become a statistic."

I force my wobbly legs to stand and move toward the door. Before I walk out, I turn and say, "I already am."

Chapter 3

Four years later

Nate

I swear, if that damn phone rings one more time… "Omen, am I going to have to kill you to get some sleep?"

Capt. Chase "Omen" McDaniels, my superior officer, and my brother in battle. Only, in the last couple of days, we've learned that not all battles are fought in the desert. Some have to be fought in your own hometown. And this battle was brought to family, which called down the fire from the Cowboys From Hell. Omen, Shark, Hyper, and myself.

Omen called us in for a domestic hostage situation when Sam, the love of his life, was taken by someone wanting revenge against him. We got her back, but I don't think it's over.

"Sorry to interrupt your beauty sleep, princess."

"Kiss my ass. How's Baby Sister?" He pauses a moment before answering. "The nightmares have started already, Squid."

"Fuck… She's a tough one, though. When I walked in, she wasn't freaked out; she held up as good as any of us. You should have heard her; strung up on that hook, naked, after enduring god-only-knows-what, and the only thing she was thinking of was helping you."

My thoughts go back to that day. I'll never

be able to forget the look on Sam's face as we watched the video feed. I've never felt as out of control as I did when those bastards tied her up and cut off her clothes... Those guys were pretty big. "Chase, is Sam… ok? I mean those guys…" I can't even say the words.

"She's all right. They weren't planning to do… that… until I was tied to a chair and forced to watch. Thanks to you and Hype, they were all dead before they got the chance."

I close my eyes; relieved she was spared that nightmare. I had been blaming myself for not being able to get her out sooner. Even though I had never met her, she's like family because she's so important to Chase. Since Chase is a brother in battle, I'd lay my life down for Sam just as quickly as for him.

"Rangers don't let brothers down, man. You know we've always got your back."

"I know it. And I owe you my life for saving us both."

"As I recall, your ass didn't need much saving. It was all Hype could do to keep you from killing Grip."

"Yeah, well. She's the only reason I didn't. Once he was down, I needed to get back to her. That's partly the reason I called. I've managed to convince Sam to stick with me until we can figure out who else is stirring this shit up. We're heading out to her place to pick up her clothes and computer. Will you go ahead of us and check the place out?"

"You got it."

I close my research and hop on my Softail, heading toward Sam's house. For the first time in a long time, I find that I enjoy the drive. This cool weather and fall color sure beats the hell out of South Florida. There, the colors never change, and there's only one season; hot as hell. Georgia is not so bad, but there's just something about the Alabama hills in the early morning light. Right before the sun comes up, the tops of her Appalachian Mountains are crowned in a thick mist. I know why Chase loves it here and why it's been hard for him to stay away for so long.

When I near Sam's place, I drive by slowly and turn around a few houses down. This isn't exactly recon in Afghanistan, but I only know how to do my job one way; the right way. I pull into her drive and make my way to the rear garage area. Being in jeans and a t-shirt instead of tactical gear, I feel vulnerable. Still, I tuck my Sig in the waistband of my jeans and walk around the side of the house. The garage door is locked, so I move on to the front. As I turn the corner, I hear an engine and assume it's Chase. I walk back around to get a better view and instantly go on alert when I see it's not Chase's truck.

I detect long dark hair, so not Sam either. It could be Chase's sister, Ava, but that wouldn't make sense. Besides if it was Ava, Shark would be with her. I bound up the stairs to have an elevated position and rest my hand on the butt of my gun.

Almost before the car stops, this petite creature with luscious brown curls jumps out of the car. I nearly swallow my tongue. She's in a short back power suit and fuck-me heels. Whatever silky shirt thing she's got on under her jacket is teasing me with a spectacular view of her cleavage, thanks to the elevated position. I forget my gun in favor of fantasizing about holding something else.

This tempting creature smiles at me, and I descend the stairs to meet her. Right as I reach the bottom step, the little minx pulls a gun on me. I nearly blow like a teenager right there.

"Put your hands where I can see them!" Her smile disappears, and just like that, the minx becomes a tiger. I hold my hands up and take a seat on the stairs. I'm sure she'll think that it gives her the advantage of height over me; though really, I just want a better view of those legs. I mean, damn, business suits aren't supposed to look like that.

"What's your name, Chief?" No response. "Darlin'?" Ooh, that's a nasty look. Ok, Chief it is. "You're shooting form is pretty good; the Sig's a good choice. I just can't imagine where you keep it in that outfit."

She hasn't opened her mouth again, but her eyes are saying a whole hell of a lot. Mostly, "Eat shit and die."

"So, who are you, Chief? You're not a cop, I'm guessing not ex-military either... Just a little hint? No?"

"Shut your mouth before I shut it for you."

This could be the sister. Strange, she doesn't look anything like Sam. Sam is pretty, sweet, and quiet. This woman... she's fire in a bottle. It's clear that her personality is more assertive and confident, but I'm more intrigued by her gun skills and what would have made her acquire them. She doesn't just know how to handle her firearm, but has obviously spent a lot of time training with it. A lot more than your typical permit holder.

There's something else there... it's in her eyes... I see a real fear there. Something in her past made her like this. The thought of someone hurting this woman pisses me off. My fury must show on my face as her eyes widen and her stance tenses. Come on, Squid, cool it. You're scaring her. Keep selling the jokester routine to keep her calm.

The rumble of another engine is heard coming down the drive. I itch to position myself into a ready stance, but can't move for fear of spooking her. When the engine turns off, a door opens, and I hear a deep, booming laugh. Fantastic.

Chase stumbles out of his SUV laughing so hard that he's struggling to breathe. Dumbass.

Sam jumps out and runs toward us, calling the woman's name. Erin… I like that.

When Sam reaches Erin, I look over to her and feel a huge grin growing on my face. She looks a hell of a lot better than last time I saw her. I give her a wink and resume my new favorite hobby: Erin watching. "She's hot. Can I keep her?"

Sam shoots me a pleading look and reaches up to place her hand on Erin's arm. "This is Squid. He's with us." Chase seems to be suffocating himself over this. I'm ready to throw a large rock at him. Eventually, he pulls his head out of his ass and steps in front of Erin to keep her from shooting me.

Erin hugs Sam, then pulls her away to talk privately. Grinning widely, I say to Chase, "I've got to get me one of those." He shakes his head and replies, "She'd chew you up and spit you out."

"Oh, goody… So, tell me, Omen, who is that hellcat?"

"That… is Sam's older sister, Erin."

I roll that thought over in my head just for a moment. "You know, you and I just might end up being family when all this is over." Chase seems to think I'm kidding.

The ladies make their way back toward us, and I watch Erin the whole time, earning her death stare once again. As a group, we move onto the porch and Erin goes to unlock the door.

Chase stops her from opening it in favor of taking the point position, still choking back laughter.

When he opens the door, his laughter instantly dries up, and he draws his Beretta. Turning to me, he commands, "Keep them out here." just before he runs in, I get a glimpse inside and draw my own weapon while directing the ladies away from the door.

I get the feeling that the only reason Erin is allowing herself to be herded away like this is the death grip Sam has on her arm. "What the hell is going on?" she demands. Challenging her angry look with one of my own, I answer, "Chase is having to finish the job I was doing when you got here." Seeing her slightly panicked look at my sudden change of demeanor, I try to diffuse the situation. "I'm not angry at you. You were protecting your sister. I'm angry that this shit won't end. It's taken too..."

Sam takes off toward the door before I can stop her. "NOOO!" she bellows. Erin and I both run after her, but Chase is there and catches her in the living room.

Damn. This place is wrecked. Chase tosses a pissed-off look my way over not having any warning, but there wasn't much I could do while held at gunpoint. "What the hell, Squid? I thought I sent you to check out the place."

"You did. About ninety seconds after I got

here, this little spitfire showed up and pulled her gun on me. I spent the next fifteen minutes staring at her big, beautiful… eyes until you showed up."

Erin apparently doesn't appreciate my defense and launches at me. Poor Chase. He has to catch her now, and it's obvious that she already hates him. "Knock it off, Squid. Go check the place out." I look over to Sam and feel like a dick. She looks done.

I turn away from the group and start searching the house. Omen would have cleared it for the obvious, but that's not what he sent me to find. He must suspect something more sinister under the surface.

I don't find anything until I hit Sam's bedroom. My initial scan doesn't pick up on anything... until… There's something wrong with the bed. It's made, but the pillows look like they were placed by a man instead of a woman.

Slowly, I pull back the covers and expose part of a message. This has gone far enough. I head back to the main room and motion for Chase. When he follows me back to her bed, I pull the covers all the way back, revealing the whole threat.

I'm coming for them.

Sam. Ava. Erin

"The fuck you are. Who the hell is this, Omen?"

"I don't have the first damn clue, but we're

gonna find out. Did you find any devices?"

"None of the obvious kind and I don't have my equipment to do a sweep."

"I don't like this setup. Let's go."

We rejoin Sam and Erin, who are sifting through broken frames to collect pictures. I jump in to help while Chase leaves; I assume, to call Colonel Avery.

He comes back with a box, and I collect all the rescued pictures. "What's our next move?" He looks my way but doesn't answer. Instead, he takes a deep breath and turns to Erin.

Omen looks nervous. Captain America never looks nervous. Whatever he's planning, he's got my full attention. "Erin, you're going to need to pack a bag and come with us."

Holy shit! He just chummed the water.

With barely a whisper, she answers, "I need to what?"

"I have reason to believe that you are in danger. We need to go to your place and gather some things for you to come stay with us for a while."

Now here comes Jaws... "Just what the hell is going on here? First, my sister gets kidnapped, her house is trashed, and now you want me to drop everything and go with you? From what I can tell, we were fine until you showed up. Maybe you just need to disappear, Ranger!"

Chase runs his hand through his hair in frustration and readies his booming Captain

McDaniels voice, "Look, either you can pack a bag to come with us or Squid will be going with you. Your choice." She steps up toe-to-toe with him. "Just who the fuck do you think you are?"

I can't help it. I cover my heart with one hand and wipe my brow with the other while pretending to go weak. So inappropriate and not a good time, but I'm in love.

Sam steps in. "Erin, listen. Stuff is going on that you don't understand. Please, do this... for me." Erin turns to Sam. She seems to be weighing her options against her love for her sister. Then, her eyes and her voice soften for her younger sibling. "I can't just disappear. I'll lose my job." Realizing the choice she's left with, she drops her head in resignation.

I feel like I've won the lottery and don't even try to hide my delighted laugh. Everyone turns to me, and I give Erin the perfect, raunchy response, "Come to daddy."

"Ugh." She sounds excited about this.

With a little bow, I kindly offer, "This way, milady." In return, she politely answers, "Fuck you."

Anytime, Sweetheart.

She storms past me, and I follow without so much as a backward glance. Without a word, she jumps in her car and speeds off. I had no expectations that she would make this easy. Game on. I stroll up to my bike and climb on, placing my phone on its mount. I take off then;

easily following the tracker I slipped in her pocket.

This is going to be fun.

Chapter 4

Erin

"Ugh." Haven't Sam and I been through enough? I realize life is never easy for anyone, but you'd think that we'd have had more than our fair share by now.

"This way, milady."

"Fuck you." I turn and leave Sam's house, not stopping till I'm sitting in my car. If that asshat, Chase, thinks that he can order me around, he's lost his mind. The fact that I appeared to acquiesce to his demands means precisely dick. I have no intention of being under the control of another man ever again.

Without another thought of this Squid idiot, I pull out and head in the general direction of home. Despite my feelings toward these unwanted men in my life, I do have a strong sense of self-preservation and find myself hesitant to go home. I make a quick decision and hit the call button on the steering wheel to call Lee.

Lee answers, concern clear in his voice, "Hey, Sweetie, any news?"

"She's banged up, but all right. What are you and Arthur doing right now?"

"Arthur's out. I've been at home waiting to hear from you. You want to come over?"

There's nothing more I would like than to spend a quiet afternoon hiding out with Lee, but

I keep hearing Chase's voice in my head warning me of danger. I wouldn't want to put Lee in that position. "Can you just meet me at Newk's?"

"I'll be right there."

When I walk into Newk's ten minutes later, Lee's already seated and stands to give me one of his super hugs. "I ordered you your usual."

"Thanks."

"So, spill before you explode."

I relay everything I know about Sam's abduction, rescue, her house, and Chase's orders. I don't even bother to mention Squid. After I unload, Lee gets all protective. "You'll come stay with Arthur and me."

"Lee, no. You know I can protect myself, and I don't want to chance bringing something to your door. You know I'll be… oh, god."

"WHAT? WHAT IS IT?" All the color drains from his rosy cheeks.

"How the hell did he find me?"

"WHO, DAMMIT?" He starts looking around for an ax murderer. Squid saunters up to the table. "Erin," he addresses me coolly. Lee stands up to meet the proposed threat, but I place a hand on his arm. "Lee, meet Squid. He's a part that I left out… intentionally." Squid only smiles, takes the seat next to me, and begins picking at my salad. Lee eyes Squid with a suspicious glare until I roll my eyes and explain his presence.

"By the way, I'm not calling you Squid. It's a stupid name, and no, I'm not interested in how you got it."

He extends a hand to Lee. "Nathaniel Erickson, but my friends call me Nate."

"Are you really her bodyguard?" Lee asks.

"Until my colonel is sure she's no longer in danger."

"You just make sure you do a good job."

WHAT? The look I give Lee is incredulous. "You're on his side?"

Lee just shrugs his shoulders. "What? Don't ask me to be mad about this. I'm relieved that someone's got your back. If you'd had better backup four years ago..." He stops at the sharp shake of my head. Nathaniel's eyes narrow at the exchange, but he doesn't press.

I've got to get out of here before things get any worse. I stand and give Lee a hug and a kiss on the cheek and turn toward the door. Halfway there, I turn and notice that Nathaniel isn't following me, but standing there talking to Lee. I march right back over to them, grab him by the shirt, and drag him toward the door. I do *not* need him learning anything about me.

Once we're outside, I pull him around the corner of the building and lay into him. "It's clear that I'm not going to be able to get rid of you, *Nathaniel*, but stay out of my business." I let him go and head back to my car.

I sit there for a moment and calm myself

down. When a loud motorcycle pulls up behind me, I give up being calm and crank the car.

Finally home, I stop to check my mail and push the button to open my garage. I hear the loud rumble of his bike and see a flash as he speeds around me, blocking the opening. The sudden move forces me to slam on the brakes.

He steps off the bike, walks over to my car, and looks at me expectantly. I reluctantly roll down the window as he leans down. With not a single trace of humor, he says, "The first step in protecting you is to check the house *before* you go in. Please stay here and keep your doors locked." He doesn't wait for a response, but turns and enters the garage with his weapon drawn. I roll my eyes and reach for the door handle, and the memory of what happened to Sam gives me pause, and I keep still.

While he's gone, I think about that last exchange. There was no goofy grin, no sarcasm; he was all business. It's strange; I've never known someone that was a goofball that wasn't *always* a goofball.

I watch as he enters the house through the garage, then a few minutes later, he exits the same way. Only then, does he move his bike, and motion for me to park my car inside the garage. I do not take orders from him. I hop out of my car and march up to where he is waiting. "You've checked the place, found nothing, and now you can leave."

"Not happening, Chief. And, before you threaten me, hear me out. If you make me leave, I'll have to report it to Chase, and he'll tell Sam. Then, you know what she'll do. Now, I don't know you, but I do care a lot about Sam, and she doesn't need this right now. If you're not a total bitch, you feel the same way about her which means you're stuck with me." I want to claw his eyes out, but he's right. "You… care about my sister?"

"As if she were my own." He crosses his arms and lifts his chin in challenge. So… Squid the goofball is just an act… Smart. I'm sure that makes people underestimate him. I won't be making that mistake again.

I get back in my car and pull into the garage. After pressing the button to lower the door, I tense as I watch Nathaniel duck under the shrinking opening. He's trapped in here with me, or rather, I'm trapped in here with him.

Inside, I'm cursing Chase, Sam, and this idiot for putting me in this situation. I force myself to calm down and think this through. Sam knows that I can't handle being close to a man, so for her to insist on this *protection,* she must really be scared, and she must really trust this man. "Shit."

I look in my rear-view mirror and see him smirking at me. Sure, I can look at hot guys and joke when we're in public, but I'm alone with a man in my house. The last time that happened, my life changed forever. I give him a one-finger salute as he moves toward my door. "You getting out or are you gonna sleep in there tonight?" Angry at myself and him, I suddenly push open the door which slams into him. He grunts and steps back, then I climb out of the car and march inside the house.

Refusing to show a trace of the fear that I feel, I don't stop till I'm on the far side of the large kitchen island. When he enters the kitchen from the garage, I lay into him. "Look, I don't know you, and I don't trust you. Sam obviously does, or you wouldn't be here. And, the only reason I'm agreeing to this is because I don't want Sam to be worried. My rules here are simple; stay away from me, or I'll shoot your balls off." His only acknowledgment of my house rules is that stupid smile of his.

Not interested in his company, I go into my room and lock the door. I need a shower… and to make myself as unattractive as possible.

Once I'm scrubbed free of styling products and makeup, I step out in a ratty t-shirt, worn jogging pants, and pile my hair into a messy knot on top of my head. My unwelcome houseguest is sitting on my sofa, doing something with some computer equipment. I go to the fridge and pull out some sparkling water before flopping down in one of my chairs. He starts to ask me something, "You hun…" but stops when he looks up.

I guess my plan worked. I'm not the polished diamond he thought he saw earlier. He shakes his head and begins again, "You, uh, hungry?" I wasn't before coming back out here, but I must be now; I swear I can smell garlic. Since my imagination leaves me craving Italian, I answer, "I'm going to order out for some pasta."

"No need. I found a jar of marinara in your cabinet that was only expired by a week. I tried some and lived to tell about it, so I guess it's fine. I improvised on the garlic bread. We've got garlic-toasted hot dog buns."

No way he just said... Somewhere in the world, Massimo Bottura just shed a tear.

Ignoring my expression, he heads to the kitchen, finds plates, and serves up the unorthodox meal on the bar. With an inward sigh, I stand and join him in the kitchen.

He doesn't seem to need help finding anything, so I just stand there and watch. The man is boyishly handsome with wind-blown hair, tan skin, bright smile, and sparkling hazel eyes.

He's an unusual man; a chameleon. At first judgment, he was immature; a tool. When he smiles, his eyes dance in a most disarming way. At the restaurant and outside the garage, he was something totally different. He wasn't smiling, and his lethal edge was glaringly obvious.

It makes me feel exhausted. One, because it's hard to keep up with him. Two, because it seems so easy for him to turn it on and off.

This mask that I wear isn't easy, but it's strong. It employs anger and indifference as its main defense mechanisms. The only problem is that it takes a lot of energy to keep up those defenses.

Returning my focus to the unorthodox chef, I can't hold back a laugh when he opens the oven. He really wasn't kidding about the hot dog buns…

I clear my throat and turn away from the scene, angry with myself for allowing that crack in my armor. Needing somewhere to place my attention, I open the fridge and pull out the makings for a salad. "You want any of this?" He looks up and wrinkles his nose, "Not big on rabbit food. Thanks, though."

I give an indifferent shrug of my shoulder and make myself a salad, trying really hard to ignore his muscular arms and chest in my floral apron.

Nate

When Erin stormed into her room and slammed the door, I had to wipe a bead of sweat from my brow. I was sure she was going to fight me about staying, so I played the only card I could; Sam. It's obvious to me that Erin cares deeply for her younger sister. It's equally obvious that she was trying really hard to come off as a bitch. It isn't genuine, though. I think it's all an act; her shield to keep people at arm's length.

Actually, I'm pretty sure I saw flashes of fear… She doesn't want me here because she's afraid of me.

It doesn't make sense to be afraid of a man you just met… unless… it's not just me. Something about her reaction to me is reminiscent of women and girls in Iraq and Afghanistan. They seem to fear all men because women there are treated like possessions, and many face daily abuse.

The thought of someone treating Erin this way pisses me off again. Who hurt this woman? I send a quick text to Chase, "What happened to Erin in the past?" The reply is almost instant. "How should I know? Even if I did, it wouldn't be my story to tell."

There's got to be something. I could find out pretty quick, but for some reason, I can't bring myself invade her privacy like that. I abandon that train of thought and go into the kitchen to find something to eat.

Opening her fridge, I have to laugh at the sad state of affairs. She makes Old Mother Hubbard look like the local Publix. Her pantry isn't much better. I manage to find something I can throw together and get to work.

The makeshift dinner is done, and I'm checking the temporary security camera feeds when I hear her emerge from her room. I begin speaking to her over my shoulder, but when I turn toward her, my brain turns to goo. She's cleared away all the tough-bitch exterior and is wearing worn clothes, is fresh-faced, and has this messy hair business going on. The sight makes me think I've died and gone to heaven. I manage to mentally roll my tongue back in my head and break my gaze to reactivate my brain cells. After a few seconds, I manage to sputter through asking if she's hungry.

I tell her about the craptastic dinner I've made, then go into the kitchen to serve up two plates. When she hesitates before joining me, I place the plates at the bar as far apart as they can go. She relaxes a bit, and my suspicions are confirmed. Someone has hurt her and made her afraid of men.

She moves around me, giving me a wide berth on her way to the fridge. She offers to prepare us both a salad, but I decline and take my seat. When she climbs up on her barstool, she tucks her left foot underneath and draws the other knee up to her chin. I sense that she's creating a quasi-barrier between us. I should take the hint, but I'm too stubborn.

We're nearly finished with dinner when I make a first attempt at friendly conversation, "So, Chief, tell me about yourself."

She doesn't even look up. "No."

I think to myself that it wouldn't be any fun if this was too easy. "I can talk about me if you like."

Still doesn't look up, "No."

"You know, any other guy might be discouraged by your efforts to shut them down." Now she looks up, "But you're not, right?"

"Not even a little." She gives an exasperated shake of her head, climbs down from the barstool, and takes care of her dishes. "Thanks for dinner," she says as she walks to her office.

To her back, I call out, "Admit it. You loved the garlic hot dog buns!" She gives me nothing.

I deal with my own dishes and make a check of all the doors and windows. With everything secure, I sit down at my computer to check the cameras and motion sensors I installed while she was in the shower. Operational and clear. I'm checking emails when my phone rings. "All good here, Omen."

"I'm kind of surprised to find you're still alive..."

"You know women can't resist me." I don't continue, and Omen lets me hang.

"Speak up, Squid. You got kind of quiet there. Or is it that you've found one woman that can resist you?"

"Shut up. I've got shit to do. I'll check in tomorrow morning at seven."

"...Make it nine." The man has his woman back... Message received.

Shortly after nine, I hear Erin making noise in her office. She's tossing things around and cursing. What could have her so wound up this late on a Saturday? I walk in and tap on her shoulder. In a flash, she's turned around and has me backed up against the wall with a box cutter at my throat. Her eyes are wild, and she's breathing heavily. After a brief moment passes, she drops her hands and backs away. "Don't… you ever… do that… again."

"I'm sorry. I didn't mean to scare you. I forget how quiet I move sometimes. I should have knocked." She looks embarrassed. "No, I just… Don't do it again." With that, she rushes out of the office and closes herself off in her room.

Damn. I feel like an ass.

I gather my stuff and head into the guest room. I strip down to my boxers and climb in the bed. It's too early to sleep, so I pull out my laptop and do a search on Erin's name. The first link is for some interior design award she won for some big project she did. Strange… She doesn't have any social media accounts. With my access, I could easily look deeper. I start to, but hesitate again. For some reason, I can't do this to her.

The next morning, I've put in a floor workout, showered, and dressed before I hear any stirring in her room. I head to the kitchen to make some coffee, not knowing what to expect of her today. None of my alarms went off during the night, but I didn't expect them to. To attack so soon, while everyone is on alert, would have been stupid.

While making my second cup of coffee, I hear the tapping of heels coming into the kitchen. Without turning, I ask, "Going somewhere?"

"I need to go to my office." I turn around then. I was expecting, or hoping, to see her in another one of her power suits. Instead, she's in tight jeans, cream sweater, and high-heel, half-boot things.

"Going to work on a Sunday?"

"Yes, on a Sunday. In case you've forgotten, I've been a little distracted by life-or-death situations lately and am behind on my work. I'm not planning on staying there, I just need to pick up some submittals a contractor left for me."

I push off the counter. "Let's go then." She is about to object, but I put up my hand to stop her. "Non-negotiable, Chief." I follow her to the garage, thinking about how I'd love to put her on the back of my bike. She glares at me as if she knows what I'm thinking. "Hey, either you ride with me, or I ride with you."

She rolls her eyes and says, "Get in the car."

Erin is quiet on the drive to her office. I spend a few minutes checking for updates from the team or my contacts. I wish I had new information; something more to give Chase, but nothing I've tried has turned up shit. I've hit a dead end and don't know where to go from there.

With nothing more I can do at the moment, I sit in silence and study Erin's profile. After a few moments, I hear, "What are you staring at?"

"Well, you, obviously." She rolls her eyes.

"Why? Because you think I'm *pretty*?" Oh… that mouth.

"You know you're gorgeous; but no, I'm wondering why you're so afraid of me. Is it me, or is it all men? I suspect it's all men, and, I'm wondering who it was that made you that way." She slides a glance my way and says nothing.

Erin

I'm glad to see my building ahead. Despite the fact that Sam trusts this guy, it's still difficult being closed up with him in such a small space. Not to mention, he sees too much that I'm trying to hide. I don't answer his questions, but it doesn't seem to matter. It's like he already knows everything I'm refusing to say. Surely Sam wouldn't have told him about my past. Even thinking that makes me feel guilty. Still, his observations hit too close to home.

Because it's Sunday, there are available spots on the street at my building on North Twentieth Street. The doorman, in his 1950's bellman uniform, greets us with a smile.

Nathaniel walks beside me step for step through the corridor. When we reach the firm's door, I punch in the code and enter the reception area. I notice a couple of pots of Forget-me-nots on the reception desk and fight the urge to turn and run. The only thing that stops me is knowing I'd get the third degree from my shadow.

I rush to my office and grab the folder of submittals and just as quickly, rush out the door with him on my heels. If he's noticed my change in demeanor, he hasn't said anything.

Back out on the sidewalk, I can't help but look around as if Jack will be standing out there ready to pounce. Come on, Erin. Nobody's called you, so he's still in jail. So, he somehow pays for the flower delivery. Big damn deal.

I don't mean to be so paranoid, but ever since the three-year mark of his sentence, I've been holding my breath and jumping at shadows. Eve had said that he could be released after only serving three years of his sentence. That means that any given day could be the day he gets out. And, the more time passes, the worse I get.

From behind me, someone grabs my elbow, and I go full-on fight-or-flight. The folder of submittals goes flying, and I scream. "Whoa! Hold on there! It's just me. You sort of zoned out for a minute." Recognizing Nathaniel's voice brings me out of panic mode, and I stop fighting.

Embarrassed yet again, I bend down to pick up the scattered papers, and Nathaniel stoops to help. After standing back up, I pull out my keys with shaking hands and unlock the doors. Nathaniel has a concerned look on his face and reaches out his own hand, silently requesting the keys. Without the slightest hesitation, I drop them into his palm. He then unlocks the car and opens the passenger door. I move on autopilot; climbing in and sitting silently.

On the way back to my place, I can see him stealing glances at me. His curiosity wins out, and he asks, "What the hell was that all about?" When I don't answer, he continues, "You ran out of there as if the hounds of hell were on your tail. You mind explaining that?"

"It's none of your business."

"Look, I can tell you're afraid of something. I noticed how you flinched when you saw the flowers at your office. Tell me what's going on and let me help you."

"Why? Why would you want to help a total stranger?"

"Sam cares about you. I care about Sam. If something happened to you, she would be devastated. Besides, you have a live-in bodyguard right now. You ought to take full advantage of me while I'm here." He waggles his eyebrows at me.

This guy is insane... Despite the fact that I know he uses his sense of humor as a weapon, I can admit that it still works. He may change personalities like I change shoes, but he doesn't seem fake. I'm positive that each persona he presents is equally him and equally honest.

It's because he's so brutally honest that part of me is convinced I could trust him. But... if I did tell him what keeps me up at night, he might pity me. I can't stomach pity. I saw it enough in the hospital, from the police, and the lawyers. So, I keep my secrets and stare out the window to hide my embarrassment.

We pull in my drive about fifteen minutes later, and Nathaniel presses the garage door opener. Nothing happens. With a frustrated sigh, I reach over to do it myself. Still nothing. "My batteries must be dead." He doesn't look convinced. I reach for the door handle to go open the door manually, but Nathaniel grabs my arm. "Wait! Let me go and check out the house. You stay here."

"Yes, Sir." As soon as he's cleared the corner of the house, I get out anyway. I've gathered my things and have just made it to the front porch when I hear raised voices. What the hell? Some asshole is in my house.

I creep up the front steps and lay my things down on one of the rocking chairs. Peering into the open door, I see Nathaniel arguing with someone I don't know. I hear Nathaniel call him Avery just before I burst into the room demanding to know who this guy is. As soon as Nathaniel turns his attention to me, Avery draws a large knife and shoves it into Nathaniel's stomach.

Avery pulls out the bloody knife and Nate falls to his knees. He turns again to me, and I'm frozen in place. He's mouthing something, but there's only a loud ringing in my ears. I watch as Avery starts to move in my direction and the ringing stops. Nathaniel's eyes are pleading, but I still can't move. He yells out, "ERIN, RUN!"

Snapping out of my trance, I regain control of my legs and turn away from Avery. I run for the porch and my gun, but don't make it very far. Something hits the side of my head, and everything goes black.

Chapter 5

One Month Later

Erin

Sam looks like an angel. I'm standing beside her, holding a beautiful bouquet of flowers. I can hear the preacher saying something about matrimony, but I'm not listening. I can only watch Sam and Chase. The looks on their faces sprout a deep longing in me. Will I ever get the chance to have that with someone?

It nearly breaks me, remembering that she almost lost him again. She pined for him ten years before finding out he only stayed away to protect her. When they did find each other again, the danger he thought had passed, came roaring back. She was taken, and he sacrificed himself to protect her once more. His efforts nearly killed him, but he survived.

I'm grateful that we all survived that nightmare. I was lucky. I only received a concussion. Sam had some pretty bad cuts, but they have all healed.

Chase wasn't the only one we almost lost, Nate nearly died as well. *"Erin, run!"* I can still hear his desperate scream in my head. I look over to him, and his gaze is on me; piercing in its intensity.

Nate and I haven't spoken since we all made that trip to Fort Benning three weeks ago. Feeling too skittish to drive myself, I had wanted to ride over with Sam, but she and Chase were going early to handle Chase's rental house. So, Nate stepped up and offered.

I had been reluctant to accept as I was regularly seeing flashbacks of him bleeding out on my floor and looking so pale in the hospital. I suppose I felt guilty; even now. I had tried so hard to push him away and, in the end, he was trying to save me.

If I had only listened to him and stayed outside, he wouldn't have been distracted and could have taken Avery out before he could hurt anyone else.

"Erin, run!" I give a little shake of my head to stop the flood of memories and focus on Sam's wedding. I make the mistake of looking up at Nate again, and he's still staring at me; his brows furrowed in concern.

Get your shit together, Erin.

"You may kiss the bride." My gaze snaps back to Sam, who looks beautifully in love. After a not so chaste kiss from her husband, I return her flowers to her, and the festivities begin.

The next three hours are a whirlwind of hugs, pictures, and congratulations. After the sun sets, we gather for an intimate dinner in Chase's grand rotunda to celebrate the new couple. While the meal is being served, my phone vibrates with a message alert. Figuring it's probably work, I ignore it.

The rest of the evening is filled with laughter

and dancing. All of Sam's new brothers take a turn dancing with her, and I gracefully accept a request to dance with Chase. The rest of the time is spent dancing with Cle, Sam, and Ava.

As one upbeat song ends, an unusual track begins to play. It's like one of Sam's hard rock bands gone soft, and by all appearances, the song is special to the new couple. As I'm watching them, lost in each other, Nate approaches me from the side. "Dance with me, Chief." I should say no, but my body won't let me. I let him pull me close, and we start moving.

There's something about the look in his eyes and the unusual song that is slightly hypnotic. I don't catch all the words, but the song is talking about becoming someone's darkness.

Lips brush against my ear as he says, "You look beautiful tonight." The sensation of his breath on such a sensitive area sends a shiver down my spine.

I know he's a good man, but that's not my problem. It's my response to him that scares me. I'm not ready for this.

After the song ends, I escape back to the safety of female company, reaching up to touch that ear on occasion.

When the party dies down later that evening, I hug Sam goodbye and threaten Chase again for good measure. We all watch as they are whisked away in a limousine on their way to Lake Tahoe.

After seeing Cle off, I set out to help Ava, Chase's sister, clean up after the intimate reception. She shoos me away claiming the caterers will clean up, she's just waiting on them to finish so she can lock up. The man called Shark is hanging around, seemingly waiting for Ava, who shows no interest in the guy. Weird. I thought they were a thing.

All the others except Nate have left. And, yes, I've begun calling him Nate. After someone nearly dies for you, you can officially consider them a friend.

I hear footsteps coming up behind me, and I hold my breath. Dammit, Erin, it's not him. He's still in jail. Keep it together. I relax when I recognize Nate's voice, "Can I take you home?" Turning to face him, I ask, "Isn't that in the opposite direction of where you're going?"

"Actually… I'm in a hotel in Soho."

"Of course, you are. Could you be any more obvious?"

He tilts his head to the side. "Of course, I could, but then you'd slap me… Come on, Erin. It's late, and you must be tired. Let me take you home."

I huff out a breath and give in, "Fine." We say our goodbyes to Ava and Shark then climb into Squid's Range Rover.

I'm feeling melancholy and keep pretty quiet on the ride home. I'm happy for Sam, but sad that she's moving to Georgia. It's not the other side of the world, but life is changing, and now I have to share her with someone else.

For the last few years, I've had only Sam, Lee, and Sherry that I've felt comfortable talking to. After Jack, I wouldn't trust anyone new and pushed everyone else away. It's really going to be hard losing Sam across state lines.

Wanting to think about anything besides Sam moving away, I pull out my phone to check the text message I got earlier. I freeze when I see it's not from my boss, Lee. It's from Detective Peyton.

CALL ME!. He got out today. I don't know how the hell it happened without me knowing, but he's out.

If Nate noticed my sharp intake of breath, he didn't say anything. I don't want him to see me afraid. He still doesn't know about Jack, and I want to keep it that way. I hated seeing pity in the eyes of the lawyers and police, but coming from Nate, it would wreck me.

I look at Nate's profile again. He's got sharp eyes but is quick with a laugh. He may be a joker but is insanely intelligent. He made me laugh. He helped me forget. If only for a very short time, I wasn't looking over my shoulder or checking my locks a dozen times. I could relax around him like I hadn't been able to do for a very long time.

Three weeks ago, his entire team received commendations and promotions, and I knew our time was ending. I would have to go back to being vigilant since he would be gone. So, I pushed him away like everyone else.

When we pull into my drive, I don't move. I see every dark place and imagine a monster is hiding there.

Nate is already out and walks around to my side to open the door. When I don't immediately climb out, his brow furrows, and he asks if I want him to check the house. "...Yes."

It makes me angry that I'm allowing myself to depend on him for safety once again, but I'm still in shock over the message from Eve.

Nate reaches for my hand, and I allow him to help me out of the Rover. Still dazed, I don't drop his hand as we walk up the path to the door. When we make the turn to the front porch, I stop dead still. My heart starts beating wildly, and I begin breathing too fast.

Nate, noticing I've stopped, turns back to me with concern etched on his features, "Erin, what's wrong?"

Flowers. Beautiful and terrifying flowers on my stairs. Forget-Me-Nots. Please, god no. I take a few steps backward, ready to turn and run.

Noticing the direction of my gaze, Nate turns and spots the flowers. He sprints to the stairs and bends down to inspect. Finding nothing alarming, he returns holding a business-card-sized envelope.

I don't need to read it. I know where it came

from. "Erin, what's going on? Are these the same flowers I saw at your office?"

My mouth opens and closes like a fish out of water. I can't get the words out. I take the envelope from his hand and cautiously open it as if Jack himself could be in there.

I open the tiny card and see the familiar script. The message inside is seemingly innocuous, but I see it for the threat that it is, "I haven't forgotten you."

The note slips from my hand and flutters to the ground. I back up a step then another as Nate bends down to retrieve the note. "What the hell?" The rising panic crests and I run. I don't know where I'm going, I just have to run. I can hear someone calling my name, but I can't stop. I've got to get away from here.

Strong arms wrap around me from behind. I fight, and I scream, but I can't get free. We stumble and hit the ground. "ERIN!... ERIN! LOOK AT ME!"

Nate… it's Nate, not Jack.

I'm not sure what happened next. The only thing I am aware of is Nate carrying me and yelling into his phone.

Jack was here. He was released from prison, and he came to my house.

Nate

When I hand Erin the tiny white envelope, she's white as a sheet. After the card slips from her fingers, I reach down to pick it up. This is not some sweet little note. "What the hell?" Erin begins backing up and takes off running like the devil's on her heels.

I call her name, but she doesn't even register my voice. I catch up to her, but she's not stopping. I throw my arms around her to make her stop; to keep her from falling and breaking her neck. She starts fighting against me like I'm the devil that was chasing her.

To keep from hurting her, I take an awkward stance, and she throws me off balance. As we're going down, I twist my body to take the brunt of the impact. "ERIN!... ERIN! LOOK AT ME!" She finally stops fighting. Stops moving altogether.

I pull out my phone to call Hyper and put in my earpiece. I shove my phone in my pocket and pick Erin up, then take off running to my truck.

"What's up, Squid?"

"Get over to Erin's house NOW!"

I can hear Hype's voice stiffen. "On my way. What's going on?"

"I have no fucking clue. There were flowers on Erin's stairs, and she went batshit when she read the attached card. She's passed out, and I'm getting her out of here. I'll call you when I land somewhere."

I had been bluffing about the hotel in Soho. Even if it was true, I couldn't take her there.

There's no way I could carry an unconscious woman though a hotel lobby without someone calling the police. What are my options? I don't want to involve anyone else while I have no idea what is happening. I can't take her back to the guest house in case the source of all this shit tries to follow me. So, plan B it is.

I head north on 65, hoping I won't have to go far. Just north of Birmingham, I spot a couple exterior-corridor hotels in a city called Fultondale. I pull in the first one and ask for adjoining rooms on the bottom floor.

Erin's still out when I back into the parking spot right outside our rooms. I unlock the door and prop it open before rushing back to get Erin out of the truck. I carry her in and lay her down on the bed so I can evaluate her condition. Not sure how she can breathe in that super tight, fancy gown, I remove it and get her under the covers.

After checking her vitals, I decide she's in no medical danger and try to determine what this is I'm dealing with.

She was fine at the wedding, during the reception, and on the ride home… until she looked at her phone. After that, she went quiet. The answer has got to be in an email or text she read while we were driving to Homewood. I go out to the truck to find her phone, but it's not there. "Shit!" I left her bag and phone on the ground at her place.

Just as I'm about to call Hyper again, he rings my phone. "Squid, there's nobody here, and her place is locked up tighter than a drum. I found the flowers and the note, but nothing else."

"Find her phone. She dropped it, and I didn't go back for it. We'll find what we're looking for on there. I'm at a Days Inn in Fultondale. Back building."

"Be there as soon as I can."

I go back in and check on Erin again. She's still out. I grab my bags out of the truck and pull out a t-shirt for her to put on. I lay it on the bed beside her, then go to the adjoining room to wait for Hyper.

I've just about worn a hole in the cheap carpet when Hype calls. "I'm at the door." When I let him in, he looks angry and confused. I imagine it's partly due to the way I look. I'm still in my tux which is now torn and dirty from struggling with Erin on the ground. "What the hell is this, man?"

"I don't have the first damn clue. You got her phone?"

"Yeah. Her phone and her bag." He tosses the phone to me and places the bag on the small table inside the door. Again, I'm reluctant to pry into her life, but whatever got to her must be bad.

I take a minute to explain what happened and he just shakes his head. "You said she started freaking out when she checked a message on her phone?"

"Yeah." He looks at me expectantly when I hesitate. "Hype, she's a civilian… and Sam's family."

"Exactly. The way I see it, we should do whatever we can to make sure she's all right. And… I know you don't want to call Sam on her wedding night. Look, you should either wake her up or check the phone."

"Dammit. You're right, but I'm not waking her up." I check the lock screen on Erin's phone. It's print-protected; easy enough.

What's it going to be Nate?

It only takes a second to decide; I go back to the room where Erin's sleeping and place her right index finger on the reader.

As I walk back to the other room, I'm opening her messaging app. It only takes a split second to find what set her off.

"What the fuck!" I pull my satellite phone from my gear bag, then key in the number of the message sender. Hyper reaches for the phone to read the message. As my call is going through, I hear him swear just as loudly. It occurs to me that I want Hype to hear this conversation, so I put the call on speaker.

"Peyton here."

"Detective, my name is Nathaniel Erickson. I'm a friend of Erin Westin…"

"IS SHE OK? WHERE IS SHE?" she

interrupts.

"She's in a safe place, but she's not ok. I need you to tell me what's going on."

"Not over the phone. I'm coming to you. Where are you?" I look to Hyper, and he shakes his head. "Detective, with all due respect, we're at a safe house, and I don't know you. I'm not giving our location to anyone that I don't know personally." When she doesn't respond, I get suspicious. "You can try to trace this number, but it won't work. I'm no amateur."

"What are you?"

"Very capable. Now, are you going to tell me what I need to know?"

"I want to talk to Erin."

"No."

"No?"

"No. She blacked out, and I think it's in her best interest to let her sleep."

"Isn't that something a doctor should determine?"

"I'm a combat medic. So, you either start talking or I'm hanging up."

"Shit!... I can't do that to her. If she hasn't told you, she doesn't want you to know… Can you keep her safe?"

"We're captains in the US Army; Rangers. As I said before; very capable."

"Call me when she wakes up." She disconnects the call before I can say anything else.

I sit down hard on one of the chairs and scrub my hands over my face. "Shit. We can't do anything until she wakes up." Hyper shakes his head at me. "No, we *can* do something, you just won't."

"It's late. You sleep for a while, and I'll keep watch. You can take over in four hours."

Chapter 6

Erin

I'm running in the dark. I've got to get away. He catches me, and I'm screaming as we fall to the ground. He's clawing at my clothes as he covers my mouth. The awful dream wakes me, and I'm left in a cold sweat. Jack… He's out. Those assholes let him out without telling me.

When I open my eyes, I don't recognize where I am. What happened? I was at Sam's wedding, then Nate drove me home where I found the flowers. Jack had been at my house. I ran away… but… don't remember anything after that.

Careful not to make a sound, I slowly turn my head to look around. It appears as though I'm in a cheap hotel in an adjoining room with the connecting door standing open. I don't hear any voices, but I can hear a shower running.

I take stock of my situation. The only thing I'm wearing under these covers is my panties. It's a relief that despite my state of undress, I'm still covered here. There's a t-shirt on the pillow next to me. I reach for it and slip it on, being as quiet as possible. Something about the shirt smells familiar. It's a comforting smell… Nate. He must have brought me here.

I sit up on the side of the bed and test my legs. Everything feels normal. My stomach growls, and I wonder how long I've been out.

Guess it's time to find out.

I make my way to the other room and hear the shower turn off. There's a large form in the bed, and the sight throws me until I recognize the sleeping profile. I breathe a sigh of relief when I recognize Hyper.

When I first met him the day Nate was stabbed, he scared the hell out of me. He yelled at Sam for not cooperating with the doctor and nurse that wanted to stitch up the cut on her head.

The sound of a door latch catches my attention. The door to the bathroom swings open and Nate walks out wearing nothing but a towel. His eyes turn dark and his jaw tenses when he spots me standing there in just his t-shirt. The obvious desire in his eyes changes to something else when he spots Hyper's sleeping form.

Nate walks over and grabs my hand on his way into the other room. As soon as the door is closed, he turns and says, "What is going on, Erin?"

Instead of answering him, I demand, "Where is my phone? I've got to call someone."

"Who? Detective Peyton?"

"How did…? You hacked my phone."

"I'm sorry, but when someone freaks out over a message and blacks out over some flowers, the time for secrecy is over. It was either call her or call Sam."

"What did she say?"

"Not a damn thing. She did demand that I tell her where we are, but I declined. After what I saw last night, I wasn't telling her anything until you gave me the green light." He reaches for my hand but pulls back at the last second. "Erin, you're safe here; with us... with me."

He was protecting me… again. He and Hyper both were protecting me… without a single clue about what the threat might be. One or both of them could have been in danger, and they would have had no idea what to watch out for.

I don't want either of them to get hurt because of me; equally as much as I don't want them to learn about my past.

That leaves only one path to take. They won't understand, but I have to do it. "Where's my phone?" Nate obviously doesn't want to hand it over but gets up to retrieve it from his bag.

When he hands it to me, he doesn't let go for a moment. "Whatever this is, we can help you, Erin. Let me help you." He lets go of my phone but doesn't remove his gaze from mine. The look in his eyes begs me to trust him. "I… I'm sorry. I can't."

I unlock my phone and call Detective Peyton. "I'm texting you a location. Can you come pick me up?"

"Hold on… Ok, I got it. I'll be there in ten minutes."

When I end the call, Nate goes to his bag and pulls out two pairs of jogging pants. He tosses one to me and turns around. I turn and slip them on, pulling the string at the waist tight to hold them up.

When I turn back around, Nate has pulled on pants as well. It's clear that he's not happy with my decision. He opens his mouth to say something, but Hyper walks in the room. "Hey. Look who's awake. How you feeling this morning?"

Nate angrily jumps in, "She's leaving." Hyper looks at me, worry etched all over his face. "I saw the note and what it did to you. Dealing with this on your own is not a good idea."

I lift my chin. "I can take care of myself. And I won't be alone."

"She called the cop." Now Hyper looks hurt. "Erin, you're family now. We take care of family. You can trust us."

"I know, but this isn't something you can fix."

"But the cop can?" The hurt is clear in Nate's voice.

My phone beeps with an incoming text, and I'm grateful for the interruption. *I'm outside your room.*

I look out the window and spot Peyton and McKenzie in their navy sedan. It only takes a moment to gather my dress and shoes before I'm reaching for the door handle. Nate places his hand over mine to stop me. "Erin... please stay." His eyes plead with me.

I drop my gaze to the floor. "I can't."

He lifts my chin, forcing me to look at him. "Should you need us, both our numbers are programmed into your phone. Just... please be careful. We'll be close." With that, he backs up and lets me leave.

Seeing me walk out, McKenzie gets out and opens the back door for me. As much as I want to, I don't turn around and face the two men standing in the doorway.

Peyton turns around and gives me a visual inspection. "Ok. First thing; are you all right?"

"Yes. I'm fine. Just panicked a little last night."

"Now, who were those men, and how did you end up here?"

"My brother-in-law is a Ranger. Those guys are his best friends and are in his unit. One of them took me home after my sister's wedding last night. When I got home, there were more flowers on my stoop."

Mike swears. "Damn, he didn't waste any time. Did it look like he'd been inside?"

"I didn't get that far. I froze when I saw the flowers. Nate checked them out and brought me the card. Then, I sort of flipped out."

"Let's head over to your place to check it out. I want to see if he left evidence this time.

We'll need to apply for a restraining order as well. That will help us if he keeps this shit up."

Before long, we've pulled in my driveway and are climbing out of the detectives' car. Mike goes to the trunk and pulls out gloves and a dusting kit while Eve gets a camera.

After a few minutes, it's obvious that they haven't found anything. "No prints?"

Mike answers, "Nothing. Either he didn't try anything, or he wore gloves. Give me your keys." I hand them over and watch as yet another man sweeps my house before I can enter. I don't like how often this is happening.

Eve leads me to the living room and takes a seat. She looks ready for the barrage of questions I'm about to throw at them, but I wait until Mike is finished before opening my mouth. When he sits down, Eve begins to explain, "We don't know why he was released early, why none of us were notified, or where he is. As of right now, there isn't even an order for him to register as a sex offender." I jump up and begin pacing. "What!?"

"That isn't all... because he never had visitors, sent or received letters, made any calls, and has no known acquaintances, we have no idea where he could be."

"The only thing any of us knows is that he was at my house last night."

"That about sums it up... Erin, there were no conditions on his release. Regardless of what we know and believe, the judicial system sees him as a free man who's paid his debt to society. We can't touch him. Now, until we can get some answers from the DA, we'd feel better if you didn't stay here by yourself. I'm guessing since Sam got married yesterday that she'll be gone for a while. Is there somewhere you could stay for a few days till we get this figured out?"

"I could stay at her house in Bluff Park."

"By yourself?" When I nod my head in answer, Mike jumps in, "That would be the first place he'd look. Not to mention, it would be better if you weren't alone."

Eve seems to be considering something. "What about that man I spoke with last night? He seemed..."

"NO. Absolutely not."

"Why? Is there something wrong with him?"

"I just don't want him to know, ok?"

Mike gets that sympathetic look on his face. "Look, you can't just hide..."

Eve interrupts her partner, "Shut up, Mike. Erin, go pack some stuff and come stay with me. Just until we get our answers and can get the restraining order." At my look, she adds, "It's either me, Mike, or we call your sister."

"All right, fine. I'll be right out." I march to my room and grab a bag. I stuff in some everyday clothes and grab some work suits. Another bag gets my bath stuff and make-up. I grab my laptop bag, and that's it. I start to walk out of my room but realize all I'm wearing are Nates clothes and not even a bra. I change quickly and head back out. Fortunately, Sam had picked me up yesterday, so my car is still here.

Thinking of Sam not being here makes my eyes misty. I close my eyes and think back to yesterday's wedding prep at the spa. While her make-up was being done, I kept teasing her about sex with Chase just to see her turn red. Eventually, I caught the evil eye from the make-up artist. Apparently, I was making her job difficult.

Not to be outdone, she returned the favor by teasing me mercilessly about Nate while my own face was being done; something only Sam could get away with.

God, I wish she were here. I've itched to pick up my phone to call her a dozen times, but I can't do that to her. If there ever was anyone that deserved a fairytale wedding and honeymoon, it's Sam. No, I've got to face this on my own.

I suck in a deep breath and realize I'm being chased out of my home for the second time by this asshole. As I enter the living room again, the somber looks on the faces of the detectives kills any good mood the memories of the wedding brought. Welcome back to my shitty reality.

Outside, Mike helps me load my bags in my car, and I mentally run through what I've got. My favorite heels are in the car, I've packed my Nikes, booties, and I'm wearing my favorite flats. "I guess that's it." I go back up the steps and lock the door, then climb in my car to follow them to Eve's place.

She doesn't live too far from me. It's a beautiful house on East Fairway Drive in Crestline. Stepping out of the car, I think to myself that being a detective must pay better than I thought. Noticing the look on my face, Eve shrugs her shoulders and explains, "It was my parents' place. When my mom died, it was easier to give up my lease and move in here than sort, pack, and sell her stuff and the house."

Mike offers to get my bags, but not before I see him slip a key to Eve. The same key she hands to me minutes later. It looks as if there is more to the detectives than a professional partnership. Great. That means that my presence here will be keeping them apart for appearance's sake. If I didn't feel awkward enough before…

I've got enough travel points to stay in a hotel for at least a week. Maybe I should. "Detectives, I can…"

Eve puts up her hand. "Stop… just… stop. McKenzie, can you wait in the car?" He nods and gets in the department car.

Before she can lay into me, I go on defense, "Eve, we both know this is not your job." She recoils as if I'd slapped her. "How can you say that to me? This isn't about the job. This is about a friend that needs a safe place to stay for a couple of days. Someone in my justice system screwed this up, and I'm not willing to stand by and watch it bite you in the ass. Now, shut up and listen. I'm sure you're familiar with the area. Everything you need is in walking distance, and the police station is behind those trees. I've got to go back to the station for a while. Get settled in. There probably isn't any food here, but Taco Mama is two blocks away; across the street from the police station, and they have a great pomegranate margarita." I smile to myself; I'm familiar with their margaritas.

Before she leaves, she shows me how to set the security system. I can imagine that her system is significantly better than mine. "I'm sorry I have to run out and leave you like this. I'll be back as soon as I can."

"Forget it. No one would ever look for me here. I'll be fine."

As odd as it is to be alone in a strange house, I try my best to ignore it and pull out my laptop. As long as I've got nothing else to do, I may as well work on the space plan for the Pinnacle tenant build-out.

It's been five hours since Eve left and I've just about got the layout finished when my phone chimes with a new message. Expecting it to be Nate, I'm kind of shocked to see Hyper's name on the screen.

"You good?"

I type back, "Yeah. I'm safe. Nate still mad?"

"Only cause he's worried."

"I'll be fine."

"I'm worried too."

"There's a police station fifty yards from me."

"Day or night, Erin."

"Thanks, Hyper."

My focus broken, I stretch out my stiff muscles and look at the clock. Nearly two. It's time for a taco basket and pomegranate margarita.

I close the lid to my laptop and run a brush through my hair. When I spot my reflection in the hallway mirror, I cringe a little but head out anyway.

The walk through Crestline is pleasant. I should venture out here more often. Lee talks about a restaurant named Lapaz all the time. If I'm still here tomorrow, I might check it out.

When I walk in Taco Mama, the place is pretty busy. I order my usual and look for an empty table, but quickly see that I'll have to wait. No worries; it's a common occurrence here that never takes more than a few minutes. Looking around the restaurant, I spot Jess Whitman.

My vision blurs, and I feel a little dizzy. She was a good friend… until she wasn't. After the attack, she gave Mike and Eve some bullshit story about me and my proclivity for kink.

I might not be as pure as the driven snow, but my sex life, whatever it was or is, has never been a topic of conversation with anyone besides Sam. Part of me believes that she had a thing for Jack and wasn't happy with the attention he was giving me.

Our eyes make brief contact, and her face drains of color. I smile my most saccharine smile and watch as Jess clumsily gathers her things and rushes out the door. Satisfied with that lying bitch's reaction, I patiently wait for her table to be cleaned off and take a seat.

As I wait for my lunch, I pull out my phone to check messages. Sam has sent a few pictures showing the fall foliage around Lake Tahoe. I text back, "Don't you have better things to do that don't involve messaging me or wearing clothes?"

"Who says I'm wearing clothes? How are things there?"

It's killing me to keep secrets from her. Especially when just talking to her would help me calm down. "Fine here. The usual construction headaches. Now, get back to making up for lost time."

"With pleasure."

Eww.

Seeing nothing else that needs my attention. I set out to people-watch until I have tacos.

In Homewood

"Where the fuck is she?" Jack pulls down the binoculars and stares at Erin's empty driveway.

"I know she's been here; the flowers are gone... Her sister... She's at that bitch's house." Jack tosses the binoculars to the floor of the car. "That stupid cunt screwed everything up. If she hadn't shown up when she did, Erin and I could have been living the good life on the beach instead of me going to prison." For him, the perfect end to the day would be killing Sam and taking Erin. He gets to walk away with his woman and be rid of the bitch that got in his way. He looks up Sam's address and slowly pulls out of his spot on the street.

When he arrives at Sam's house, he swears loudly when he sees the For-Sale sign by the mailbox. "Shit!" He drives out of the neighborhood to plan his next move. "I wonder..." He pulls up Lee's firm's website. Erin's picture is still shown under Lead Designer. "No problem, I'll see you at work tomorrow."

Erin

After filling up on tacos and queso, I walk around Crestline Village to see what has changed since I stopped working in this area. After visiting several of the shops, and killing as much time as I can, I visit the market and pick up a couple of things before heading back to Eve's house. All the lights are on when I get there, and I walk in noisily to keep from startling her.

Eve is sitting at the bar with Mike eating Chinese take-out. They both look up as I walk in. "You smell like tacos," Mike accuses. "Jealous much?" I toss over my shoulder. Expecting a little resistance, I add, "I'm going to turn in and get some work done before bed… I'm going to work tomorrow."

Eve shrugs her shoulders, "Good. You know what to do if shit happens. I'm off the next two days and refuse to leave the house."

"I'll bring food then. I'm a pretty lousy cook, but I can do something. Is there anything you won't eat?"

"No healthy shit."

"So, tofu it is." I see her shaking her head and close the door, but not before I see her smile for the first time.

Nate

"This is bullshit, man." It's nine pm, nearly twelve hours since she got in that car and left. After checking out of that hotel, I haven't done jack-shit except to head back to Chase's guest house. And pacing. I've done plenty of that. That, and sitting on my ass.

In yet another failed attempt to calm my nerves, Hyper explains, "Look, she's safe enough tonight. She's with that lady detective and seems to be settled in for the night. Tomorrow she'll be at work in that secure building. Besides, you could save yourself all this drama if you'd just…"

"NO! I'm not digging into her background. You putting that tracking app on her phone was for her safety, but I won't invade her privacy like that… I want her to trust me. Whatever happened to her has destroyed her ability to trust people, and I won't perpetuate that… Stop trying to calm me down. It's not helping. In fact, each time you try, it just makes me more…" The grin on his face brings a quick end to my outburst. "You dick. You've been riling me on purpose."

I've got to do something before I lose it. "I'm going to swim a few laps... asshole" I leave the room to grab some shorts and a towel, then head out the door. When I get to the pool, I can see the steam rising from the heated water and look forward to some physical effort. I quickly strip down and pick up the shorts. "What the hell?" Nobody's home anyway. I toss them back on the chair and dive in, thankful for the heated water in this November chill.

Cutting through the water, I stretch out all my muscles and start to relax. A few minutes in, I start to think about Hyper's efforts to push my buttons. I don't get why he's doing it unless… he knows. He's figured out that it's not just a mission this time.

Plenty of times on missions, I've used charm and flirting to obtain information or compliance from a mark. A month ago, things started out with me doing the same thing to Erin. Somewhere along the way, it changed into something else for me. Still, just what Hype thinks he'll accomplish by dicking me around… I don't know.

After about an hour, I climb out and dry off; the warm water making the cool air feel even colder on my skin. "This sure as hell isn't Miami." I throw my clothes back on and walk back to the guest house. In the living room, I find Hype sitting down with a beer watching football. I decide to join him just to have the distraction. When I stretch out my legs, he offers me a beer. "You're still a dick… even if you're right." In answer, he raises his beer to me, then takes a draw.

After the game, I force myself to sack out. As soon as I've finished checking my security, my phone indicates that I've got a message. Surprisingly, it's from Erin. "Thanks for helping me last night. I wanted you to know that I will be going to work tomorrow and that I'll be staying with Eve again."

I want to see her. Not about protection or trying to convince her to confide in me. I just need to see her for my own sanity. I tap out a quick reply, "Want to do lunch?"

She doesn't reply right away, and that makes me antsy. I feel like a stupid teenager waiting for her to answer. "Dude, get a grip. You're a grown-ass man." I toss my phone on the nightstand and get into bed.

That night, I don't have any disturbing wartime dreams. Instead, I dream that I'm trying to find Erin. She's been missing for days, and I've exhausted every lead. Every trace, tip, and sighting leads to a dead end. I have this dream three times during the night, and it wakes me up each time. After the third time, I give up and drag myself out of bed. It's almost five anyway.

Grabbing a towel, I head to the pool again. Once I reach the patio, I see a pile of clothes on one of the chairs. "Damn, man. Are you in there naked?"

"So, what?"

Groaning, I strip and dive in the lighted pool. "Just keep your ass on that side. I don't want to see your junk."

"I can see how my junk would make most men feel inadequate."

"Fuck you."

"So… what are you going to do about Erin?"

"Well, there's only so much I can do if she doesn't want my help."

"That's not what I'm talking about, and you know it. What are you going to do after we nail this bastard? I know you're not just going to walk away and forget her. Are we going to have another Omen on our hands?"

"Hell no. I'm not going to wait ten years."

"Good."

I take a few more laps, then head back to the guest house to shower and dress. Only then do I allow myself to check for Erin's reply. "Pick me up at noon, or we can meet somewhere."

Hmm. Meet her somewhere so she can leave at will, or pick her up and have a captive audience? No contest. "I'll pick you up."

Downtown Birmingham

Jack pulls in the parking deck across the street from Erin's office building. He's early; hoping to get a spot on the south-facing side to watch for her. Just before eight, he spots her walking to the entrance. The white-haired guy she works for catches up to her and they walk in together. Now all I have to do is be ready to follow her home; wherever that is.

At noon, she walks out and greets some guy before climbing in his Land Rover. Who the fuck is that? She doesn't get to move on to another man. As much as I want to find them and kill the poacher, I have to wait. They'll be back. She has to come back to get her car. Then, I'll learn all I need to know.

Nate

"So, where are we headed?"

"Feel like Italian?"

"I'm game."

"A hidden place called Gianmarco's then. I'll tell you how to get there."

She wasn't kidding about being hidden. This

place is off the busy Greensprings Highway, right in the middle of a neighborhood. It must have a stellar reputation, or no one would ever know to come here.

Once we're inside and seated, I have to remind myself to take it easy on her. As much as Captain Erickson wants to grill her, Nate has to remember that he's here as her friend. That's what she needs more than anything else. "You... doing ok?"

"Yeah, I'm fine. I miss my bed, and I miss Sam. What about you? I would have thought you and Hyper would be back in Georgia by now. What are you guys doing?"

"Swimming... and playing charades mostly." She nearly spits out her drink.
I only sit there and smile innocently. She's trying to look annoyed, but her eyes are sparkling with laughter.

"We don't have to be back for a few more days..." My laughter dries up, and I give her a pointed look. "Really, we're just hanging around here in case you need us."

The change in her demeanor says she wasn't expecting that. Her eyes mist up, and she looks away. I guess her and Sam have been on their own a long time and aren't used to having backup.

Now that she knows we're on call, I change the subject, "So, what's it like staying with the detective?" Erin recovers, and a ghost of a smirk crosses her lips. "As bad as she eats and as little sleep as she gets, I'm surprised she's still living. She's ok, though. I've known her for a long time. We've become friends of sorts."

"What about McKenzie? He a good guy?"

"Yeah, he's fine. He and Eve are a thing. Me being there is cutting him off, but he's not complaining. Still, I'll be glad when I can get out of their way and go back home."

Here's the soft opening I was hoping for. "What's the hold-up on that? If it's a security issue, I can fix that."

"I might take you up on that. I can't stay with Eve forever." So, basically, I got nothing new from that whole exchange...

The rest of the meal and trip back to her office passes without any awkwardness. I pull up
to her building and ask, "To give the detectives some alone time, we could do dinner tonight."

"I would, but I've already told Eve that I'd cook for her." As disappointed as I am, seeing the genuine letdown on her face gives me an ego boost.

"No offense, but... ok, this is really going to be offensive, but based on what I saw in your kitchen, I don't think that's a good idea. Murder by dinner is a crime."

My joke earns me a smack to the arm, but it's worth it because I also get a glimpse of her beautiful smile. "Maybe tomorrow, asshole."

Chapter 7

Erin

It was hard wearing a mask all day today. Thank god Sherry was visiting build sites all day. One look at me and I wouldn't have been able to hide anything from her. I could tell Lee was suspicious, but he didn't pry.

After leaving work, I stop by the grocery store and order an idiot-proof dinner kit from the seafood counter. Confident in my ability to turn on an oven, I grab a bottle of wine and head to Eve's house.

An older model Ford SUV pulls out behind Eve. *"I'm almost disappointed. She's making this too easy."* Pretty soon, it becomes evident that he won't be able to get to her tonight. *"I didn't expect to be following her to Crestline."* His truck sticks out among the expensive cars of the neighborhood and will be too easily remembered. *"That's all right, though. Now that I know where you're staying, I'll just find better wheels and fit right in."*

When I walk in the house, Eve is sitting at the bar pecking at her computer. I've never seen her out of her serious detective clothes. The yoga pants and sweatshirt make her appear so much younger. Her long red hair is even pulled up in a messy bun adding to her youthful appearance.

She looks amused as I turn on the oven and search the cabinets for a pan. Finding what I need, I remove the sauce bowls from the carefully assembled bags of salmon, vegetables, and couscous.

"Don't look so nervous. All I have to do is bake them for twenty minutes, transfer them to plates, and pour the sauce over them. Even I can manage that."

Eve stands and grabs glasses and a bottle opener. "Just in case, we'll go ahead and start on this." She opens the bottle of wine and pours us both a glass.

"So… how long have you and Mike been *together*?" Her head snaps up, and she has this stunned look on her face. "How did you know?"

"I saw him give you the key that you put in my hand." At the shake of her head, I add, "Hey, I'm not judging. It's good that you've got somebody you can talk to; somebody that understands your life."

She turns and taps her fingers on the gleaming countertop. "Speaking of…"

I put up my hand to stop her, "That's off-limits."

"Uh-huh. Fair is fair. This guy that was guarding you… he's not like other limp-dicks that can't handle shit. This guy was ready to take me on just to protect you. Which begs the question… Why are you here with me instead of him? Or better yet, why doesn't he know about Jack?"

"Eve, you know how people treat victims.

After all these years, even Mike still treats me like glass. I don't want Nate to see me as damaged." She drops her head in disappointment, then reaches in a drawer for a corkscrew. Without looking up at me, she expertly opens the bottle of wine and her mouth. "Damn, for such a smart woman, you can be pretty stupid. The way I see it, you should just tell him and find out for sure. Either he's chicken shit and runs, or he doesn't, but you pushing him away like this guarantees that he'll walk. What have you got to lose?"

I stand there quietly as I mull over her words. "I should have known better than to stay with a detective. Wipe that smug look off your face and pour me another glass."

Twenty minutes later, the oven timer goes off, and I pull out our dinner. Wow, it looks edible. I'm rather proud of myself. I transfer everything to plates and pour over the sauce. Eve refills the wine, and we laugh and talk over dinner. We keep talking until we've emptied our plates and the bottle. By this time, it's getting late. I start to clear away the dishes, but Eve stops me. "You cooked; I'll clean."

"Sounds fair. I'm going to bed." As I'm walking to the guest room, Eve tosses out, "You know I'm right about him." I don't turn around, but answer, "I know."

The next two hours are spent going back and forth on telling Nate or not. I've just about convinced myself to talk to him, but then balk when I start thinking about how to tell him. I can just see all the disastrous scenarios playing out in my head. We go out to dinner, and I drop my bomb, "You seem to like me. Before things go too far, you should know I'm being stalked by a man that drugged, then raped me four years ago. Now, how about dessert." Or, I could just unload all that on him first thing when I see him next, then watch as he stumbles over himself to get away from me.

Not liking any scenario and angry at the situation, I lie down to try and get some sleep.

After tossing and turning most of the night in the unfamiliar bed, I'm still grumpy in the morning. When I'm dressed, I stomp around the kitchen, fixing some coffee to snap me out of this mood. Eve emerges just as the machine is finishing and watches me, amused, until she really looks at me.

I fill up my travel cup and walk out to my car with Eve following me the whole time. "Erin, I'm sorry I pressed last night. It's just that… I know people. This Nate guy is one of the good ones. Give him a shot, I'll bet my life that he'll face this shit and not only stick around but have your back."

Then with a smile, she adds, "Besides, I need your ass out of here soon so I can get some." I so did not need that visual. "Oh, god! I'll find a hotel for the night. Bye, Eve." She watches as I back out of her drive, then turns to go back inside.

I'm going to do it. Today. I'll call Nate and have him meet me at my house after work. If I'm going to do this, I want to be in my home, my haven where I'll be the most relaxed.

Somehow, just deciding to talk about this with Nate makes me feel optimistic, and I drive the rest of the way to the office feeling almost cheerful.

The detective walks back around the house and through her front door. As she turns the lock, she's confident that she's finally gotten through to Erin. *She's going to tell him.* She steps to the side to set the alarm and thinks to herself, *God, I hope I'm not wrong. Erin needs someone that can stand up to her and make her happy.* She pictures the fierce man standing in the hotel doorway and laughs to herself, *I'll bet my badge; he's that someone.*

Raising her hand to the control panel, her smile fades as she feels a breeze when there shouldn't be one. The hairs on her neck stand to attention, and a feeling of dread fills her.

Eve never noticed the figure waiting on the back deck or his move around the house to the open entry door.

She readies herself as much as she can without her service weapon. Hoping to have the element of surprise, she braces to turn and attack.

"Hello, detective." He's a lot closer than she thought. By the time she turns around, it's too late. The needle has already gone into her neck. She looks at the black mask covering her attacker's face, but it doesn't matter; she knows who it is.

She falls limply into his arms. "It's nice to see you again, Eve."

Erin

The office is blessedly quiet. I quickly lose myself in projects. The work I did at Eve's is uploaded and updated with the finish selections Lee left for me. The ability to have control over something is quite a change from the last few days, and I find it comforting.

Walking to the conference room for the regular Tuesday staff meeting, Sherry catches up to me. "Hey, you. What happened yesterday? You ok? It's been so long since we've gone on one of our lunchtime shopping sprees that it feels like you're breaking up with me."

I look at my long-time friend. We went through design school together. It was a second career for her, but I was just a kid. Still, we hit it off and have been friends ever since. It's been great to have her as a friend. After losing my mom so young, I was sort of lost navigating adulthood. Sherry has always offered sound advice when needed without the overbearing meddling that family can sometimes involve.

As her kids and I got older, she would show me pictures of her grandkids from Michigan and lament about not seeing them enough. Then she got the idea to tease me about having babies that she could see all the time. After the attack, she visited me in the hospital and is one of the few that know what happened. Since then, she doesn't tease me anymore.

I whisper back, "I'm sorry, Sherry. I've been hiding since Sam's wedding. After that mess a month ago, things have gotten worse… They let Jack out Saturday."

"Oh, honey." She wraps me in a warm hug, and we take our seats for the meeting. "Where are you staying?" Before I can answer, Lee speaks up, indicating the meeting has started. I whisper to Sherry, "Let's do lunch today, and I'll catch you up." She nods, and we turn our attention to Lee.

After the meeting, Lee follows me to my office. He offers me a hug and fresh coffee. "Got time for an update?"

"Sure, I've finished the space plan, finish plan, and the elevations." I show him the new plans and tell him that the specification writing has already commenced. Once that's done, he leans back and crosses his arms. "Now, the real update."

I fill him in on everything that's happened since Saturday night. "I'm hoping to have some answers about all these fuckups today.

Regardless of what I find out, I can't stay with Detective Peyton forever. I'm going to have my security improved and move back home. McKenzie is working to get restrictions placed on Jack, and I'll get a restraining order as well… And… that bodyguard…"

My phone beeps with an incoming message. "Hang on. This could be news. It's Detective Peyton."

"New info. Please come home right now."

"Lee, I'm going to have to take an early lunch. Could you tell Sherry I owe her lunch tomorrow?"

"Sure, sweetie."

Walking to my car, I begin thinking of my home security, then of Nate's offer to help beef it up. I still have to call him. Maybe we can discuss the security after I tell him everything… that is, if he doesn't run away.

When I pull into the village, I get a bad feeling in the pit of my stomach. I've had one before, and I ignored it. It turned out to be the biggest mistake of my life. Deciding not to ignore this one, I pull into a parking spot in the Village and open the messaging app on my phone. "On my way. Should I bring lunch for you and Matthew?"

I hold my breath for the reply after using the bogus name.

"No. he ran out and picked up a pizza."

I fight down the rising panic. No! Please, not

Eve. I pick up my phone and call Mike. Before he can speak, I'm screaming, "Jack has Eve! You've got to get to her house right now! Please, he'll hurt her!"

"Erin, what's going on? Where are you?"

"I got a text saying to come home right now. Something didn't feel right, so I texted her asking about lunch for her and Matthew. I got a reply from her phone saying that *Matthew* picked up a pizza. It's a trap. He's there, and he's going to hurt her. You've got to do something!"

"Erin, listen to me. Do not go to Eve's. If it is Jack, I don't want you anywhere near there. Where are you?"

"I'm in the village."

"Go to the village police station. I'll call this in. Stay with the officers. Do not go anywhere alone."

I put my car in park and dash across the pavement to the station. I burst through the doors and scare the receptionist half to death. "Detective Mike McKenzie from Homewood PD is calling in a hostage situation on East Fairway Drive. I can get your officers through the security there."

I know Mike wants me to stay here, but he can just be pissed at me. I'll stay with the officers, but I am going to help Eve.

The receptionist sits there, shell-shocked, and doesn't move. I open my mouth to yell at her again, but loud sounds coming from the back stop me. Apparently, the word from Mike has just come in as a few officers and plainclothes rush out into the reception area. The desk cop shouts to them about what I said, and one of the plain-clothes officers comes up to me. "I should leave you here, but I promised McKenzie that you wouldn't leave my sight. Since my partner isn't here, I have no choice but to go to the scene. So, you're going to have to come with me. Stay behind me at all times." He gently grips my elbow and we rush out after the other officers.

Given that the house is just through the trees, I lead them across the street, and they surround the house. The officer that is still holding my arm silently leads me around to the front of the house where the door is standing wide open.

Through the opening, I can see a bloody Eve tied to a chair in the middle of the entry hall. Her head is bowed, and I pray that she's just unconscious. The cop senses that I'm about to scream or take off running to her. He covers my mouth and wraps an arm around my waist. I should be hyperventilating at the alien touch, but can only focus on the pool of blood under Eve. The cop leans down and whispers in my ear. "Settle down. She's alive; I can see her chest moving. Let these guys clear the house so we know it's safe to enter. I've already got an ambulance on the way."

The strong man pulls me away to near the front sidewalk and introduces himself as Det. Nick Owens. It seems like it's taking an eternity for the police to clear the house.

My guardian turns to me, "Who did this? What's going on?" A familiar voice behind me answers. "I suspect that it's a man named Jack Rogers." Mike walks into view and gestures to me with his chin as he continues, "He's after Erin here, who is in the protective custody of Detective Peyton." He turns fully to the Village detective, "Nick, tell me where Eve is."

The familiar way in which Mike addresses det. Owens tells me they know each other. Mike takes a step toward the house and Det. Owens puts his hand on Mike's chest. "Mike, we've spotted her, but we can't move until the house is cleared." As soon as Owens gets that out, one of the uniforms jogs up to the man, "Detective, there's no one else here."

Just then, the ambulance pulls up. Mike stares at it for a second, then looks back to Owens before running to the open door, "EVE!" The local detective runs after him, and I follow suit.

Mike is kneeling beside Eve when I reach the door. I see the devastation on his face as he lifts her hair to look in her eyes. He carefully touches her face and is whispering to her.

I look away from the scene, the pain of what I brought to her weighing heavily on me. The emergency medical team finally makes it inside and shoves Mike out of the way.

I don't know what the extent of her injuries are and start to ask, but Owens pulls me back out of the house. Realizing what is happening, Mike thunders, "NO! Let her go! She stays with me!"

We watch as the medics cut Eve's ties and gingerly lift her to the gurney. When they lay her down, they assess her abdomen and face. From where I stand, I see three fingers on her left hand have been splinted, and various gashes have been bandaged.

Looking over her bloody and battered body, my eyes fill thinking about what must have happened. She was tortured, made vulnerable for the sole purpose of getting to me. When my eyes reach her bruised face, her eyes are open and trained on me. She whispers, and I have to get close to hear, "Talk to him. You need his help." She turns to the other side, "Mike." The paramedics let him come to her side, and he caresses her face. "I'm right here, Eve."

I continue to watch as Eve is carefully strapped down. The paramedics announce they're ready to leave and load Eve into the ambulance. One turns to Mike. "Detective McKenzie, we're headed to UAB. You can follow us there."

Mike calls into the back, "Eve, I'll be right behind you." Then he drags me back to Detective Owens. Once we're standing beside him, Mike gets nose-to-nose with me, "You call those Rangers. This fucker isn't playing." At Owens' confused look, Mike grabs his shirt to pull him close and explains, "She's got a protective detail coming. A couple of Army Rangers named…" He looks expectantly at me for their names, so I supply them, "Erickson and Maxwell." Mike looks back to Owens and continues, "She doesn't leave your station without them."

Owens nods, "Got it."

The ambulance pulls out, sirens blaring, and Mike takes off running for his car.

Down the street

"That bitch. That beautiful, smart bitch." Jack knew that any reply to Erin's message would be risky, but he didn't expect a test. As soon as the message was sent, he knew he'd fucked up. He saw it in the detective's eyes when he asked her who Matthew was. Realizing he had been made, Jack took the only play he had and ran out of the house. Thirty seconds more and he would have been stuck in the house as it was surrounded by police.

Instead, he only watched as they loaded Eve in the ambulance and the others led Erin away.

Feeling oddly proud of his prey, he smiles.

Nate

My forehead is leaning against the cool tile as the hot spray works on the tight muscles in my neck. I hate this feeling. Pre-mission nerves are bad enough, and they only last a couple hours. Worrying about Erin has been going on for two days. I feel like I'm going to snap.

I shut off the water and step out to dry off. As I'm walking into my room, my phone begins to ring. As soon as I see Erin's name on the screen, I'm fully alert again. "Erickson."

"Nate?" She doesn't sound right. I hear a strange noise, then, "Shit, get a chair and some water." All my senses go on high alert at this point.

A tense moment passes before a male voice comes over the phone, "This is Detective Nick Owens from Crestline PD. Who is this?"

"Nathaniel Erickson."

"Ranger Captain Erickson?"

"The same. What's happened?" As he speaks, I'm throwing on my jeans and shoes.

"There's been an incident involving

Homewood Detective Eve Peyton. Her partner has requested a protective detail for Ms. Erin Westin. I need you and Captain Maxwell to report to me immediately. We're at the Crestline police station."

"We'll be there in forty minutes."

I grab a shirt and run out to alert Hyper. I find him in the kitchen, putting away some bottled water. "Hype, we've got to go. Something's happened." He stops what he's doing and immediately heads to the door. "Is Erin ok?"

"I don't know."

"Where is she?"

"Crestline PD." He tosses me the keys, "You drive. I'll navigate."

I'm flying down the interstate, through the mid-day traffic and we make it in thirty minutes. It seems Crestline is a very high-end suburb of Birmingham; not at all what I was expecting.

In Crestline

Jack waits in a rented Audi SUV on a side street in Crestline Village. With those pain in the ass detectives out of the game, he only has to wait for Erin to walk out of the station and follow.

As he's waiting for Erin to emerge from the station doors, a Range Rover skids into the station lot and a very angry-looking man gets out. It's the same asshole from yesterday…

wait… he's not alone. "Who the hell are these guys? Whoever they are, they're really starting to piss me off." Jack starts the engine and pulls out to leave the area. Turning left on the cross street, he drives past the market where he spots Erin's car. Making a quick decision, he pulls in an open spot beside her and slips a GPS tracker under her back wheel well. Time to regroup.

Nate

When Hyper and I walk into the reception area of the Crestline station, we don't even give our names before the receptionist picks up the phone and says, "Detective Owens, the Rangers are here."

A tall man with blond hair and dark blue eyes walks into the room a moment later. He eyes us warily for a second, then says, "I'm Detective Owens. Can I see your military IDs?" We hand them over, and he gives them a cursory glance. His nonchalance makes me question his abilities until he walks over and asks the receptionist to check them out. That's better.

Hyper must come to the same conclusion as he decides to engage the man, "What happened Detective?"

"First of all, I'm only talking to you because McKenzie is a friend of mine and he vouches for you. He called in a hostage situation at a nearby house, involving his partner, Det. Eve Peyton. Before the call from him came in, Ms. Westin had shown up here claiming the same thing. Mike said he wanted her to stay here, but she said she could deal with the home's security.

I sent several officers ahead to surround the house, and I escorted Ms. Westin around front. When we arrived, we found Det. Peyton, badly beaten, on display in the entryway. We checked the house, but no one else was there. When Mike showed up and saw the shape Eve was in, he decided to follow the ambulance to the hospital. His last instructions before he left were that Ms. Westin could only be released to your custody. Not officially, but as her protective detail."

Hyper and I exchange a glance. This guy's made of some bad shit if he's going to stage an attack on a cop across the street from a police station.

The receptionist walks up and hands our IDs back. "They check out." Owens nods and leads us into the bullpen. He stops outside a closed door and looks solemnly at us. In a lowered voice, he tells us, "Detective Peyton was tortured. Why, I don't know. McKenzie says it was a trap for Ms. Westin, but that doesn't make sense to me. I've learned that Ms. Westin had been staying with Peyton and would have returned after work anyway."

"It's something we see in combat. A soldier is always on alert, but when you receive a distress call and see an injured friend, the natural reaction is to zero in on them, breaking your situational awareness, and making you vulnerable to ambush."

He scrubs his hand over his shadowed jaw, "If you and McKenzie are right, then what does this fucker want with Ms. Westin?"

I look to Hyper. It's become painfully clear that this whole situation is much more than we imagined. Hyper answers, "It appears as though only Ms. Westin can answer that. If it's all right with you, we'll get her out of here, get her looked over, and check in with McKenzie." It's obvious that he's not happy letting us leave without more information. I figure he's only doing it because he's got some assurances from the other detective.

"You just tell him to keep me in the loop." He opens the door, and Erin stands up. Seeing her safe after fearing the worst is like a sucker-punch to the gut. I want to grab her and run away, but I'm certain she wouldn't appreciate the display.

She lunges toward the door. "How is she?"

"We don't know anything yet." I turn to Owens. "I won't tell you where we're going, but here's my number. You won't be able to trace it."

When we walk out of the station, Erin turns in the opposite direction of the parking lot. "Whoa, whoa, whoa. Where are you going?" I jog over to where she is. "My car. It's still parked at the market." Hyper says, "Give me your keys." Her eyes narrow to angry slits at his demand, and she looks poised to argue. Before she has the chance, Hyper speaks up, "Erin, he got to the cop." He holds out his hand to Erin expectantly; still, she hesitates before finally handing them over.

Hyper turns to me and says, "You know where I'll be." I nod and add, "We won't be far behind."

As Hyper is walking away, I grab Erin's hand and head to the truck. It's a short walk filled with horrifying images of what could have happened if this man had gotten his hands on her. I don't know who he is, but if he's bold enough to attack a cop fifty yards from a police station, he's one dangerous bastard.

Reaching the passenger side of my truck, my nerves get the best of me. I wheel her around and pull her to me, wrapping my arms around her. I bury my nose in her hair and breathe in the scent of her till the tension coiled inside begins to melt away.

I've flirted and teased her plenty, but have never made a move on her before. The only reason I'm doing it now is because today scared the shit out of me. Surprisingly, she doesn't pull away, but grips me just as tightly. It seems that she's just as shaken as I am, realizing how different the situation could have turned out.

When I feel the choking fear fade away, I lean back to look at her face. She's not crying, but her eyes are red. I brush her hair out of her face, "You're all right, Chief."

She shakes her head. "He could have killed her." I grip her chin, forcing her to look square at me. "He could have killed you."

Worked up all over again, I pull her to me again for a moment before releasing her to help her into the truck. My knuckles are white as I climb in and grip the wheel. I have got to calm myself down. She's under my protection now, and I'm going to find out what it is I'm protecting her from.

Finally on the move, I mention, "I'm sure you're not going to be able to get your stuff from the cop's house. Do I need to take you to your place to get some things?"

"If it's all right with you, I'd rather check on Eve." That's not surprising. I nod in agreement and ask, "Where did they take her?"

"UAB." Of course. I'm not from anywhere near here, but I know that hospital well by now. "We're spending way too much time there lately," I say as I pull out of the parking lot.

Chapter 8
Nate

On the way to UAB, Erin calls McKenzie to find out where Eve is. We make it through the maze of hallways to her door to find that there's an officer on guard. As we approach, the officer stiffens his stance. "McKenzie is expecting us."

"Name?"

"Erickson and Westin."

The officer turns and knocks on the door. After a short wait, Mike answers and lets us in.

Erin rushes in, ignoring Mike and another man on her way to the lady detective who appears to be sleeping. I'm about to ask McKenzie what he's learned when I notice the other man's face. He's not happy that Erin ignored him and is moving in behind her too slowly and too quietly.

This pisses me off for two reasons. One, I don't want another man touching her. And, two, she is jumpy around men and him stalking up behind her will freak her the hell out.

I swiftly move between them as I speak her name to keep from startling her. She turns at my voice and notices the other man for the first time. Her face registers recognition, then quickly turns to anger. "Officer Travis."

"Detective Travis," he corrects her as he side-steps me to stand in front of her. "Are you involved in this little dust-up today? If you are, I have some questions for you." As he finishes his little announcement, his eyes travel up and down the length of her. She bristles at his tone and his wandering eyes.

To draw his attention or his ire, I cut him off by sticking my hand out as if to introduce myself. "I'm Nathaniel. Erin's boyfriend." I steal a glance at Erin, but she doesn't object. Apparently, she's glad this guy's attention is off her for the moment. To make sure it stays that way, I continue, "Are you with the Crestline Police Department?" He reluctantly takes my hand and engages me. "Well, no. I'm in the same precinct as McKenzie and Peyton."

"She probably better take a rain check then." His face begins to turn red, but I've no intention of giving him a chance to object. "After all, this is Crestline Detective Owens' case, and I'm sure he'll want to be the first to take statements from any of us."

He's so angry that his face appears mottled. Mission accomplished, I turn around to face Peyton, essentially dismissing the prick. Not even a second passes before I hear him stomp off towards McKenzie and whisper something. Soon after that, the door closes behind him.

Peyton looks up at me and lifts the brow over the uninjured eye, "Boyfriend?" I smile in return and shrug my shoulder, "Nice job playing dead. He didn't look the type to respect an unspoken-for woman."

"You're right. He doesn't."

Mike joins us around the bed, "Now that we're all here… Officially, all that I told Owens is that you were on your way to Eve's house and something didn't seem right, so you called me. Unofficially, he knows about the trap, but has no evidence to indicate this is anything other than a home invasion."

He turns to me then, something akin to respect on his face, "I called you because you've saved her twice now..." At my look of surprise, he adds, "Yeah, I heard all about you and your team last month. It takes a hell of a man to try and save someone even as a knife is shoved in his gut."

The detective reaches into his pocket, pulls out a flash drive, and hands it to Eve. "Eve, this has become so much more than unwanted flowers, and you know our hands are tied. You are going to need some help." He places the drive in Erin's hand and quickly cuts his eyes to me before looking pointedly at Erin. "He needs to know."

Erin drops her head but nods as she pockets the flash drive.

McKenzie turns to me one last time. "She's hardheaded and strong-willed. She's not weak or fragile, and you'd better not treat her like she is." He pauses, then adds, "I will kick your ass if you fuck up."

"I would expect no less."

There's a knock at the door, and a cheery nurse walks in with a cart. "Time for vitals and some pain medication."

Erin reaches for Eve's good hand and gives it a small squeeze. "I'm sorry this happened to you."

Eve stares right back at Erin with fire in her eyes. "Don't. I'll be fine." She turns that fiery gaze on me and says, "Make sure *he* won't be." Part of me is shocked that she said that out loud, in front of her partner. It isn't anything I wasn't thinking, but she should be more careful.

The nurse, ready with her equipment and pills, shoos us out of the way, and we decide it's time to go. McKenzie follows us to the door and says, "Erin, I don't know when I'll be able to go in and get your things from Eve's."

"Don't worry about me. Just make sure she gets better."

"I'll sit on her if I have to. Now, I don't want to know where you're going, but I need a way to get information to you." I pull out a card and write a number on it. "You send a message to this, and I'll contact you."

We say our final goodbyes and leave them to rest. Walking back to the truck, I suggest that we go to her place to pick up some things since hers are stuck at the crime scene. She's adamant about not wanting to go back to her house. "Just take me to Sam's house. I've got spare things there." I can understand her reticence about going back home. She probably feels that it has been violated and no longer feels safe.

An hour-and-a-half later, we're pulling up to the guest house at Chase's place. Hyper walks out to greet us and grabs the bag that Erin's holding. "I've moved my things to the pool house so you can have the spare bedroom here."

"Thanks." She looks embarrassed and relieved at the same time.

Hyper moves to leave, but I stop him with a hand on his shoulder. In a voice only loud enough for him to hear, I say, "Have a seat. I think we might be about to learn just what we're up against."

I take the rest of Erin's things to her room and find her sitting on the bed. Uninvited, I sit down beside her. She's silent for a long while, and I wait patiently.

She sighs and says, "I guess it's time to welcome you to my nightmare." She pulls the flash drive out of her pocket and studies it. "I can't look you in the eye and tell you this story. This should have everything you need to know." She thrusts the drive at me, and I wrap my fingers around her hand, holding on for a moment. Without a word, I release her hand and leave the room, stopping for my laptop on the way back to Hyper.

Back in the living room, I show him the drive and motion for him to follow me into the kitchen. I don't think Erin can hear us in the living room, but I don't want to take any chances.

We sit down at the table, and I plug in the drive. The only thing on it is a folder labeled Case File:152836-PM. The numbers don't mean anything, but when I open it, there are several other folders; witness interviews, hospital reports, detectives' notes, DA charges… I was never enthusiastic about learning Erin's past, but now, I've got this sick feeling building in my gut.

I look at Hyper, and he just shrugs his shoulders. "Where do we start?" I ask. He answers, "I guess with witness statements."

I open that file, and the first thing I notice is a file named; Samantha Taylor. This shit feeling I have just got worse. I open the file, and we begin to read. What I find there knocks the wind out of me. It's all I can do to stay seated. I clench and release my fists the whole time I'm reading, but it does nothing to calm the growing rage. I force myself to read Sam's entire statement, but that's all I can handle.

Hyper notices my distress and offers, "You know the what and the who. Why don't you let me sift through the rest?" Grateful for the reprieve, I get up and grab a bottle of water from the fridge.

I walk outside and try to figure out what to do next. I mean, I was in the Middle East. I saw women that were viciously gang-raped, only to be beaten or killed by their families for their impurity. Those victims that survived were never the same again.

This explains why Erin is vigilant about self-defense and is nervous around strange men. It doesn't explain why she was determined to hide this from me. Analyzing her actions brings back McKenzie's words at the hospital. *She's strong... not weak.*

Like a ton of bricks, it hits me. She's not a victim. She was victimized, but she refuses to wear that title. She's afraid that once people know what happened to her, all they'll see is the victim. That's why she's been hiding it from me. She doesn't want me to see her that way.

That's total bullshit though. Anybody that looks at that woman and thinks "victim" is a fucking moron. She's made of some tough shit; tougher than many soldiers I know. I'm convinced that she's tougher than me, and I'm done pussyfooting around her.

With a determined set to my jaw, I rush through the door and the house, back to her room. I knock twice before throwing open the door, but she doesn't acknowledge my presence.

I march right up to her and spin her around. Lifting her chin so she's forced to meet my gaze, I give her one second before I claim her mouth. Taken completely by surprise, she's slow to react.

I slide my arms around her and pull her

flush against me. Her body feels like every wish I've ever made. When her arms reach up and pull me closer, I deepen the kiss.

I'd rather cut my own hand off than let go of her, but I have to pull back so that I can get a read on her emotions. Her brow furrows because I stopped, but before I take this any further, I have to know, "Is he... what he did, the reason you pushed me away? If it isn't, tell me to stop right now." The hope I see in her eyes is all the answer I need, but I need her to say it for her own benefit.

"Those that knew... I didn't want you to look at me like everybody else does."

That's all it takes. My mouth crashes down on hers again, and I make it clear that her past means exactly shit to me. Her body relaxes against mine, but only for a second. Then suddenly, it seems as though everything she's been holding in for the last month bursts free and she becomes wild.

A thought briefly crosses my mind before I get lost in her kiss; this woman owns me.

Erin

Damn him. For the last month, I've been wishing this moment would never happen.

Erin! Run!

I tried so hard to push him away. Even so, when he was dying on my floor, his only thought was to save me. That's when I fell for him; only to face off with a killer in the next breath.

When we both survived that day, I should have stopped running. Several times I nearly let myself reach out for him, but the eventuality of Jack's release would cross my mind, and I would gather up my defenses again. I couldn't stand the thought of something happening to Nate, so I continued to keep him at arm's length.

Now, as hard as I tried to hide my past from the world, people are being hurt because of me. And, Nate is seeing every awful thing on that flash drive.

Expecting the worst, I prepare myself for our next encounter. He'll be ready with his kid-gloves and his platitudes and hang a do-not-touch sign on my neck. Well, Eve was right. "You could lose him either way, but you certainly will if you keep locking him out."

It's only been a few short minutes when I hear a knock at my door. Without invitation, it opens, and I'm being spun around.

I expected to see pity or disgust in his eyes. I did not expect to see raw hunger. He doesn't give me any time to process what's happening. He claims my mouth and pulls me hard against him.

This is a mistake, there's no way he's had time to review what's on that drive. He'll kiss me, then regret it after he learns about Jack. At least, that's what I expect to happen.

Suddenly, he pulls back and studies my face. "Is he… what he did, is that the reason you pushed me away? If it isn't, tell me to stop right now." Oh god. He does know… and he… still… he's not treating me like I'm damaged.

I don't want to say anything; to chance ruining the moment. The relief I feel is dizzying, and I can barely hold myself up. I glance up, and the look on his face is sobering. He is telling me that if Jack is the only reason I'm holding back, then it's not reason enough. When I tell him that, yes, Jack was the reason, he again greedily claims my lips. This time, I let him know just how much I've been holding back.

When Nate pulls back again, I'm breathless. He reaches up and wipes away tears I wasn't aware had fallen.

"You are not what happened to you. It might have changed you, but it is not who you are. And, fuck anybody that thinks otherwise. Now, let's go and talk to Hyper. We've got some planning to do."

Feeling lighter than I have in years, I take his hand and allow him to lead me through the house.

Hyper is sitting in the kitchen with his back to us, pouring over the files from Mike. "Squid, based on these medical reports and Erin's account, the drug in her system means she has no memory of the…" He's just turned around to find that Nate's not alone and stops mid-sentence. He jumps up so fast that his chair goes crashing to the floor. "Oh, fuck, Erin. I'm sorry. I didn't…"

I hold up my hand. "Now, don't you start. You just read that I have no memory of the attack. If you start handling me with kid gloves, I'll shoot your balls off." Predictably, both men flinch. Hyper kind of squeaks and complains, "Damn. Couldn't you have started with kicking my ass and work up from there?"

"Not my style."

He clears his throat, "Back to work then. Tell us what's not in these files."

Deep breath. I give myself a mental pep talk, then take a seat at the table. You can do this, Erin. "I met Jack at a trade conference. He was a rep for one of the flooring companies exhibiting that day."

I continue with the story the same way I had told the detectives four years ago, then pick up where the files left off. "The judge set bail, and Jack got out. Within a couple hours, the first flowers arrived at my house."

Hyper has been furiously scribbling notes, but stops and looks up, "The same flowers that were on your porch Saturday night?"

"The same. Until the trial, I would find the flowers at my home and my office. When I moved out of my house and in with Sam, it didn't take long before they were delivered there as well. Eve and Mike knew, but since he wasn't textbook stalking me, there wasn't anything they could do. Eve told me to do what I needed to protect myself, so I bought a gun and took shooting and self-defense classes."

I pause and take a deep breath. Nate jumps up and gets a bottle of water from the fridge and hands it to me. After a sip, I continue.

"After the joke of a trial, Jack was only given five years." I shake my head, remembering the look in the DA's eyes. "I was supposed to be notified before his release became imminent; as were Eve and Mike. That obviously didn't happen. So, Jack was released a year early, without notification, without requirement to register as a sex-offender, and is now in the wind. Eve found out Saturday and tried several times to reach me. As you witnessed, I finally saw her message about fifteen minutes before finding the flowers and card."

Both men swear, and Nate jumps up and begins to pace. "I can find this guy...."

Hyper calls him, "Squid."

"...should be easy. I've got..."

"Nate." Once again, Hyper's attempt to get Nate's attention fails.

"...surveillance, financials..."

"CAPTAIN ERICKSON! Stand down!"

Nate looks up then.

"You know we can't do that. We're not hunting insurgents here. This is an American citizen that the courts have decided has paid his debt. We go down that road and get caught, we're in deep shit with the Army. If that happens, Erin's here without back-up."

"He's right, Nate. It's just like before. He hasn't done anything that we can prove, so no one can touch him." He doesn't look convinced so Hyper tries again, "We can't go after him. I hate it, but until he tries something, we're powerless."

Nate lashes back at Hyper, "He's already tried something! You didn't see what he did to Peyton!"

"Shit. Man, you know what I'm talking about. You're so far out of range on this. You're not thinking straight. You've got to focus. We'll do our jobs right, this guy will fuck up, and we'll put him down."

Nate scrubs a hand over his face. He's still on edge but sits back down beside me.

Hyper stands and picks up my keys. "It's been a shit day. I'm going to take Erin's car and be seen around Homewood. The windows are tinted dark, and I want to see if I pick up any tails. I'll report in later and bring back some food." He walks out the door, not waiting for any argument.

Once he's gone, I don't know what to do with myself. I feel out of sorts. The worst parts of my life have been excised and are on display.

Yes, Nate held and kissed me passionately *after* finding out about what Jack did. But now, he's angry and all over the place. He hasn't even looked at me since I finished filling in the blanks.

Feeling raw and exposed, I stand, wanting to hide away in my room. I take one step and hear a strained voice say, "Don't."

Nate grabs my hand. "Don't push me away again." He looks up at me, and I see no pity in his eyes. It's pain I see in those depths. He is hurting for me; for what I went through, and is afraid I'll shut him out again.

He really isn't like anyone I've ever known. I'm filled with a desire to know the depths of this man. I move back to him and stand between his knees. The pain that was so evident on his face slowly turns to desire. Sensing my intentions, he leans back, and I lower myself to straddle his lap. He reaches for me and pulls me against his chest, and we stay like that for a long while.

After what feels like an hour, I sit up and grasp his face in my hands. Who is this man that is willing to fight to keep me safe? I stare into his eyes as though I'll find the answer there. Finding nothing, I decide I don't need an answer and softly touch my lips to his.

Nate lifts his hands to grip my hips and pulls me forward. My hands move from his face to his shoulders as his tongue teases the seam of my lips. I open up to him and desire, hidden away long ago, comes raging back as never before.

I press myself against him and inwardly groan at the sensations coursing through my body. Oh, how I've missed this; being held and touched. The thought has me pulling back. "This feels good. Too damn good." I'm not sure if it's him or just that it's been five years since I've... been close to anyone. "Is it you or am I that desperate?"

I feel the laughter vibrating his chest. "I know one way to find out." He slides his hand around the back of my neck and pulls me back down to him. The man can kiss. And, when his expert lips move to my neck, it's no time at all before he finds a sensitive spot that was long since forgotten.

Within seconds, my insides are melting. Yes, this feels way too damn good, and yes, it has been a long time, but it's definitely Nate that has my body singing.

Nate shifts his position, and his hungry mouth returns to my neck as his hand moves just under the hem of my shirt.

As the heat from his hand sears my bare back, he presses against me, and I lie back on the sofa.

In this position, I begin to get these flashes in my head. They're like a horrible sense of déjà vu. I hear moaning and grunting and feel helpless. In an instant, I'm fighting to escape; lashing out in fear. "Stop! Don't! Let me go!" I'm clawing and wrestling for my freedom; hearing nothing but screaming in my head.

The next thing I know, I'm crashing into the floor, struggling to draw in enough air. Someone is calling my name, but it seems far away. After a few times, I realize I know that voice. Slowly, I look up and see Nate standing across the room. He looks like he's seen a ghost. At that moment, everything comes rushing back. We were… and then… oh, god.

Mortified, I cover my face and apologize, "Nate." I let out a sob. "Nate, I'm sorry."

He rushes over and picks me up off the floor. Sitting back on the sofa, he pulls me into his lap and presses my head against his chest. "Erin, no. God, I'm the one that's sorry. I didn't think. Are you all right? What happened?"

"I don't know. It's never happened before. It was you, then it was like I was trapped in a nightmare and it wasn't you anymore."

"Did I do something to scare you? Has this ever happened with another lover?"

"I don't know, no. I've not been with anyone since… I've had nightmares before, but not during the day. Not like this."

"These nightmares, are they just nightmares, or is it possible they could be memories?"

"I don't know that either. I've assumed they were just nightmares since the doctors told me I likely wouldn't remember what happened."

"Well, maybe…" Nate's phone begins to ring, interrupting him. Hyper's name appears on screen, so Nate answers it on speaker. "I've been around Homewood for a while. I haven't picked up anything, so I'm heading back. I'll grab some food on the way back."

"Got it."

After the call, all I want to do is run and hide, but Nate grips me tighter and simply rubs his hand up and down my spine.

Homewood

Jack activates the tracker placed in Erin's car. "What the hell is she doing in Springville?" He pulls up the location on the Google Maps satellite view to see that it's not a densely populated area. There's nowhere to park and watch the property without looking out of place. Looking closer, he spots a dirt road that seems to access the back of the property but decides to wait until nightfall before checking it out.

With a couple hours to kill, he grabs a bite to eat. Jack picks a place and checks his appearance. Satisfied, he goes in and immediately catches the attention of a young, blond waitress. Inwardly, he groans, but pastes on a smile and somehow makes it through dinner without shoving his fork in her throat. She makes it obvious that she's interested, but she doesn't have Erin's long, dark hair or her powerful presence. She's got an annoying, bubbly laugh which is nothing like Erin's melodic sound.

Despite the mismatch, he briefly considers taking her anyway; just to take the edge off. It has been four years. By the end of the meal, he decides she's not worth it and is just grateful to not have to listen to her anymore. In his car, he pinches the bridge of his nose to release some of the pressure, then checks the tracker again. He instantly perks up when he sees her car pinging in Homewood.

Jack cranks the car and turns in the direction of her signal. The bitch at the restaurant left him edgy, and he is aching to get his hands on Erin. He'd even settle for getting a glimpse of her tonight. He tells himself, "Not too close, Jack. She'll be too much on alert today. Just a look. That's all you get."

By the time he catches up to her signal, she's pulling into the Publix parking lot. Perfect. He can easily park and sit without being noticed. Now to find the spot with the best vantage point to see her coming out of the store.

He finds a spot that allows him to see both the entrance and her car. Several minutes are spent watching the door with no sight of her. He begins to get antsy when he spots movement near Erin's car. This big bastard is walking near her car, then… opens her trunk! "What the hell?"

The guy places his bags in the trunk, then turns toward the driver side. This is one of the guys that came to the station today. Jack grips the wheel of his car until his knuckles turn white, and he watches this man drive off in her car.

Confused and angry, Jack decides it's time to get a closer look at things. He doesn't move from his spot for a long while. He wants to see if this man drives the car back to Springville.

Forty-five minutes and three stops later, the signal leaves the Homewood area and eventually takes the on-ramp to I-59 North. "Looks like I'm going into St. Clair County."

Remembering the dirt road and the woods, he looks down at his attire and decides he needs a change if he's going to crawl around in the dirt. He pays a visit to Alabama Outdoors to find what he needs and is climbing back in his car as the sun begins to fade.

Chapter 9

Nate

Seeing Erin afraid and scrambling off the couch hurt as much as that knife to the gut did. I hate that my touch triggered shitty memories for her. And, I'm certain those are memories and not just nightmares.

That reminds me, I need to look over the medical reports. I want to know what drug she was given and how quickly she metabolized it. If she is remembering parts of the attack, it's possible he used two different drugs at two different times.

It's also possible that since her memory has been triggered in a wakeful state, her nightmares could worsen. As much as I want to blame myself for bringing this to the surface, I did not do this to her. These memories would have come out eventually.

What I do know is that I can help her through it. I've worked with enough soldiers with PTSD to know that she can make it. Especially with someone like Sam on her side.

She stopped shaking a while ago but is still on my lap with her head on my shoulder. I want to be careful with her, but McKenzie's words keep coming back to me. She's not weak, and I won't allow myself to baby her. I just need to act normal, and right now, normal should be hungry.

"You hungry, Chief?" She doesn't look up, but responds with a weak, "Yeah."

"Come on. Let's set out some plates. Hype should be on his way with some food." Together, we set the table. She's quiet but seems to appreciate me not pressing her.

When Hyper returns, we all sit down to eat. I determine to keep the conversation light considering Erin looks wrung out. Hyper and I share stories about Chase and the rest of our group. Erin talks about Sam and someone named Cle. If I'm not mistaken, there was a Cle at Sam and Chase's wedding. Hyper perks up at the mention of this Cle woman and even begins to ask questions about her... Interesting. Erin tells us that she's CIA. Impressive.

Once dinner has been cleared away, Hyper excuses himself to the pool house for the night, and Erin excuses herself to take a shower. I take the opportunity to set the security system and check the motion detectors I used to create a hundred-foot perimeter around the guest house.

House secure, I plant myself on the couch and turn on some music. Nothing seductive, just soothing. It's been a shit day, and we could both use some chill.

I'm going through the medical reports in the files McKenzie gave her when Erin walks in the room. She's dressed in grey leggings, and an oversized sweatshirt that says Roll Tide across the front and her damp hair hangs in a long braid. Her eyes are downcast, and her mood is subdued. I can't handle that. It's not at all like the Chief that I know.

"Come here so I can kick your ass."

That catches her attention. Her eyes are on fire as they drill into me. "Excuse me?" I pull out a deck of cards and a jar of pennies the guys and I play with on occasion. God, I hope this works. "Let's go, Chief."

She juts out her hip and crosses her arms across her chest. "What makes you think I know how or want to play poker?"

"Oh, come on. It's the South and you were raised by your dad, a Navy man. You know how to play, so sit your ass down." The corners of her lips turn up just enough to know that I've got her. She walks over and picks up the cards, then sits down and begins to shuffle like a card shark.

We play long enough for me to learn that I never want to play her for more than pennies. And, long enough that all the stress of the day is no longer weighing down her shoulders.

At eleven, she yawns, and I suggest we turn in. "I'll be in the room right across the hall, and my door will be open if you need me."

"Nate… thank you." She kisses me on the cheek and walks to her room, but hesitates by the door as if she can't decide what to do.

She eventually does go in but leaves her door open as well.

The guy at Alabama Outdoors was incredibly helpful outfitting Jack with the right apparel and gear for a night hunt.

Jack makes a quick stop at the untraceable house owned by one of his family's shell corporations. There, he switches into his new hunting fatigues and moves all his gear to the truck. All except for the deer urine the guy sold him. Jack only bought it to keep up his cover story. He told the guy that his gear was stolen and he needed to replace everything except his guns. To that end, a hunter *not* buying something to mask his scent would have appeared suspicious.

Jack makes the drive to Springville and finds the dirt access road he spotted on the satellite view. Once he's satisfied that his truck is hidden from street view, he steps out and dons his gear. Night vision, binoculars, and a listening device he had stashed away with some money, IDs, and other things.

Jack walks into the woods and takes up a position behind a fallen tree on the northwest corner of the property. He has a clear line of sight to all three of the structures the satellite view showed but is closest to the guesthouse since it's the most likely candidate. Beyond the main house, there's what appears to be a pool house and a small guest house at the edge of the woods. Now for the hard part… waiting patiently.

After about an hour, he sees the big guy from earlier leave the guest house and walk across the property. The man enters the pool house and turns out the lights. So, it's just Erin and the shorter guy. That makes things a bit easier.

Liking his odds, Jack decides to make his play. He moves back to the truck to collect the rest of his gear and plan his next move. As he turns, he sees a light come on in one of the back rooms of the guest house. A shadow crosses the window, but he can't tell if it was her or not. Liking his proximity to the window, he decides to scope it out before returning to the truck.

As he's creeping closer to get a better look into the window, Jack feels something that shouldn't be there. He briefly turns on the flashlight he's carrying and looks around. A fucking tripwire? Who are these assholes? Alarms start going off in his head, and he turns and runs full tilt back to his truck.

He jumps in the cab; thankful he had the forethought to back the truck down the rutted road. "Dammit!" Gravel flies as he careens down the makeshift road.

Nate

"What the hell?" My phone is sounding off that one of my wires has been tripped. I open my computer to check the cameras, but the battery light is blinking. "Shit! Dammit!" I never plugged it back in after sifting through Erin's files.

I pull out the back-up battery from my pack and shove it in the port. By the time I pull up my surveillance systems, there are no motion signatures detected. It could've just been an animal, or it could have been a zombie hoard, and I'd have no fucking way of knowing.

As much as I want to put on my night vision and check it out, it would mean leaving Erin alone, and there's no way I'm chancing that.

I plug in the laptop and opt for leaving it on through the night. If I get another alarm, I'll call Hyper to stay with Erin so I can do a sweep. Otherwise, I'll check out the area at first light.

Sometime later, an unfamiliar sound wakes me. It sounds like it's coming from Erin's room. I climb out of bed and walk quickly, yet silently, to her open door.

With the moonlight spilling in through her window, I can see her clearly. She's tossing around on her bed in obvious distress. After a moment, she sits up with a gasp, and I call out to her. "You ok, Chief?"

She jumps but doesn't scream out in fear. "Yeah. It was just another nightmare."

"You want to talk about it?"

She sits there and stares out the window for a beat before she answers. "It was different than the others. Usually, I only get impressions of… of… being under someone and scared. This was worse."

"It could be a memory. I've got an idea." I make my way to her bed and shoo her over so I'll have some room to sit. Picking up her phone, I grab her finger and use it to unlock the screen, earning me a side-eye stare. I find the voice app and start recording.

Erin nods her head in understanding and begins, "In the dream, I'm at my old house. Jack is there, and I'm angry that Sam is running late. I've been handed a glass of wine, but want to keep my wits about me and only take a couple of small sips. When he's not looking, I pour the rest into a plant. Pretty soon, I start to feel funny, but I'm in control. He must believe that I drank it all and feels comfortable enough to start talking. The things he's saying… they're awful. He mentions a brother, Spencer. And, that Spencer is living it up waiting for us in Hilton Head. I don't know what that means, but I don't like the sound of it. I reach for my phone to call Sam, but he knocks it out of my hand. That's when I begin fighting, and he realizes I'm not incapacitated enough. In our fight, we fall to the floor, and he grabs my hands and holds them above my head with one of his. With the other, he reaches into his pocket and pulls out a syringe. He uses his teeth to remove the cap and stabs the needle in my thigh. Everything goes black at that point."

"Erin, I'll bet anything that this is a memory. It would explain a couple anomalies I found in the medical report. The part that scares me is what he said about his brother waiting for you. This could be more than an obsessed stalker. We'd better get this to McKenzie first thing in the morning. He'd be able to check into the brother and find a connection. Since they didn't find any family before, it's possible that Jack Rogers isn't the name he was born with."

Erin shudders at the possible implications of this new information. While this could prove to be important, it has disturbed her deeply.

I want to offer to stay with her, but I'm not sure that's the right move. I'm also not sure it would be the wrong one. As hard as it is, I decide the best course of action is inaction. For her to be comfortable with anything tonight, it has to be her decision. I have to be careful how I proceed, "Is there anything I can do?"

"No. I'm sorry I woke you. I'll just try to go back to sleep."

"Sure, Chief." I back out of the room and climb back in my own bed.

For the next half hour or so, I'm pouring over the possible reasons this Jack fucker would be *delivering* Erin to his brother. None of them are good.

Tired of pouring over worst-case scenarios, I'm grateful to hear a sound at my door. Erin moves to my bed, and without a word, I lift the covers in invitation. She climbs in and lays her head on my shoulder. Wrapping my arm around her, I squeeze her to me, and she lays there silently for a while before her breathing changes, and I know she's asleep.

Erin

What is it about this man that makes me feel better? He's a clown, but he's fierce. Arrogant, but caring. Independent, yet protective. And, I've never felt so relaxed as I do tucked under his arm like this.

I wrap my arm around his bare, impressive chest, but he doesn't move. It's amazing and confusing at the same time, but lying here with him like this, I feel all the anger and fear draining away.

The last thoughts I have before falling asleep, are that I could be falling for Nate, and hoping it's not a mistake.

The next time my eyes open, I'm surprised to find that I haven't moved a muscle during the night. Usually, I wake up in the aftermath of Hurricane Erin.

I carefully roll over and stretch out like a cat; scratching my belly. A low growl beside me says, "I can get that for you if you like." With an eye roll, I answer, "I'm good."

"But I'm sure I'd be better."

"Have you always been such a cocky bastard?" I ask as I roll over onto my stomach.

"Only when I was sure I could back it up." With that retort, he pops me on the ass and jumps out of bed. A moment later, I hear the shower running and force myself out of bed.

Back in my room, I find the usual damage from Hurricane Erin that I didn't create in Nate's bed. I straighten everything up and think about work today. I don't want to call in because the 3form rep is supposed to meet me at ten. She's going out of town tomorrow, and I need to get some specs for an unusual installation before she does.

I pull out some simple slacks and top and opt for some black flats. Perfectly normal for work attire, but will stand out compared to my usual power outfits. I head into the bathroom to apply some makeup and assess my tresses. My hair is dry, so I remove the braid and finger the soft waves left. It'll do. Makeup, teeth, and I'm done. Now… coffee.

In the kitchen, I find Nate and Hyper catching up on whatever it is they discuss when I'm not around. Nate looks at me and frowns. I ready myself for the fight, thinking he better not even… "I had hoped you would call in today, but I was prepared in case you didn't."

Wow… It seems he knows me better than I realized. "All I ask is that you follow a few safety protocols." I start laughing, and Nate looks confused. "What's so funny?"

"If Hyper doesn't stop holding his breath,

he's going to pass out." Nate glances his way and bursts out laughing himself. Hyper mumbles something about women and coffee.

"Ok. So, what are my rules?" Since Nate is still laughing, Hyper head-slaps him and begins listing the rules. "Squid will take you to work, and one of us will pick you up. Is there somewhere to eat in your building?" At the negative shake of my head, he continues, "Have something delivered or call one of us."

"Isn't that a little entitled; me calling one of you because I'm hungry?"

"We'll be in Homewood, so no, it's not a big deal. We just don't want you out without one of us right now."

"Not even in a group?"

"I'd rather you didn't. If this guy has balls enough to attack a cop, your friends would be nothing. I'm sure you don't want to risk any of them."

Lee and Sherry's faces pop into mind. "No, I guess not." Nate walks over to hand me a travel cup and squeezes my shoulder. "You ready?"

"Yeah."

On the way in, Nate asks about the projects I'm working on. I point out some of the buildings I've done work in and tell him my favorite story of how during one project, a client made an odd request for a change in one of our renderings.

"What was it?"

"We sometimes place human analogs into 3D models to show scale. One of the client's executives asked that we… shrink… the nose on the human analog."

Nate turns to me looking incredulous. "You've got to be shitting me. Do they not like money?" I shrug my shoulders, "The architect I was working with on the project was having trouble keeping a straight face during the exchange. As soon as we left the meeting, I started cracking jokes. By the time we reached the ground floor of their building, I had him in tears."

"Colorful job you have. Pun intended."

"God, you're so corny."

"God… Wow, I've been promoted. Up until now, I was just a Captain," he says as he pulls under the portico at my building. Groaning, I ask, "How does anyone ever take you seriously?"

He turns serious and says, "I can be persuasive." He then grabs my hand and asks, "Do you trust me?"

Wide-eyed, I stutter, "I… wait. What are you going to do?"

"I need you to trust me."

"You haven't given me any reason not to, so yes, I trust you." With that, he gets out of the truck, walks around to open my door, then reaches for my hand to help me down. I look over and see Lee near the door with Sherry a few steps behind him.

Without warning, Nate pulls me to him and bends me over backward before kissing me passionately… next to this busy Birmingham street.

The sudden change in him paired with the rush of desire brought on by his kiss has short-circuited my brain. When he lets me back up, he whispers in my ear, "Trust me." Nate reaches in for my bag and hands it to me. "Call whenever you're ready to leave." Then with a wink, he's gone.

Lee and Sherry haven't left their positions near the door and are shamelessly gawking. After Nate climbs back behind the wheel, Sherry begins to fan herself, "I need a cigarette." As unsteady as they are, I force my legs to carry me to the door.

Lee decides to join in the teasing, "I want one of those."

"You've already got one. Now, move."

They both follow me to my office, but Lee gives Sherry *a look,* and since he's the boss, she reluctantly walks away.

"Wasn't that the guy…"

"Close the door."

"Oh, shit." He closes the door and takes a seat in one of my guest chairs.

"Jack Rogers was released Saturday without any warning." I stop him from his building outburst. "And, some things have happened since then that have made me nervous. As a precaution, Nate is sticking close for a while."

"Sticking close? Just how close? I've never seen a bodyguard put on a show like that before." When my only response is blinking eyes and a blank stare, his eyes go wide in understanding. "It *was* a show. You think this monster is watching you?" I give him a slow nod. "He's been to my house. I went to stay with one of the detectives, and she was attacked in her home as a means of setting a trap for me."

He stands suddenly and looks worried, casting nervous glances my way. It's odd, he's never behaved like this before.

"Is it… safe for you to be here?"

"With all the security of this building, I'm…" My voice trails off, and my heart breaks the moment I realize what he's asking. What he really wants to know if the people here are safe around me.

As much as it hurts, it's a fair question. I've dealt with more than my fair share of psychos since coming on with this firm. Lee has a company to run and employees whose protection he's responsible for. And, knowing that Jack has been here delivering flowers, the threat is tangible.

"Lee… say what you need to say, and I'll get my things."

He looks as miserable as I feel. "It'll just be a leave of absence."

I drop my head in shame. "I understand. I'm sorry I've put you in this position."

"Dammit, honey. Don't think for a minute I blame you. You'll beat this, and you'll be back." He comes around the desk and pulls me up into a giant hug. It's not fair, but since when has that mattered to my family.

I want to be angry and fight being forced to leave a job that I love, but I can't do that. I love Lee like a brother. Remembering how beaten Eve was; it would kill me if something happened to him or Sherry.

He releases me and looks me in the eye. "I know you're going to be fine and that you'll be back." He leans down to pick up his coffee and messenger bag, then turns for the door.

After he's gone, I look around the office. I'm not the most sentimental person, so there isn't much to pack up. All I have here are the framed accolades on the wall.

I grab an empty paper box and throw those in before sneaking out the back entrance into the main hallway.

Wandering around the lobby, I end up in the building's small coffee shop. I've been sitting here a few hours when I get a text from Nate, "Feel like lunch?"

"Yeah." Within seconds, I receive his reply, "I'll be out front in fifteen minutes."

Chapter 10

Nate

Pulling away from her building this morning was fucking hard after kissing her that way. It was meant to be for show, but I couldn't convince my dick of that. All I wanted to do was toss her back in the truck and run away with her.

It wouldn't have worked though. She would've kicked me in the balls and lectured me about this being her life and her decisions to make.

So, instead of doing I wanted, I climbed my ass back up in the truck and drove away with a raging hard-on. It wasn't that I was trying to torture myself or tease Erin. My hope is that the man after Erin was watching and is enough of the obsessive and jealous type and that he'll come after me for what he sees as poaching on his woman.

To focus myself and help with my… condition, I change the temperature control from heat to cold and drive to Homewood to meet up with Hyper and McKenzie. The address I was given ends up not leading to the station, but an apartment building. The nice kind with a doorman. I walk in and tell the doorman I'm here to see Mike. When I give him my name, he nods. "He's expecting you. Have a good day, sir." I give him a little salute on my way to the elevator.

When McKenzie answers his door, he steps back, and I walk in to see Hyper, Owens, and Peyton sitting there. "Glad to see you looking a little less knocked around." She half-smiles and McKenzie motions for me to sit down.

Owens is the first to speak, "We didn't get shit from Eve's house. No prints, no eyewitnesses, and none of the residents' cameras caught anything. He was wearing a mask so Eve can't make an ID." Noticing her defensive body language, he adds, "Let's say, we don't have an ID that would hold up in court. Mike?"

"Nothing. No prints at Erin's house, the flowers, or the card besides those we can eliminate." He looks back and forth at me and Hyper. "What about you guys? Anything?"

Hyper goes first, "I've been driving her car around town since yesterday just to see if it attracts any attention. So far, nothing." Hyper looks to me. "I've been making some public displays to draw him out or make myself a target." For that, I receive some curious stares, but I shrug them off. "It'd be nice if I could kill him in self-defense. Outside that, I may have something, but I'm not sure how reliable it is."

Four sets of eyes widen, and they wait for me to share. "After reviewing Erin's medical reports and her own accounts of nightmares or flashbacks, it seems as though she could be remembering some useful details about the attack."

Owen's looks suspicious, "How is that possible? I read those same reports."

"Erin told me that the night Jack attacked her, he gave her a glass of wine. She didn't want to become impaired, so she only took a couple of sips and poured the rest into a plant. After several minutes, Jack must have assumed she was out enough to make some incriminating comments. He told her that he had a brother, Spencer, waiting for them in Hilton Head."

There's a chorus of swears in response to the revelation, but I just continue, "It was after this confession that he put his hands on her. He realized he had screwed up when she began to fight back. He subdued her, then pulled out a syringe and injected her with the ketamine. She was out in seconds."

Mike jumps up, visibly upset, "Why the fuck didn't this come out earlier? Did she think we were just playing games?" Assuming the question is directed at me, I give the best explanation I can. "Something triggered a flashback that freaked her out and last night, she woke up screaming and told all this to me. She said she's had vague nightmares of the attack, but never remembered anything specific before. Again, this could be nothing, but it feels solid."

Peyton and McKenzie begin a frenzied conversation between the two of them, then Peyton looks up. "At his arraignment, Rogers showed up with a black eye and scratches on his arms that we didn't see when we arrested him. I wondered how he could have gotten them, being in isolation, but didn't ask because I really didn't care."

Attempting to steer the conversation back to the present, Mike speaks again. "His records showed no family, and he had no priors. And, believe me I looked. It seemed impossible that someone with such a clean record would rape and attempt kidnapping as their first offense, but there was nothing."

Hyper jumps in to say what everyone else is thinking, "Assuming he did, how the hell was this guy able to obtain a solid enough alias that you guys couldn't shred?"

McKenzie looks defeated, "I don't know, but we sure as hell know where to start looking now." He stands and indicates this meeting is over.

Hyper and I walk out together and are silent until we reach the parking lot.

"This isn't just some horny local that's target-locked on Erin."

I blow out a deep breath, "I know… We've got to look at this from another angle. No way some Joe Blow has the connections to secure such an unbreakable identity just for the purpose of stalking a woman. This guy is some kind of pro… and he's patient." All of a sudden, the security breach last night seems more significant. "Hype, last night, something tripped one of my wires, but because of a battery issue, any signature was gone by the time I pulled up my system. Are you sure you haven't picked up a tail?"

Angered by the accusation, he moves to stand toe-to-toe with me. "Watch it, Squid. How do you know he hasn't picked up on you? You're the one that's so distracted that you fucked up your own security system. Maybe I need to be the one guarding Erin. At least I'd be paying attention to what's going on around us instead of watching her ass."

I clench my hands into fists, ready to clock the bastard, but he doesn't back down. During the tense stare-down, I'm reminded how the man in front of me has put his life on the line for me; more than once. "Fuck, but you're right."

I scrub my hand over my jaw and back up a step. "This guy has some serious backing to fool the cops... So, if he's not following you..." As one, we both turn toward Erin's car. Knowing what I'm thinking, Hyper asks, "Is it in your truck?"

"Yeah, I'll get it."

Within minutes, our sweep finds a tracker placed on Erin's car. I pull out my phone and take a picture of it. "What are we dealing with here?"

"Damned if I know. You know what this means though. He already knows about Chase's place. We can't be sure, but this paired with the security breach, we have to assume he's already tried to gain entry there."

I know he's right. "Probably, but I'd still rather take my chances there than anywhere else."

"Agreed. I'll head back to Springville and work on additional security measures. You hang around the city and wait for Erin… Do we leave this thing on or destroy it?"

"I'm thinking that he won't know we've found it. If we leave it, we might be able to use it against him."

As Hyper drives off, I glance down at my watch and see that it's half-past eleven. I pull out my phone and text Erin about lunch. After a brief exchange, I head north through downtown in the direction of her building.

When I pull under the portico, I watch as Erin steps out carrying a white box. What the hell? I open the door intending to round the truck to her side, but she pretty much sprints to the truck and hops in. "Get me the fuck out of here."

"Yes, ma'am." I turn that truck north and get her the fuck out of there.

A few miles down the freeway, I ask, "You want to talk about it?" She's quiet for a moment but eventually answers, "I was asked to take a leave of absence. My presence is putting the other employees in danger."

"That's rough. I'm sorry."

"If I thought what happened to Eve would happen to Lee or someone else there, I'd walk away willingly. So why does being forced out feel so shitty?"

"Because you're a fighter… You want to go to Georgia?"

"Wait. What? What airplane did that jump out of?"

"Well, your immediate calendar just cleared, Sam and Chase will be on base in three days. How about a change of scenery?"

She laughs to herself and thinks about it for a minute. "Why the hell not? Turn around and head to my house. I'll call Mike to see about getting my stuff from Eve's."

"Yes, ma'am." I take the next exit and jump back on the southbound ramp as she's talking to Mike. After she disconnects the call, she turns to me and reports, "He said everything is boxed up and is in his office."

"Great. We'll run by there before heading to your place." Using the steering wheel button, I call up Hyper, "Change of plans, we're going back to base. Get packed up."

"What about Erin?"

I glance her way, "She's coming with us."

By the time we get back to the house in Springville, it's almost three. Erin goes into her room to pack up the few things there. Hyper was packed and ready when we got there.

"What about her car and the tracker?"

"I don't know man. Did you learn anything about it?"

"It's sophisticated, but that's all I know. This is normally your job."

"We'll leave it. I'll call Mike and tell him to come get it. Then, it won't be anywhere near Erin, and we get to be helpful to his investigation."

I head outside and call up Mike. "McKenzie."

"It's Erickson. We're packing up and taking Erin out of here. We located a tracking device on her car, and we're through fucking around in the dark." The detective swears under his breath. "Have you gotten anything useful from the info I gave you this morning?"

"Not yet. It's gonna take some time. I want that tracker."

"I knew you would. I'll text you the address where you can find it... Mike, find him."

"I'm doing my best. That little shit is going to pay for what he did to Eve and Erin."

"Damn straight."

Back inside, I pack up my stuff and equipment, and we're ready to go. While Hyper and I load the bags, Erin stands back and laughs. "Nate, why do you have more stuff than Hyper and me combined?" Hyper pretend-coughs to cover a laugh. For that, he gets an obscene gesture, and Erin gets my petulant face, "It's ass-saving, monster-killing equipment. Now, get in the truck. Hype, we'll check in with you later."

Erin

An hour into the drive, I'm questioning my impulsive decision to leave everything behind to go with this man. "I can't believe I'm running away."

"I don't see it as running away. I see it as choosing a battlefield where you have the most advantage."

"Unfamiliar surroundings. What kind of advantage does that present?"

"You mean besides a shit-load of Army Rangers?"

"Ok, dickhead. Let's try and remember for a second that I haven't spent the last several years on an army base and don't know where soldiers crash or stash women while they're practicing beating the shit out of other soldiers."

Trying not to laugh, I apologize to her, "I'm sorry. I've got a two-bedroom house on base. No one can get within a mile of us without being inspected and having their ID checked by some armed-to-the-teeth guards. As a matter of fact, my house is in the same village as Chase's. You and Sam will be within walking distance of each other when she gets back."

Oh... I hadn't thought of that. When she finds out I'm staying with Nate, she's going to give me all sorts of hell. Of course, when she finds out why I'm staying with Nate, it will be much worse. It will be what it will be, I guess.

When we get to the Fort Benning area, Nate stops at a grocery store so we can pick up a few things. Back at the truck, he sheepishly informs me that he'll need to take my weapon. "Don't look at me like that. Base rules dictate how guns are transported onto the premises; unloaded and secured. You'll get it back anytime we leave the base. Now, hand it over."

I pull it from my holster and release the clip, dropping it in his outstretched hand. After that, I clear the chamber, locking the slide, then hand it over. He opens a safe hidden in the dash and places my M&P Shield in with his Beretta. The ammo goes into a lockbox under his seat. I'm not happy, but I don't appear to have any choice.

After going through the gate and the required security check, finally, we pull into his driveway. It's long since turned dark, and the area is quiet.

His is a small house, but it's got a lot of architectural interest. It's white with a terra cotta tile roof that gables on all four sides. The front porch is screened-in, and there's even something called a sleeping porch in the back.

We get our stuff in the house and sit down to eat the dinner we picked up on the way in. While we eat, he gives me some history about the base and the Rangers. I've never been interested in that kind of thing, but oddly enough, I find it fascinating.

After I've finished eating, I sit back and watch Nate for a while. There are so many questions swirling around my mind, but one keeps coming to the forefront. I draw my knees up to my chest and ask, "Why are you doing all this for me?"

He looks at me as if he's confused by the question, but then I see the hurt on his face. "I would've thought that part was obvious."

"Not to me, it isn't."

He stands and moves to the hallway, pausing with his back to me. "Maybe you should open your eyes sometime."

I'm left sitting there with his words playing on a loop in my head. *Open your eyes... Erin, run!... You're all right, Chief... You are not what happened to you... Don't push me away again.*

In my mind, I can see his smiling face, him in protective mode, pride and respect in his eyes during my show of strength, his fear when I was in danger, and the pure desire on his face when he held me close.

I've been stupid. No, not stupid; scared. I've managed to project Jack's face on every man I meet, even Nate, and that's not fair. Nate is crazy sometimes, but he's a good man that has proven his worth time and time again.

Almost on their own, my legs stand and move toward Nate's room. Half-way there, I stop at the bathroom door when I hear the shower running. I close my eyes and take a deep breath, then, before I can change my mind, I open the door. Through the shower glass, I can see Nate.

He stands there, unmoving, with his hands braced against the wall in front of him. His muscles are tense, and his eyes are closed as the water runs over his face. I move closer and grab the handle to the shower door. The rush of cool air makes him open his eyes. He turns to me, shocked, and asks, "What are you doing?"

I don't answer. Instead, I step inside, fully dressed, and lay my head against his chest. "I do see you… and I'm tired of running."

I lift my face to look into his eyes. He moves a lock of wet hair off my face, then drops his hand to cup my cheek. "I would never hurt you."

"I know." Rising on my toes, I press my lips to his. Nate responds by wrapping himself around me and spinning us so that his back is pressed against the shower wall. My heart bursts when I realize what he's doing. He's giving me the comfort of not being trapped. The gesture brings tears to my eyes and makes me want to give so much to this man.

I step out of his grasp and reach for the hem of my soaking shirt, pulling it over my head. It makes a wet smack as it hits the shower floor. My leggings and panties are the next to go. In a stirring display of self-control, his eyes never leave mine.

When I reach around and unclasp my bra, his eyes are molten. Once the bra has joined the rest of my clothes, I take his hand and place it on my breast. His eyes close briefly, then he turns off the water and reaches for a towel.

He reverently dries me off and then himself. As soon as he's hung up the damp towels, he bends down to pick me up. Moving to his room, he doesn't stop until we're at his bed.

One arm pulls back the covers, then he lays me down. After walking around to the other side, he climbs in beside me and pulls me back against him, wrapping an arm around my waist. "Don't you want..."

"We will. There's no need to rush anything."

I'm partly disappointed and partly relieved. I would have given myself to him, but he's giving me something even greater. He's showing me that having my body isn't his end-goal; having all of me is.

We lie curled up on his bed for a long time. Nate draws lazy circles on my middle while we talk. We talk about everything and nothing. I learn about his life and family in Miami; he already knows about mine from Sam.

After a while, my terrible day takes its toll, and I turn over and fall asleep with my head against his chest.

Nate

She's, once again, sleeping peacefully in my

arms. Not for protection or because of some nightmare, but because she wants to be here. This woman that once threatened to blow my head off is naked and asleep in my arms. I can't explain it, but somehow, just her lying here with her warm, soft skin against mine feels better than any sex I've had before.

I now completely understand why Chase would never pick up women. After Sam, no one else could measure up. I wonder at what moment he knew Sam was it.

Chuckling to myself, I think back to the moment Erin held me at gunpoint. That was my moment. I knew that from then on, there would never be another woman for me either.

I press my nose to her hair and decide that Erin is my new favorite smell. I need to find out what shampoo she uses and buy a case of it just to make sure she never runs out. I want to breathe in this scent every night when I go to sleep.

Every night… except when I'm deployed. It occurs to me that for the first time in my army career, I hate the idea of having to go overseas. But… that's because I've never had something I wanted to stick around for. Until her.

Somehow, this train of thought reminds me about the shit we're in and that we need to come up with some sort of plan tomorrow. I tick off a list of contacts that I need to make in the morning. I need to check in with McKenzie to see if he got anything off the GPS tracker from Erin's car. Playing a hunch, I've got an FBI buddy that I want to ask about any human trafficking activity in the Carolinas. If he has anything, I'll have him contact Peyton and McKenzie.

Last, I need to check in with Shark. There's something wrong with that bastard. All day Saturday he was acting like a whiny little bitch when he should have been all over Ava; who wasn't giving him the time of day. Man, if he's fucked up with her, I need to start planning his funeral and find a good attorney for Chase. Of course, before either of those things, I need to sell tickets, because that shit will be epic.

With that thought in my head, a smile on my face, and a soft woman against me, I fall into the best sleep I've had in a long time.

Homewood

"What the hell?" Jack checks the signal again. "The tracker is at the fucking police station? That son of a bitch must have found it." He takes a breath to calm himself. "It doesn't matter. They can dissect and study that thing all they want; it won't tell them anything."

Still, he's frustrated knowing that he lost her.

Determined to pick up her trail again, he decides to visit the most likely places she would go. Jack turns his car in the direction of her house first. Finding no one there, he makes the long trek to that big house in the country. He parks his car in the wooded lane, then cuts through the woods in the dark.

There are no lights on in the big house, pool house, or the guest house. The only car on site is Erin's Audi. Deciding to chance it. Jack makes his way to her car, then to the house she was staying in. It's empty. "Where are you, dammit?"

On the way back through the woods, he pulls out his phone. "Tell me where she is."

The man on the other side of the call pauses before answering, "I don't know."

"Track her phone or something," he demands.

"Man, you know I can't do that. I'd have cops at my door in like, five minutes. Why don't you just find…" Jack hangs up, uninterested in hearing what the other man has to say.

"Sweet Erin... You keep running. It'll just make finding you that much more satisfying."

He makes his way back to the hidden road, angry at himself and his coward of a brother.
He decides that it's time to take this up a notch and thinks through a few ideas on his way back to the city.

Chapter 11

Nate

For the second time in my life, and the second day in a row, I wake up with a woman in my bed. Just two days, and I'm hooked.

Staring at her sleeping form, I begin to notice things about her that were never obvious before. They're small things, like the way her long lashes fan out over her cheeks, the barely visible freckles on her nose, and most of all, how young and innocent she appears in sleep.

These small, delicate features are at odds with the tough veneer she presents. She flat out refuses to show any hint of vulnerability. No, that's not quite right. She refuses to acknowledge having any vulnerabilities.

My training taught me that there is no fear that can't be overcome by preparation, and I'm certain the self-defense classes Erin took would have taught her the same thing. The difference between us is that I'm able to evaluate a situation for potential danger and respond accordingly. Erin lives under the fear that monsters are everywhere, hiding in plain sight, and keeps herself constantly on alert. That kind of life takes its toll on a person. Mainly through isolation and distrust.

Erin stirs beside me, and I find myself looking into her emerald green eyes. I am humbled that she now looks at me without suspicion in her eyes. "Do you know how beautiful you are?" She laughs, "You know, if you had led with that a month ago, we might have gotten to this point a lot faster." I lift a skeptical eyebrow in response. She laughs even harder and says, "You're right, it would've made things worse."

"You hungry?" When she nods, I stand and reach out my hand, smiling impishly. She glances down at my morning wood and shakes her head. "You might want to put that up first." I respond with a hearty laugh and grab some sweats from the dresser. After slipping them on, I toss her one of my tees and head to the kitchen.

One pot of coffee, some eggs, and toast later, Erin goes to take a proper shower, and I start making calls.

"McKenzie here."

"Mike, it's Erickson. How's Eve?"

"She'll be fine. She's still pissed as hell though. Should I ask where you guys are?"

"On-base at Fort Benning."

"Well, damn."

"I thought you'd approve. I'm assuming you found nothing useful in the tracker."

"You assumed right. It's a real piece of work. Certainly not by amateurs. And, before you ask, we haven't found anything on this Spencer guy or an alternate identity on Rogers."

"I think I can help with that. The involvement of another player smacks of human trafficking. I've got a contact in the South Carolina FBI that I'm going to run these names by. It's not much to go on, but at least he can tell us if someone up there is on their radar. What else is going on down there?"

"Not much. Owens has closed the case on the home invasion based on lack of evidence. If Rogers had mentioned Erin while torturing Eve, we would've had enough to get a warrant, but since we have no idea where he is…"

I can tell he has more to say but is stalling. "Spit it out, Mike."

He blows out a frustrated breath. "We can't do anything unless and until he makes a move on her."

He's not telling me anything I don't already know, but it still pisses me the hell off. "So, either she's bait, or she's a prisoner. You know damn well she's not going to let anybody keep her locked up, and I refuse to dangle her in front of this bastard just so we can get a shot at him."

"Then, we keep working this brother angle and hope something turns up… Erickson?"

"Yeah?"

"Don't end up in the news."

Mike signs off, and I send an email to Jim Krantz, my friend in the FBI. Hopefully, he'll be able to find something we can use to tie up Rogers before he makes a run at Erin.

My last task is to text Shark, "What's up your ass, bro?" His reply is terse, "Leave it." My god… it *is* Ava. Chase is going to kick his ass.

I'm laughing to myself when Erin walks in. Her hair is in a pile on top of her head, and she's wearing leggings and another Alabama sweatshirt. "What's so funny?" I wonder if I should say anything, but hell, "Shark pissed off Ava, and now Chase is going to kick his ass."

"What did he do?"

"No idea."

Not intrigued by the drama, she sits down at the table and stares right at me. "What does Mike say this morning?"

I don't want to dump this on her right now, but the look on her face says she'll stab me if I try to bullshit her. So, with a clinical detachment, I relay to her the call to Mike and the email to Krantz. During the update, she shows no signs of being agitated at the news, but I guess she's had a lot of practice over the years. "So, what do we do now?"

"We… are going to get out of here and have some fun. I've got a friend with a lot of river property at an inlet, and I want to spend some time outside in this fall weather."

"I hope you don't mean fishing."

There are a great number of things I love about Alabama and Georgia, but fishing isn't one of them. "Chief, I'm from Miami. Unless your catch can pull you over the side of the boat, it don't count as fishing."

That draws a rare smile from her. "So, who

is this friend of yours?"

"Shark, actually. He spent some time in this area growing up. The property is rough, but it's got a great bike trail leading to a central clearing and pier. It's where I like to hang out when I've got some off-time."

"Let's go then."

We separate to dress and gather things for a picnic. Pretty soon, the cooler is packed, and we're ready to spend a day in the woods… Well, I'm ready for the woods. Erin just walked out in tight jeans, a cream-colored sweater, and her hair falling around her shoulders in loose curls. To myself, I whisper, "Down, boy."

About twenty minutes later, we pull off the road and drive the dirt path to Shark's equipment garage. When we reach it, I park and open the roll-up door. There are peddle bikes on a rack and a few dirt bikes parked against the wall, but I zero in on the four-wheelers with cargo racks.

I tell myself that's the more practical choice, even as I imagine Erin pressed against me with her arms around my waist. I'm sold. I grab the keys to the ATV and drive it outside.

Once we've got everything loaded and the garage is secure again, we set out on the trail to my favorite refuge.

The ride out is easy. Shark does a good job keeping the trails clear. With Erin holding on tightly to me like this, my only complaint is that the ride isn't longer.

All too soon, we break into the clearing, and I can hear Erin gasp and I say, "It's beautiful isn't it?" There are a million different colors in the trees. That's why I love it here. Especially in the peak of the fall season. "Yeah. I mean, my dad's place at the lake is great, but this… this is magnificent."

I park the four-wheeler next to the trees and climb off. I watch, amused, as Erin turns in a circle to survey the spot. "I would think that with you being from Miami, this would all be boring to you."

"Then you'd be wrong. Miami's great and all, but everything there is pink, mint, and baby blue stucco."

Erin gives me a strange look. "It's ironic. In Miami, everything is so vibrant and alive, but the colors are all the same. Up here, it takes the leaves dying to create this masterpiece."

With a sly smile on my face, I poke fun at her. "That's deep, Chief."

She groans. "Shut up."

I take her hand and show her around. The clearing features a large gazebo with built-in seating, and there's pier big enough to host a party.

We walk hand-in-hand down to the pier and sit on the swing. Erin looks along and across the river. The property across from us is heavily wooded as well. "I can see why you like it here.

It's quiet and private."

"It does give me a place to practice my pick-up lines without being interrupted."

"Ugh, you are such a child."

"All part of my charm… Really though, I think it's just the peacefulness of the water."

She hums her agreement and lays her head on my shoulder. "That's how Chase met Sam, you know? She said he stumbled on to our dad's pier looking like a whipped pup. He just sat there for hours before saying a word."

"I didn't train with him, but Shark told me about that day. Some kid in Ranger training was struggling in the mountain phase and was getting razzed pretty bad. Chase and some of the other guys pepped him up; convinced him to keep trying. The next week, he took a fall and broke his neck. Chase took it hard. Our CO knew about Chase helping the guy and granted him leave when that phase was over. The minute Chase got the green light, he took off. Didn't even bother changing out of his training uniform. Now that I think about it, I guess it's a good thing Shark didn't own this property at that time, or Chase might have never met Sam."

We sit there for a while longer, then Erin stands and walks in the direction of the ATV. Taking the hint, I get up and follow. When we reach it, Erin grabs the blankets, and I handle the cooler.

Wanting her to pick a spot, I wait for her to

move first. She bypasses the gazebo to spread the blanket on the pristine bed of leaves. I set down the cooler, and we both work to unpack lunch.

Once we finish the simple meal of sandwiches and chips, we both work to clean up. Well, I try to help, but I can't tear my eyes away from her. Even completing the simplest of tasks, her movements are so graceful and tempting. I'm helpless to do anything but stare.

She's almost finished when the wind catches a napkin, and she chases after it on all fours. I don't realize I've been chuckling to myself until she turns and gives me a squinted-eye stare. "I'm sorry. It's just after the first time I saw you, I never imagined that you would be the type to play in the dirt."

"I'm not playing in the dirt, I'm crawling around on a blanket."

"It's just that you're so… cute."

She takes on this mock sweet voice and places her hand at her neck, "Why Squid, that's the nicest thing anyone's ever said about me." Then, of course, she rolls her eyes and turns back around to finish packing.

God, I love that mouth. I sneak over till I'm on my knees behind her. "I never expected you." I want so bad feel her in my hands, to pull her against me, but I don't want to scare her. In my head, I'm begging her to show some sign, to make some move that says I can touch her.

She grants my wish when she leans back against me and tips her head against my chest. I reach up with my hands to caress her arms, then move one hand to her middle, slowly slipping it under the hem of her sweater.

Her skin is so warm and soft, and I'm already high on the feeling of her. Inch by inch, my hand slides up until my fingers barely brush the fabric of her bra. I swallow hard when she lets out a long sigh.

In one motion, she turns her head as my hand lifts to cup her breast. Her green eyes open, and I stare into them as I lower my mouth to hers. If I was concerned about being slow and careful, I shouldn't have been. She's not hesitant in the least and even pushes her breast farther into my hand.

Hoping I'm reading her right, my hand leaves her breast to join the other at the hem of her sweater. I slowly lift the fuzzy thing and miracle of miracles, she lifts her arms for me to remove it completely. When it's off, she leans forward to grant me access to her bra clasp.

It takes me several seconds to remove it as my hands are shaking. Once the thing is gone, she leans back again, and I take her into my hands. The cool fall air has done its job, and I brush my thumbs against her hardened nipples as I gently massage the soft mounds.

In no time, she begins to writhe as if she wants more. I can give her more, but only when she tells me, she wants it.

I swear she must be reading my mind. No sooner than the thought enters my mind, she's spinning in my grip and wraps her arms around my neck. She latches onto my mouth like a starving woman. Like a starving man, I give just as good as I get until she leans back and yanks my shirt over my head.

Curious, or maybe desperate, to see how far she wants to go, I lay back so that she's on top of me. Her hair falls over us like a curtain, and I love it. I reach up and grip her ass to pull her right over my pulsing erection.

She suddenly sits up, straddling my hips. Her eyes are on fire, but she seems nervous for a second. That is quickly replaced by a fierce determination. Quietly she states, "I want you," but repeats it with more resolve, "I want you."

"I'm right here."

Now that we've voiced our collective intent, she looks less sure of herself. To put her at ease, I place my hands behind my head. To anyone else, it would look like a casual move, but she knows why I'm doing it. I want her to know that she's got all the control here.

She visibly relaxes at the display of surrender and places her hands on my chest. My eyes nearly roll back in my head at the feel of her hands on me. She has yet to touch me in an erotic way, but her caressing me like this is fantasy enough considering I never thought I'd get this far.

After exploring the scar Avery gave me, her hands move to my belt. All earlier hints of hesitation are gone. She makes quick work of my belt, button, and zipper. She tugs at my jeans and boxers as I lift my hips off the blanket to help her remove them completely.

In a choked voice, I grit out, "Condom." She answers with, "Pill."

Pill… but she hasn't… At my shocked expression, she rolls her eyes. "That's not all they're used for."

I guess they left that out of our combat medical training.

Once I'm completely bare, she stands and sweeps her gaze over my whole body. She seems to linger on my erection, the corners of her mouth turning up ever so slightly. I'm already enjoying the view from down below, but my mouth dries up when she begins to peel off her jeans and panties.

Before my eyes have had their fill, she lowers herself to straddle my hips and leans down to kiss me again as if to reassure herself that she's ready. I don't permit myself to say a word. I'm afraid that the wrong thing would come out and spook her, so I keep my mouth shut.

Eventually, she maneuvers herself so that I'm lined up to her entrance. She closes her eyes, which I'm certain is a bad idea, so I break my silence, "Chief, look at me." Her mind must have been going to a bad place as her eyebrows are drawn together. Hearing my voice, her eyes snap open to find mine, and I see relief there.

While holding my gaze, she slides backward, pressing herself onto my hard shaft. When she's fully seated, her eyes drift closed again, but this time, it's not in fear. It's pure ecstasy broadcast from her face. I can appreciate the sentiment; sex has never felt this good before. It's not just that this is the first time I've gone bare; I feel this woman everywhere. I breathe her in like air, the essence of her seeps into my skin. This woman, only this woman, reaches the deepest, the Darkest Part of me.

I open my eyes again, and my gaze wanders from her face down to her breasts, and finally to the point where we connect. Hidden from the rest of the world on her hip is a tiny tattoo. It's a delicate script that says "breathe & live." It's a reminder to me of how amazingly brave she is. She is a survivor, a fighter, and she has given her trust to me. This moment will forever be etched in my mind as one of the most important moments of my life. She has branded me, and I belong to her.

The thought of her claiming me stokes my desire, and I'm beginning to have trouble keeping still. I'm dying for her to move, but I will not rush her. Finally, she braces her hands on my chest and, ever so slowly, she lifts herself, then sinks down again. After she's done this several times, she demands, "Nate… put your hands on me."

I pull my hands from behind my head and place them on her thighs, sliding them up to grip her hips.

Pairing my strength with hers, I lift and lower, increasing her speed until she's panting. I know she's relieved that she was able to do this, but I don't just want this experience to be cathartic. I want it to be so damn good, that it chases all her ghosts away.

With this in mind, one hand moves from her hip to work my thumb against her clit. I can tell she likes that; she lets me see it, and she lets me hear it. My eyes alternate between watching her bouncing breasts and her face. Her breasts are sensational, but I don't want to miss the moment the pleasure from orgasm washes over her.

With my hand adding to the sensations, it's not long before she climaxes. The look on her face is the most beautiful thing I've ever seen. The absolute best part is hearing my name whispered from her lips.

After bringing her pleasure, my hand returns to her hip, and I continue thrusting until I feel my release bearing down on me. It only takes a few more plunges before I'm bellowing her name.

Erin crashes down on my chest, utterly spent, and I don't mind at all. In fact, the only thing I'm capable of right now is pulling the spare blanket over the both of us.

Erin

Lying here on Nate's chest, I feel more at peace than I have in the last four years. My whole body is tingling and feels like jelly.

No longer in the heat of the moment, I shiver in the cool air. Nate pulls a spare blanket over us and begins to caress my back. "You ok, Chief?"

"I'm more than ok." He rolls us so we're lying on our sides and the movement dislodges him from inside me. Nate reaches over to move some errant hair off my face and tucks it behind my ear.

"Thank you," he says.

Thank you? I've never had that response from a lover before, and it confuses me. "Thank you for sex?"

"Thank you for trusting me." Overcome with emotion and unable to respond, I move closer to him and close my eyes.

I'm not sure how long we lie like that; I guess I dozed off. When I open my eyes again, the sun is setting behind the trees casting long shadows over the ground.

I look up and see that Nate fell asleep wrapped around me. I gently nudge him awake. "Mornin' Chief."

"Time to go, soldier." I reach over and collect my clothes as he splays out on the blanket, stretching his muscles. "That's quite a body you've got there." He grins wide, "Thanks for noticing."

I realize too late that I've made a mistake. As soon as those words leave his mouth, he starts flexing. Typical. Impressive, but typical. Spotting his shirt behind me, I pick it up and toss it at his face.

We dress quickly due to the falling temperature, then the cooler is packed, and blankets folded. With one last look around, we hop on the four-wheeler and start back. I ride the whole way with my arms around his waist and my cheek resting against his back.

Too bad the ride couldn't be a little longer.

Homewood

Jack waited in his spot across the street from Erin's office today, but she didn't come in. Frustrated, he called in posing as a carpet rep. "I'm sorry, Sir. She's taken a leave of absence. Sherry Stanson has taken over her projects. Would you like me to transfer you to her office?"

Through gritted teeth, he replies, "Sure." In order to avoid suspicion, he waits for the call to be transferred, then hangs up.

His next call is to his brother, "Have you found anything yet?" Jack is pacing the floor having lost his patience. "Nothing. There aren't any social media accounts to track."

"I know that, dammit. Tell me what a third-grader can't find."

"I can tell you that she hasn't used any of her bank or credit cards since the day before yesterday. She's totally off-grid."

"Somebody knows where she is." Jack ends the call and throws his phone across the room. It smashes into pieces, but he doesn't care. Burner phones are easy to come by.

Resuming his pacing, he considers all the possibilities again. "It can't be the meddling bitch sister. She's still on her honeymoon. If they'd come back early, I'd have seen them." Other than the sister, Erin has no family.

There were two people in her office she was particularly close to that are a possibility. Her boss, whatever his name is, and that older woman. "The Erin I know wouldn't have left her position willingly, so that means she was forced out. That scratches out the boss."

He can't exactly call the office again and speak with the woman whose name he can't even remember. But then… with those two big men she was with, why the hell would she trade them in to hide out with a defenseless lady? He stares at the TV in the cheap hotel room. The local news is on, but the sound is muted.

"Fuck!" Jack is poised to throw a lamp through the screen when a picture of Detective Peyton is shown. It's captioned with, "Investigation into the home invasion of Homewood Detective Eve Peyton suspended due to lack of evidence."

"That's it." Those detectives know.

Chapter 12
Homewood

"Homewood PD. How can I help you?" asks the bored receptionist. "I need to speak with Detective McKenzie please."

"What is this concerning?"

"I was told to contact him about any activity at a neighbor's place. Her name is Erin Westin."

"Just a minute, Sir."

"McKenzie here."

"Detective McKenzie, my name is Stuart Schultz. I'm visiting my grandmother who lives next door to an Erin Westin. Erin went out of town and asked my grandma to report any activity at her house to you. I haven't seen anything personally, but my grandma wanted me to contact you. A little while ago I ran out to the store, and while I was gone, a tall, blond man who introduced himself as a friend of Erin came here and asked if my grandma knew where Erin was. She said no, and he left. When I got back, Grandma told me what happened and what Erin said and asked me to call you."

"Thanks, I'm glad she did. Did the guy give her a name?"

"She said he introduced himself as Tim."

"He didn't give a last name?"

"No. I'm sorry."

"Tell her she did just fine. I'm going to come by and look around Ms. Westin's place. If I brought a picture, do you think she could tell me if it was the guy or not?"

"Grandma, do you think you could identify this Tim guy in a picture?... She says, yes."

"Great. I'll be by within the hour."

"Detective… are we in danger? Should I take my grandma out of here?"

"No, this is just a case of a man being too interested in a lady that is not."

"Good. Thanks. We'll be waiting for you."

"See you soon."

Mike gathers his phone and keys and heads to the front of the precinct. Before he rushes out the door, he thinks better of it and checks in with the dispatcher who's familiar with the situation. "Stan, I'm heading out for the night. I'm going to run by the Westin place to check out a suspicious person reported."

"Got it. See you in the morning."

The drive to Erin's house takes only ten minutes. There's only one house close enough to be labeled a neighbor, to the left, as the right side is only a wooded lot.

From the driveway, there doesn't seem to be any sign of disturbance or attempted entry. A closer look doesn't reveal anything either.

The detective walks over to the neighbor's house and rings the bell. The man that answers the door is a thin guy with dark hair and a longish beard. His eyes are aimed at the floor, and he fidgets nervously. "Are you Detective

McKenzie?"

"Yes."

"You must be Stuart."

He nods and asks to see McKenzie's ID. Mike hands it over and thinks to himself that this guy looks like a video-game-playing basement dweller.

The shy man hands Mike his ID back and backs up into the house. Normally, the seasoned cop would step into a person's personal space to assert control of the conversation, but he's afraid this guy might faint. "Would it be all right if I spoke with your grandmother now, Mr. Schultz?"

"Sure, she's in the kitchen fixing some tea. It's right through there."

When McKenzie walks through the doorway, the guy gives him a wide berth. Mike almost chuckles to himself, but somehow keeps it in check. After passing through the opening to the kitchen, he swears at his own stupidity and the two bodies on the floor. Before he can even turn around, something crashes into the back of his head, and he collapses to the floor."

Jack quickly ties McKenzie up and searches him. Keys, phone, notepad. His phone is fingerprint locked; easy enough. He puts it down and flips through the notepad. The last page with any writing lists a Capt. Nathaniel Erickson, Fort Benning. The name means nothing, but it could be one of the guys with

Erin.

Jack pulls out his phone. When Spencer answers, he talks fast, "I need you to find out who a car is registered to. Can you do it?"

"Yeah. That's easy. Send me the tag number."

Jack sends Spencer a picture he took of the truck Erin was riding in. He walks back over to the unconscious detective and pulls out his pistol. Screwing on the suppressor, he pulls out a chair and takes a seat. While he's waiting on Spencer, he'll find out what he can from the cop.

A cup of water is sitting on the table, and Jack picks it up and tosses its contents at the detective's face. Mike stirs and groans. As Jack begins to speak, he tries to look in the direction of the sound, but his vision is blurred.

"Where is she?"

It takes a monumental effort, but Mike manages a weak, "Kiss… my ass."

"Who's Nathaniel Erickson?"

"Someone I… hope you… meet."

Jack laughs, "You know, I admire you, detective. You've always had a set of brass…" Jack's phone rings, "What have you got?"

"The truck is registered to a Nathaniel Erickson. He's an Army Ranger stationed at…" Jack interrupts, "Fort Benning. Let me call you right back. I've got to handle something."

Jack rises and moves to stand over Mike. "Sorry, detective. I can't have you making this difficult for me."

His vision clearing slightly, Mike looks up the barrel of the gun, as pictures of Eve flash in his mind. He turns his head just before he hears the blast.

Jack stands there and removes the suppressor from the nine-millimeter and stuffs it in his jacket. The shot was still loud, but different enough that it could be mistaken for something else.

Jack's next move is to gather Mike's phone, keys, and notepad. Then, as calmly as he walked up the path to the house, he strolls back out to his car.

Shortly after he's pulled out of Erin's neighborhood, he calls Spencer back. "You were saying?"

"I've got an address, but it's inside the damn base… You aren't going to do anything stupid, are you?"

"Send me the address." He disconnects the call and sets out for Georgia.

A few miles away from Erin's, Jack pulls off the road into a gas station. He removes the sim card from Mike's phone and tosses it into the trash. Before pulling back out onto the street, he tosses the phone into a storm drain.

Erin

Hyper is waiting in the driveway when we get back to Nate's house. He's holding a bottle of wine, case of beer, and carry out bags with Marco's printed on them. "What have you got there?"

"I've got calzones, wings, and a salad." A salad… how sexist of him. "You can have the salad. I call dibs on the wings… if they're hot enough." He shows a hint of a smile, and under his breath I hear him say, "I should have figured as much."

All throughout dinner, the guys joke, talk sports, and speculate on what would happen to Shark when Chase gets back. For the most part, I keep quiet and listen, waiting for them to start talking about the Jack situation.

By the time Hyper leaves, no one has mentioned anything about Jack, and I am confused. Nate shuts the door behind Hyper, and I open my mouth. "What was that all about?" Now it's Nate's turn to look confused. "What?"

"I thought Hyper was over here to discuss a plan, new information about Jack, our next step... Something."

"Oh. No. The team usually gets together for dinner on Thursday nights, and we have only one rule. No shop talk." I jump up and start pacing. "So, when do we figure out what to do next? I can't just sit here waiting around doing nothing."

"Chief, we're doing everything we can. The FBI is looking into Rogers possibly having a history in Hilton Head as well as his possible connection to any human trafficking activity. Eve and Mike are working in the legal system to get information on Rogers and get some restrictions placed on him. And you, Chief, are taking a vacation in the safest possible place while the dust settles… Now, I'm going to take these take-out containers to the trash while you pick out a movie and pop some popcorn. Got it?"

I'm having trouble keeping up here. People are getting hurt, I've lost my job, and I'm on the run. I can hardly sit still, and he wants me to make popcorn? "I'm going crazy here. How can you guys just turn things off and be so calm?"

Holding the bag of trash, Nate turns around, "In my line of work, you kind of have to… Or stroke out by age thirty. Now, pick out a movie."

"Ok. Chick flick it is."

I find the popcorn and a large bowl and set about making the movie snack. The front door opens and closes, and I hear Nate groan, "You've got to be kidding. Seriously?"

"What's wrong with Iron Man?" He stomps into the kitchen. "You mean besides Tony Stark?"

"I happen to think Tony Stark is hot," I toss over my shoulder.

Nate steps in close to me and reaches around to place his hands under my shirt. In my ear, he whispers, "I can be hotter than Tony Stark."

"We'll see."

After the movie ends, Nate cuts his eyes to me and teases, "I think Pepper is hot." I don't take the bait. Instead, I walk to the hallway, then throw back, "She sure as hell is."

In my room, I take off my makeup and change into a gray cotton sleep set with a lace racerback. Ready for bed, I move to the bedroom door, heading to Nate's room. When I open the door, I let out a shriek. Nate's standing there, leaning against the door frame. "Are you coming with me, or am I sleeping in here?"

My hand lifts to my hip. "That's a hell of an assumption you're making."

"I don't think so." With that, he turns and enters his room, not bothering to close his door. From where I stand, I can see clearly to his side of the bed and watch as he strips off his clothes. Damn, but he's cocky.

Nate

Just as I'd hoped, Erin is crawling into bed with me. The day we had together was better than I could have imagined, and I'd like nothing more than to be able to hold her again.

As if reading my thoughts, she echoes them, "Today was great. You, Nate, are a good man."

"You, Erin, are an amazing woman." Instead of shrugging off the compliment, she turns it around on me. "I mean it. I'm not sure I could have done that if… How did you know how to… I was afraid I'd flip out again, but you... Who are you?"

"Not sure you want to hear this."

Her face shows defiance, and she challenges, "Try me."

So, bossy Erin is back. "In the Rangers, we sometimes get called out for rescue missions. They could be Americans or anyone. You can always tell those that have been abused. Sexually or otherwise, they're scared to death of you. Even if they know you are the person sent to get them out of hell, they flinch at every move you make.

"The worst part is watching them when they're obviously hungry or thirsty. You have food and water, but they're afraid to accept it in fear that you'll want something in return… or, that it might be drugged, which is how some of them were taken."

She nods in understanding. "We have to be very careful about how we walk, talk, and interact with them so we don't spook them. Any food or liquids we provide, we present in sealed packages or bottles. Sometimes, the rescue is so afraid that they refuse anything we offer no matter how hungry or thirsty they may be. I learned that if we leave all the food and water out in the open, eventually they'll inspect it and take some when we're not looking. The most important thing is to make the rescue feel like they're in control of what happens to them as much as we can."

"What about during the escape or dangerous situations?"

"Those are the hardest times. If the situation permits, we carefully explain our purpose and that, at times, we might have to grab an arm, place a hand on them to signal or stop them, or possibly, grab them up and run. Those rescues usually go a little easier. When we don't have time for neighborly conversation, it's a lot rougher on them. They still come around; it just takes more time for them to trust us."

She stares at me in wonder. "You really aren't what you seem. It's intentional, isn't it?"

Without answering, I lean forward and briefly capture her lips. After that, she curls against my side, and we sleep.

The next morning, we go through what has become our routine. I shower and go start the coffee. She joins me for breakfast and after, has her shower while I check in with Mike and Jim. I can't get Mike on the phone, so I send him a text and call up Jim. He hasn't got anything to share with me yet. Having not heard back from Mike yet, I try him again with no luck. Something feels off. He should be answering his phone.

My next call is to Eve. She's frantic when she answers, "Erickson, Mike's missing. He didn't come over last night, and I can't get him on his phone." I look at my watch, it's still early there. "Have you checked with the station?"

"I was just about to when you called."

"I'll hang up. Call me back as soon as you finish with them." Feeling helpless, I reach up and rub my day-old beard and consider calling Hyper. "Not yet," I tell myself. Wait for Peyton.

Not two minutes later, my phone is ringing. "What'd they say?"

"He said he was going to check out a suspicious person reported at Erin's house. I told them to send a squad car to check it out."

"Keep me posted." My next move is to call Hyper. Not that he can do anything from here, but he needs to know that something's up.

Five minutes later, Hype's walking in my door. My phone rings again before we make it back to the kitchen. "They found his car. It's at Erin's place. I'm on my way over there now."

Erin walks in at this point. Her eyes widen at Hyper's presence and our worried looks.

"Call in Owens. He can't do anything official, but he'll know that whatever this is, it's related to your attack."

"Got it. I'll let you know as soon as we find anything."

Erin's voice is nearly a whisper when she asks, "What's going on?"

"Mike's missing. His car was found at your house. They're looking for him now."

She crumples in a chair and Hype jumps up to get her some water. "Oh, god… Mike. How many people is he going to hurt to get to me?

I've got to stop this." She looks to me, her eyes pleading, "Please help me stop him." I open my mouth to say something, but the ringing phone stops me.

It's Owens. "We found Mike. He was in a neighbor's house. The residents, an elderly couple were murdered sometime yesterday. Mike is alive, but barely. He's on his way to UAB. The medics say he was shot in the head, but it looks like the way his head was turned or turning made the bullet deflect. They said it did get enough of him that it fractured his skull. They also say that he's been like this for at least twelve hours. He should be dead… He still may not make it."

"From what I know of him, he will. He's a tough bastard."

"I know I've been kept somewhat in the dark here. I think it's time somebody told me everything."

"Eve… Talk to Eve. She's probably ready to talk to anybody if they'll help bring down this son of a bitch."

"And, you… keep that woman safe. I know she's at the center of all this." I look across to her and see the tears streaming down her face. "I fucking guarantee it."

Erin looks straight at me, and I know what's coming. I lay my phone down on the table, then give her my full attention. "I'm done," is all she says. I inject steel into my voice when I give her my one-word answer.

"No."

"Don't tell me no. I'm not going to keep hiding while he hunts the people I care about."

Without breaking her gaze, I growl, "Hype, get out." She turns her face to him, "Don't you fucking move." She once again pins me with a glare, "You, listen to me."

"No, you listen! We brought you to this base because it is safe *here*. Tomorrow, Sam will be *here*. We are doing every damn thing we can do to find him, but he's a ghost, and he's not scared of anybody. This asshole has taken out two well-trained cops and will not hesitate to eliminate anyone else that gets in his way."

"What the hell am I supposed to do then? I am not a coward, and I won't just stand by why he mows people down, trying to get to me."

She's getting all worked up, and I am too. Calm down, jackass. You're not helping the situation. Softening my voice, I reply, "I know that, Chief. We just have to be smart about this. Let the police and the feds do their job. Our focus needs to be on keeping you, and starting tomorrow, Sam, safe."

She doesn't argue further but does leave the kitchen having had all she can take.

When Erin is safely out of earshot, Hyper muses, "This whole thing is a powder keg."

"I know it, but there isn't a damn thing I can do about it."

"You talk to Chase yet?"

"I'm waiting till tomorrow. After the shit he's dealt with the last ten years, the man deserves one un-fucked-up week with his new wife."

Hype nods in agreement, "What about Shark?"

"Man, I don't even know where he is. This shit with Ava's got him all jacked up. I'm sure we're going to need him before all this is over though."

The rest of the day is tense and passes slowly. Erin mostly stays in her room while Hype and I get updates from our various contacts. At noon, Hype leaves to pick up some food. While he's gone, I get another call from Eve.

Hype has just come back from the Brew Pub and is walking in the door when I disconnect the call from Eve. "Mike survived surgery but has yet to regain consciousness. The people that were killed were just unlucky neighbors. Owens thinks that Rogers killed them and posed in their house to lure Mike in."

I hear a gasp behind me. I close my eyes and drop my head. I hadn't realized she was behind me. "The Dorseys?" Hearing the tremor in her voice, I stand and gather her to me. "I'm sorry, Chief." I hold her tight while she sobs. She's devastated by the violence visited upon the innocent couple.

Chapter 13

Columbus, Georgia

Jack pulls into the parking lot of a Starbucks and picks up his phone. After several minutes of research, he hasn't found a legitimate way to get on base. And, with numerous entry points, there's no way to spot her coming or going. Even knowing that Erickson lives just inside the main gate, it's impossible to get close enough to watch without drawing suspicion.

There's got to be a way. Tossing his phone in frustration, he spots a gay couple walking out of the coffee chain.

"Damn. That's it." He picks up his phone again to find what he needs.

Three hours later, he climbs out of the cab in the front of AWOL. He took time to shop for the right kind of clothes and visit a salon to have the right look.

Peering across the street, he takes a moment to school his features. Places like this disgust him. There's only one hole a man should stick his dick into. Maybe two if you count her mouth. But, since the odds of finding a female soldier to sneak him on base are too small, this is his only option.

Taking a much-needed deep breath, he pulls himself together and walks to the door. By the time he reaches for the handle, he's gotten into character by reminding himself what the ultimate goal is.

Step one. Find a guy with a military haircut. He pastes a smile on his face and begins moving around the sickening place.

He spots a few of the right type, but they're in groups. That won't work. Soon, he eyes a built-looking guy, alone at the bar. He's got the right hair and looks uncomfortable. Jack slides up to the bar and seemingly ignores the quiet man. Evaluating the guy's body language, he decides that if he's too effeminate, he'll turn the guy off. So, he orders a beer instead of the Cosmo that his research mandated he get.

Out of the corner of his eye, he catches the guy checking him out, then diverting his gaze back to his own drink. To speed things along, he experiments with a little conversation. "Ugh, why are these guys so lacy? I mean, I'm all for being out, but that doesn't mean we have to be so camp all the time."

Having set the bait, he turns back to his beer and waits.

After several minutes and furtive glances his way, the other man speaks. "You… ah… come out here much?" Jack looks his way and smiles nicely, but not too enthusiastically. "No. I'm from Atlanta. We've got places like this, but they're too much sometimes. Know what I mean?"

"Yeah. I like to hang out and watch, but it's too over the top more often than not."

Jack wants to keep talking, but has to be careful to play this right… don't push too hard. Eventually, his patience pays off. The other guy starts again, "My name's Adam. What's yours?"

"It's Luke."

"What do you do, Luke?"

"I'm a physical therapist. What about you?"

"I'm in the Army. I'm here for sniper training."

"Wow. The Army… I'm proud to meet you. No matter who you are, it takes a lot of guts to serve. Guts that I never had I'm sad to say."

"Don't feel bad, we can't all serve. I'm sure you help people plenty. Working in the medical field is one thing that I could never do."

"Thanks for saying that. Most people I meet in my job just want to yell at me for making them do exercises that hurt."

Adam gets quiet after that, and Jack is afraid that he wasted an hour sitting here… He's about to move on to someone else when Adam suddenly speaks up, "Would you… would you like to get out of here?"

"Yes, Adam, I think I would."

Jack follows him outside and asks about ordering an Uber, all the while, hoping the other man has his own wheels. "I can drive, that is, if you don't mind riding with me."

"Not at all. Lead the way."

In the car, Adam asks, "Do you want to go to your place or mine?"

“I have a roommate at the hotel. Better make it yours.”

“It’s on base, so you’ll need your ID.”

Jack smiles brightly, “That’s no problem.”

At the gate, both men hand over their IDs and are sent through. Just inside the gate, they pass a sign for Custer Village and McGill Street.

Adam eventually pulls up to a smallish house with no lights on. “I have a roommate, but he’s on leave right now.”

Jack places his hand on Adam’s thigh and answers, “I’m glad.”

The two men exit the car, and Adam unlocks the door. Once inside, Adam asks, “You want another beer?”

“Sure. This is a nice place. I thought all military guys lived in barracks.” Adam laughs as he hands Jack the beer, “No, that’s only in training.”

Adam takes a draw from his beer as Jack makes a show of checking his wallet. “You got any condoms? I’m out.”

“Sure. Be right back.” As soon as he’s gone, Jack pulls a syringe from his pocket and doses the other man’s beer. He won’t taste anything and will be dead in minutes.

When Adam comes back, Jack comments on the beer, hoping to avoid having to touch the other man again. “This brew is good. What can you tell me about it?” Like magic, Adam picks it up and takes a long draw. “It’s called Ghost

Train. It's brewed in Birmingham. I ran across it in a beer garden during a stop on my way here."

Adam motions to the sofa and Jack dutifully joins him, sitting on the edge. Adam places his hand on Jack's thigh, and Jack takes another sip of beer, hoping the action will prompt Adam to do the same. Fortunately, it works, which will help to speed things along.

Jack watches the other man carefully and can tell the precise moment Adam realizes something is wrong. He moves his hand from Jack's leg and looks at the beer. By this point, his movements are beginning to become sluggish, and he tries to stand.

He's still too lucid and prone to panic, so Jack attempts to guide his thinking, "Hey, are you ok? You look like you don't feel so good. Have you eaten something today that could have given you food poison?" Any struggle with this guy would leave evidence, and that would be a big risk. "Maybe you ought to lie down. Should I call a doctor?"

"No. I'm sure I'll be fine." He barely makes it into the bedroom before falling to the floor.

Jack steps over him and checks the closet, carefully selecting clothes he can use to look like a typical morning jogger. He finds what he needs and even discovers a handgun in an unlocked safe. With the found items in hand, he closes the door and moves to look in a hall closet for a flat sheet. He plans to get a few hours of sleep here, and the sheet will keep him from leaving hairs on the couch cushions.

Early the next morning, Jack gathers the clothes, gun, sheet, beer bottles, and Adam's keys. He tosses everything in the trunk, and within minutes, he's driving toward Custer Village.

Once he makes the turn to McGill Street, he quickly locates Erickson's house. The black Land Rover from Springville is sitting in the driveway.

Now, all he's got to do is be ready in case they leave. From the front of the house, he can see two parking lots with a clear vantage point. There's a parking area just off the main road and at a Starbucks two blocks over. He'll alternate between the two areas, so no one reports someone sitting in their car in one spot all day.

Erin

Last night was awful. I left Nate and Hyper in the kitchen, deciding to go to bed early. It turned out to be a mistake. Every time I closed my eyes, I saw Mr. and Mrs. Dorsey's faces.

Sometime after midnight, Nate came into my room and climbed in bed with me. Though I was awake, I didn't speak to him or touch him. It just seemed wrong for me to receive any form of comfort, knowing what their family was going through because of me.

This morning, I woke up bleary-eyed and groggy. The coffee helps, but not much. Hyper drops in kind of early, and I offer to make some breakfast just to keep myself from thinking about what Jack did to that sweet couple. Hyper graciously accepts, so I pull out what I need and get busy. Thankfully, I can cook a decent breakfast.

When Nate enters the kitchen, he acknowledges Hyper and walks over to me. I'm pulled in for a hug, but it's too short. Nate's phone rings, and after seeing the caller, he pulls away and goes outside for the conversation.

Hyper, looking to be amiable, asks, "You feeling ok this morning?"

After last night's breakdown, I'm not sure what he expects. I want to be bitchy, but he doesn't deserve that from me. I sigh and say, "As well as can be expected, I guess."

"Like shit, then."

That coaxes a small smile from me. "Like shit."

Nate walks back in and relays part of the conversation he just had. "That was Chase. They'll be landing in Atlanta around three. Sam wants to pick up a few things in town, but Chase needs to get on base and do some checking on things. Why don't we meet up with Sam and keep her company while she gets what she needs?"

"I'd like that."

After breakfast, Hyper leaves to go do… something. I don't have anywhere to go or anything to do so I just hang around while Nate makes his update calls. "Mike is still out even though the swelling in his brain has gone down. We won't know for sure if there is any permanent damage until he wakes up, but his EEG looks normal, at least."

The updates on Mike make me think about the Dorseys' family again… and Eve and Mike. The anger and the grief become too much, and I escape to my room to be alone for a while. When that doesn't help, I gather some things and head to the bathroom to take a long shower.

After washing, conditioning, and scrubbing everything twice, I still feel as if I have their blood on my hands. I slam my hands against the tile wall in anger over and over again until the pain becomes unbearable. Then, I lean against the cool tile and allow myself to slide down to the floor. Tormented by my inability to do anything to stop the chaos, I lose myself to body-racking sobs.

The shower door opens, and strong arms reach for me. I'm picked up and pulled tight to a bare chest. Despite the solace I find in his embrace, I can't stop shaking.

"Let's get you out of here, Chief." He turns the water off and grabs some towels. Eyes closed, I feel myself being dried off, then carried down the hall. He places me in his bed and hovers over me. "Look at me, Chief. This is not your doing."

He lowers his forehead to mine. "Don't let him beat you this way. He's the monster responsible."

His lips find mine, but I'm unresponsive; too deep in my despair to allow myself any comfort. "Erin, you're letting him win." I know he's right and that makes me desperate to feel something besides soul-crushing grief. What would it hurt to lose myself in him for a while?

I reach up and pull him down to me and feel grounded by the weight of his body on top of mine. It crosses my mind that I should be terrified of being in this position, but the fear just doesn't manifest itself. The only thing I feel in this moment is hunger.

I kiss him furiously; as if my very survival depends on it. He responds with equal passion, lifting his lips from my own and burning a trail down my throat to my shoulder. Without me stopping him, he continues down and closes his mouth over my breast. I hiss at the contact, overwhelmed by the sensation.

He gives equal attention to the other breast, then moves down further. By the time he begins teasing my center with his tongue, I'm completely given over to his touch.

The climax quickly builds and crashes over me like a breaking dam. "Nate, please."

He climbs back up my body to take my mouth again. I force my mouth from his and plead, "I need you."

I feel him at my entrance, but he doesn't press in. He must be afraid of scaring me again. My eyes open and stare straight into his concerned eyes. "Nate. I need you now."

That ends the war waging in his mind, and he plunges deep into me. My body bows up at the incredible intrusion, and he stops moving again. My legs wrap around his waist, and I watch as the worry on his face fades away.

I moan my pleasure, and he pulls out and thrusts back into me ungently; testing my limits. "More." After I utter this one word, the dam breaks. He begins driving into me with a forcefulness I've never experienced before, and I can't get enough. He continues his punishing rhythm with abandon; past the point where another climax has me writhing beneath him. He doesn't stop until I'm depleted, and his release sends him over the edge.

He roars my name and collapses down to his elbows, dropping his head to my chest. After several moments, he rolls off and gathers me to him. Neither of us speaks; we're just two lovers wrapped up in each other, trying to keep the outside world from creeping in.

Right now, there's no mission, no deadline, and no danger. We've created this bubble where nothing exists besides the two of us, and I'm truly amazed at how safe this man makes me feel. After Jack, I never thought I'd be able to get this close to someone again.

After a while, I feel I'm back to my fighting form. I lift myself up just enough to see the bedside clock; disappointed that we have to leave our sanctuary. "It's nearly two. We should get up."

"You think Sam's going to know what we're up to?"

I half snort, "Knowing Sam, she's got a bet going with Chase about us."

"So, you're thinking that they bet on how quickly I won you over?"

"It's more likely they bet on whether I would kill you or not."

"Hmm. Wonder who won? Let's get moving. We're meeting them at four."

Nate climbs out of bed, but I'm not ready for this moment to pass yet. I need him to know what he did for me. "Nate?"

He looks back at me, a knowing look in his eye. "I told you, Chief, I've got you."

With misty eyes, I force myself to get up and deal with the signs of our carnal activity. That task taken care of, I dress and deal with my still-wet hair. A last look in the mirror shows that I'm finally presentable and walk out to the kitchen to put away dishes from the dishwasher.

During this extraordinarily domestic task, some unexpected and disturbing thoughts plague me. While this feels so normal and right, what happens in a few days' time? What if Jack is still free weeks from now? Will I be stuck here without transportation, a job? Is that a bad thing? I'm practically living with Nate, so what happens if Jack gets caught tomorrow? I have a job in Birmingham to go back to, but Sam will be here. Could I live with him? Could I live without him?

The barrage of what-ifs threatens to shred my sanity. In the end, I decide that all I can do is take things one day at a time. Anyway, it's about time to go meet Sam and Chase.

As Nate and I pull out of Benning's main gate, every uncertainty is forgotten; replaced with an excitement to see my sister. Missing her for a few days hardly compares to the torture and death exacted by Jack, but being without her makes dealing with all of it that much more difficult.

Nate and I pull into the shopping center where we're supposed to meet them and park near the entrance. As we're waiting, I begin worrying over telling Sam about all the shit that has happened. To myself, I say out loud, "She's going to flip when she finds out that I've been keeping this from her."

Nate reaches over and squeezes my hand. "You don't worry about that. I spoke to Chase this morning. He knows what's been going on and said he would talk to her. Hopefully, she'll... Hey, they're here." I follow the direction of his pointed arm and see Chase's truck.

Chase spots us, and I watch as he parks and

walks to Sam's side to open her door. She takes his hand and gives him a long kiss before stepping down from the big SUV.

Nate and I walk over to join them, and I rush to Sam, giving my little sister a great big hug. "You look beautiful. This new life looks good on you." Sam hugs me right back, "You should try it sometime."

We both stand up straight again, and she looks me over, giving me a suspicious glare. "You look… different." Her eyes look to Nate and back to me, then suddenly go wide. "You *are* trying it sometime. When did this happen?"

"We've got all the time in the world to talk about that. What I want to know is who wins the bet."

"What bet?" she asks innocently while her eyes are full of mischief. I cross my arms and give her my best bullshit stare.

"Oh, all right. It was me. Want to know what I get for winning?"

"Nope." To save myself from her telling me anyway, I turn to the men and see them shake hands and start talking in hushed tones.

"Hey, Sam, what all do you need from here?"

"Nothing that can't wait." She gives me a motherly look and continues, "I'm not going to do any yelling because I know why you didn't call. All I'll say is that I'm glad you're fine, and glad you're here. Now, let's get you back to base where it's safe. All I ask is that we get something to eat first and maybe stop and let me pick up a few groceries."

"Sounds simple enough. What about Chase?"

"Some meeting was scheduled for tonight that he's got to rush off to."

We join the men who seem to have finished their conversation. Chase gives me a one-armed squeeze, and I offer him a genuine smile. "We all set?" he asks. Receiving head bobs from all of us, he says to Sam and Nate, "This is one of *those* meetings. I don't know how long I'll be, and we're not allowed to bring in our phones. I'll call as soon as I'm finished."

Before hopping back in his truck, he leans over to Sam. "I'll see you later, Mrs. McDaniels." He kisses her deeply; then he leaves.

After he pulls away, Sam turns to Nate, "So… I hear I've won a bet." He attempts to look nonchalant, "That depends. What did you bet on?"

"Chase bet that Erin would eventually shoot you. I bet that she would eventually kiss you." Nate gives me a wicked look. For the love… this is not happening here. "The shooting thing is still a possibility and grows the longer we stand here."

They both laugh at my embarrassment, but do, thankfully, finally move toward Nate's truck. Then we have to decide on a place to go for dinner. Nate suggests Mabella's Italian Steakhouse. It sounds good to Sam and me, so we head in that direction.

After a short drive, we get to the area but run into the typical urban nightmare. These kitschy downtown places are great, but the parking sucks. We end up having to park around the corner, a block and a half away. Despite the walk, the dinner and cocktails are absolutely worth it.

We stay a little too long, and Sam and I become happily tipsy. Not drunk, but sufficiently loosened up. Around nine, Nate reminds us that we've yet to visit the grocery store. At our collective boos, he adds, "You can stay with us until Chase gets finished."

Sam and I are laughing and stumbling our way back to the truck with Nate between us keeping us straight. We've just passed an access between two buildings when I feel myself being jerked backward.

I scream out and watch as Sam and Nate turn to see what happened. Sam's face drains of all color and Nate draws his weapon; murderous intent clear in his eyes.

The voice in my ear makes tangible my greatest fear. "You didn't think you could hide from me, did you?"

Nate starts creeping forward, "Let her go."

He must see something I don't because he stops advancing. In a split second, I figure out what made him stop when I feel the barrel of a gun at my temple.

Sam watches on in horror as his free hand begins to roam over my body. "You still feel fantastic. I can't wait to have you under me again."

At his words, something inside me breaks. He can kill me, but he won't take me ever again. I start fighting, "You sick fuck, you'll have to blow my head off first." I land a few blows, but they don't earn me my freedom. He digs his fingers in my throat, and I begin to see spots.

"I've got a better idea." He aims the gun at Sam, and I see the muzzle flash before I can scream. "SAM, NO!" Time slows to a crawl as I watch Sam fall lifelessly to the ground.

"I can kill him too, or we can stroll through this alley to my car."

It's no contest. Nate is a medic. With him alive, Sam has a chance. If I keep fighting, they're both dead.

I focus on Nate's tortured face, and everything inside me goes cold. "Take care of her."

He shakes his head and yells out, "ERIN, dammit! Don't you fucking do this!"

Jack starts to lift the gun again. "NO! Nate, please… Don't let my sister die." At the sound of Sam coughing, he turns and swears. With one last imploring look at me, I give my head a negative shake, and he tucks his gun away. He swears loudly and runs over to Sam; pulling off his jacket and placing it under her head.

Thinking he's won, Jack starts pulling me through the alley, and I watch as Nate applies pressure to Sam's stomach. He pulls out his phone, and I get one last look at his face before I'm enveloped by the darkness of the alley.

Chapter 14

Nate

"Hold on, Sam!" I dial emergency and put the phone on speaker before placing it on the ground.

"911. What's your emergency?"

"My friend's been shot, and a woman has been kidnapped. Please, I need help."

"What's your location?"

"I'm in downtown Columbus on First Avenue between Eleventh and Tenth. Tell them to hurry. The asshole's getting away."

"Sir, I need you to stay calm. What's your name?"

"Captain Nathaniel Erickson, Army Ranger."

"All right, Captain, help is on the way. What's your friend's name?"

"I'm… Sam."

"Where were you shot, Sam?"

"Stomach. Please… hurry. He's got my sister." She tries to sit up. "We've got to find her."

I press on her shoulder to keep her down. "Lie still, Sam."

"You've got to help Erin!"

The dispatcher attempts to calm Sam down. "Sam, you need to calm down and try not to talk anymore. I've got police and an ambulance on the way. Captain, what can you tell me about her condition?"

"I've got pressure on the wound, but nothing to pack it with. I'm certain the bullet didn't strike the aorta or any major organs."

"Do you have medical training, Captain?"

"Combat medic."

"Sam, the ambulance should be arriving any second now, led by an Officer Stephens."

I answer for Sam. "I hear them. Thank you."

Two patrol cars and an ambulance rush up the street. Someone yells, "Captain Erickson?"

"Yeah. You Stephens?"

"That's me." The young cop carefully picks his way to where Sam and I are on the ground; gun up and at the ready.

"Gunshot wound here. She's conscious and talking. The woman was taken through there." I point at the alley access. Two of the officers take off through the access, one scans the street, and Stephens runs over to where Sam and I are to secure the area for the medical team.

Once the paramedics take over Sam's care, I move back, but she grabs my hand and whispers. "Find her."

"I swear." Then, I stand and turn to Stephens.

Without waiting on the questions I know are coming, I start spitting out information rapid-fire. "His name is Jack Rogers. Six-one, one-ninety, dark hair, trim beard. He was just released a week ago for kidnapping, assault, and rape in Alabama. The woman he took was his victim four years ago. If you contact Homewood PD Detective Eve Peyton, she'll confirm all this. The victim is Erin Westin five-six, one-fifteen, long brown hair."

Everything in me is screaming to join the search, but the first two cops return before we make it to the alley opening. "We found signs of a struggle in the grassy area and a shoe on the pavement, but they're gone."

As one, Stephens and I ask if they spotted any cameras in the area. One of the uniforms nods, but adds, "Plenty, but they all seem to be pointed at the back entrances of the surrounding businesses. None are aimed at the loading area."

I bend at the waist and let out a loud, angry roar.

Stephens ignores me and starts barking out orders. "There are four access points on Eleventh and Broadway. I want footage from every camera on this block. Mack, that's you. Stinson, you canvas Broadway. Brunson, you're on Eleventh."

Reining myself in, I pull out my phone again. This time to call Hyper. "He's here! That bastard's here, and he's got Erin!" Stephens walks over and motions to his ear. I put the phone on speaker, and Stephens demands, "Identify yourself."

"Captain Draven Maxwell, US Army Ranger."

"What the hell happened, Squid?"

"He jumped out of an alley and grabbed her, then shot Sam when Erin began fighting. He told her that Sam and I could die, or she could leave with him giving me a chance to save Sam. She gave herself up. She's gone."

"Keep it together, man. You know they're both tough as nails… Where do you need me right now?"

"Hospital. Stay with Sam. Call Shark. He needs to find Omen." I glance over at Stephens and vow, "I'm going to find Erin."

When I've disconnected the call, Stephens asks, "Who are Shark and Omen?"

"Liam Callaghan and Chase McDaniels, Rangers. McDaniels is Sam's husband. He's Secret Squirrel on base right now, and we can't contact him." He nods and motions for me to follow him, then jogs back to the ambulance.

"How is she?"

"In a lot of pain, but we got to her fast. And you did a good job before we got here."

Sam calls out "Chase…"

"We'll get him. Hype's on his way to stay with you until Shark can get him."

After that, the medics shut the doors, and the ambulance speeds off. Stephens says, "Let's go check that alley." I reluctantly follow him when my insides are insisting we not waste time looking where we know she isn't.

Because of the concrete path, there are no

signs of anything until we get to the loading area. The patch of grass is marred as if there was a fight here. Erin's shoe is about ten feet and ninety degrees from the entry point. It's broken and facing away from where the car would have been parked.

I analyze the scene out loud. "She walked backward willingly through that access."

Stephens pulls up at that, "Willingly?" I explain to him the choice Jack presented to Erin. He nods and points to the drag marks, "When they reached the grassy area, he, what, sedated her? That would explain the drag marks, but not the struggle or the shoe."

Thinking of Erin's training, I get an idea, "Whatever it was, she faked it. Look, the drag marks lead up to the tire marks. He would have tried to put her in the trunk. That's when she made her move and ran that way." I point to the direction of the fallen shoe. "Only… something went wrong. Either he tackled her, or she tripped on the shoe that broke during the struggle."

Stephens says what I'm thinking, "I guess at this point it doesn't really matter. We're just wasting time here."

I start pacing. Officer Stephens watches me warily as I talk to myself. "How the hell did he find us anyway? Mike didn't know my address, but even if he did and gave it up, that would have only led him to the nearest gate, which is

Benning's main gate. There's no way someone could be camped out there waiting for us without attracting a lot of attention. He couldn't have just waltzed on base by himself. And, there's no chance he posed as a soldier or family member."

I keep going back to the attack on Mike. Something about it... "Shit!"

Stephens comes to attention. "What?"

"Rogers posed as an elderly woman's grandson to get at one of the Homewood detectives. What if he got on base the same way? Erin was allowed on base, escorted by me... Rogers got someone to take him on base."

"It couldn't have been one of the businesses on base. They require background checks and special ID to access the base."

"No, that's not it. He met someone on the outside and convinced them to take him in..." My phone is out again. I call my MP friend, Chintzy. "Chintzy, I've got an emergency here. I need to know if you have any reports of an assault or murder with a stolen vehicle... in the last twenty-four hours."

"Hang on a sec... You're gonna owe me for this."

"Fine. Shut up and do it."

"...Ok... it looks like we've got a murder victim found by a roommate... this morning. Gun safe was open, and some clothes and the deceased soldier's car is missing."

"Anything else?"

"Nope, just that one."

"I need info on the car, Chintzy."

"I'll email you now."

"Thanks, man."

Stephens hands me a card showing his email address. As soon as I get the message from Chintzy, I forward it to him and take off toward my truck. From behind me, I hear him running after me, "Hold on. You can't just leave. The detective is going to want to speak to you."

He catches me at my truck, and I turn on him, "Look, my team specializes in hostage location and rescue. I guarantee you that I'm far better at this than your detective. Now move! Please."

Stephens backs away, and I peel out, headed in the direction of home to get to my equipment. I reach for the call button on the wheel, but before it's depressed, a call from Shark rings in. "I've got Omen. We're on our way to Sam. What can you tell us?"

"Nothing right now. Drop him off and get back to base. Bring Hyper with you."

"Squid we'll..." There's another call coming in; Jim Krantz.

Just before I transfer to the other call, I yell, "MY HOUSE!"

"Jim, please give me some good news."

"Yeah, I've got three Spencers flagged for one thing or another in the Carolinas. I can narrow it to one if I've got something to cross match."

"Look for a brother."

"Ok… Spencer One is an only child, Spencer Two has three sisters, and bingo, Spencer Three lists two brothers; one deceased. I'll send you any pics I find of the live one if you have something to compare them to."

I picture the man's face as he gropes a terrified Erin. "Hell yes, I can ID him." The wait for Jim to find something is excruciating. "Got it! Sending to you now."

Not wanting to waste a second, I slam on the brakes skidding to a stop. I open the email app on my phone and look for Jim's message. "Got him."

"Squid, you're dancing to my music now. This is big federal shit. You have to give me everything you've got on these assholes."

"The brother goes by the name of Jack Rogers. He's been in jail in Alabama for the last four years. He got out a week ago and has just taken the woman he was convicted of kidnapping and raping. If you want this, you've got it. Get your boys down here now before he kills her."

"Two hours."

"Jim, I need you to let me in on this."

"It's the woman, isn't it?"

"She's mine."

"I'll make the call."

As soon as I hang up with Jim, I'm calling Officer Stephens. "Your detective is about to get a call from FBI Special Agent Jim Krantz. Your perp is wanted by the FBI for human trafficking. They're on their way down, and I'm on my way back."

Erin

As I'm pulled through the alley, I silently pray, "Please, God, don't let my sister die." My prayer is that she'll live and have babies and be happy. My hope is that I'll get to see her again.

Jack stops next to a tan Toyota sedan. Before I see him move, he presses a cloth against my mouth and nose. I start fighting with all I've got, then will myself to calm and hold my breath. I pull at his arm over my face for a moment more, then slowly let it fall slack.

My lungs are burning, waiting for him to remove the cloth. When he finally removes the cloth, I fight the urge to gulp in oxygen and take a slow breath, so he'll believe I'm out.

I allow myself to be dragged to the back of the car and hear the trunk open. As he's positioning himself to stuff me inside, I take my shot. I land a knee shot to his groin and an elbow strike to his sternum.

While he's incapacitated, I turn to run, but the strap on one of my shoes must have broken during our struggle. The loose shoe rolls with my ankle and I end up sprawled on the ground.

By the time I look up, he's standing over me with his gun pointed at the alley. "If you make a sound, the first person I see is dead."

Utterly defeated, I stand, and he forces me into the trunk. The last thing I see before the trunk closes is the needle plunging into my thigh.

When I wake again, I'm in the back of another vehicle. The space is large and flat, and there's something hard and smooth over me. The air in here is fresh and warm, but I can't see any light coming in around the edges of my holding place. It seems that I'm in the cargo area of a large SUV. That means windows. If I can lift the cargo cover enough, I should be able to get someone's attention.

Carefully, I test the edges of the cover for latches. Finding none, I gently press up on one side while supporting the other. It doesn't budge.

I try again with both hands on one side, but it still won't move. He must have something heavy on top. Suddenly, I remember a detail about Sam's Terrain. The back seats will lay forward if I can find the latch on the seatback.

I can get my hands on the sides of the seats, but don't feel anything. Then I remember, in Sam's car, the latches are on the top of the seats. I work my fingers to the front of the cargo cover, but there's not enough space to reach through. Dammit!

All I can do is wait and plan.

I've only been awake for a couple minutes when I feel the SUV slow down. I hear a garage door opening and then closing behind me. I'm too late.

I brace myself to attack as soon as Jack opens the SUV's back hatch but hear a door slam and a raised voice instead. Jack gets out and argues with a man that entered the garage. Oh my god. Jack just called him Spencer.

I stay quiet and listen to their heated argument. "What the hell, Trey? Why are you here? Please tell me you haven't brought that bitch with you."

"Watch your mouth, Spencer. I told you I was bringing her here."

"Yeah, and I told you not to. The heat is on you enough as it is already. Eventually, they're going to know who you are, and they'll come knocking on this door."

"No, they won't. Those dipshits couldn't find their asses in the dark." I hear them moving to the back of the SUV and force myself to go limp just as the hatch lifts.

"Damn, man. You've got to get her out of here, or we're both screwed."

"No. I told you, this one's mine."

"You're fucking obsessed. Get her out of here!"

"She stays!"

"If you won't handle her, I'll do it."

Jack yells, and I hear a scuffle and the sounds of fists hitting flesh. I'm frozen in place. Peering outside of the cargo hold, I spot them fighting and see the glint of a knife. Not wasting any more time, I slip out the back and pause for a moment in case they heard me. There's an exterior door close to my location, and I decide to make a run for it.

Slipping off my remaining shoe, I creep to the door and open it just as I hear a man yell out in pain. I tear out of there as fast as my feet will carry me. I don't know where I'm going, but I can, at least, see to follow the finely graveled driveway.

I turn around to see if I'm being chased and don't see Jack or Spencer. Still, I keep running.

I've run at least a hundred yards, but have yet to find the end of the wooded driveway. Realizing I'm a sitting duck, I veer off into the tree line. I've gone at least two hundred yards when I break through the other side only to find that I'm at the point of a peninsula. I have no choice but to turn back.

Up ahead is a grouping of tall ornamental grasses, I crawl in between them to catch my breath and rest a while. My feet are raw and bleeding from my barefoot escape through the woods. Funny, I hadn't noticed until now, but they hurt like hell.

When my heart rate slows down, and I'm breathing normally, I think through the situation

I'm in. With any luck, Jack, or Trey as he was called, and Spencer killed each other. I can't count on being the case or that someone equally bad isn't next in line, so I don't want to chance going back to the house.

Besides smelling the ocean and feeling sand under me, I don't know where I am. I suspect this is Hilton Head since Jack… Trey mentioned Hilton Head and Spencer before. What throws me is the grandeur of this place. The house is massive, and the property is sprawling.

Ok. Think, Erin. I could try to find another house, but, in the dark, I could end up going in circles. I could follow the beach, but I'd be too easily spotted.

The temperature has got to be in the forties, so I can't just stay here. I've got to do something… There haven't been any sounds of someone looking for me; no feet in the brush, no cars, no nothing. What if they're both dead? I could find a phone or just take the vehicle Jack brought me in.

I can't believe I'm doing this. Without a better option, I pick myself up and slowly make my way back to the driveway, keeping to the tree line in case someone does drive by.

I've now gotten as close as I can to the garage without leaving the tree line. I wait five, ten, fifteen minutes before I feel brave enough to dart across the clearing to the corner of the garage. Dropping to my belly, I peer through the still open door, under the body of the SUV. I can't see anything from this angle. Crawling on the ground, I make my way to the doorway. I see blood on the floor, but no Jack or Spencer.

I take a deep breath to calm my nerves, then crawl the rest of the way to the driver door of the SUV, finding it open. I climb up in the cab, hoping to find keys or a phone… Nothing.

My only options now are to enter the house or walk the entire driveway to the main road… There's just no way I can go in that house. I look around for a jacket or coat and something I can wrap around my feet.

Finding nothing, I give up and turn back to the door I escaped through. At the sight in the doorway, I hang my head as the tears begin to fall. "Honey, you came back. Now, turn around and move."

Chapter 15

Nate

I march into the Columbus PD and spot Officer Stephens right away. He approaches me with caution. "Captain, you shouldn't be here. The FBI is on the way and Payne, the detective, is pissed about you leaving the scene, and about you being included in the investigation by the FBI."

"I don't give a damn what he is. He can..." Just then, a red-faced man bursts through the bullpen door and storms toward me. His greasy hair and large paunch tell me that he's long past his effectiveness as a good cop. "Stephens, is this the guy you failed to arrest for leaving the scene of a crime?" When Stephens doesn't deny it, the irate detective starts back in on me. "Who the hell do you think you are fleeing the scene of a kidnapping and attempted murder? I don't care if you are some hotshot Ranger. Stephens, take him to interrogation."

"Some other time maybe. I've got work to do."

"You? Soldier boy, you've got no authority here. You're just a witness, or maybe you had something to do with the whole set-up."

"Wow. You sound like a bitter washout." He launches at me, "You son of a bitch. You..."

An air horn stops everyone. We all turn toward the direction of the sound, and I see Jim standing there. He is quite the opposite of Payne. Being a former MP, he looks like he could still cut it. He's freakishly tall, and his skin is as black as night. The only thing that's changed are the nerdy Clark Kent glasses he's sporting. I glance down at my watch, then back at him. "You made good time." He doesn't respond, but instead, walks up to Detective Payne. "I'm Special Agent Jim Krantz. Where can we talk?"

Payne straightens himself and motions to a conference room. Gesturing to me, he snarls, "He's not coming."

Krantz counters, "I'm afraid that's not your call to make."

We all file into the room and Jim opens his briefcase and begins. "The man that shot Mrs. McDaniels and kidnapped Ms. Westin is known in Alabama as Jack Rogers. His real name is Trey Battle. He and his brother Spencer are involved in a sex trafficking ring on the Southeast coast. Their primary residence is located on Hilton Head's Daufuskie Island at Bloody Point."

Payne scowls, "If the FBI knows all this, then why are they both still walking around?"

"So far, we haven't had enough evidence to get a judge to issue a warrant to search the home of one of the wealthiest families in Hilton Head. With the abduction of Ms. Westin, we now have probable cause, if we can convince the judge Trey took her."

Jim turns to me, "And I believe that's where

you come in." If Payne's face wasn't red enough before, it's absolutely mottled now.

"I positively identified Battle as being the man that took Erin. We have a lead on the car he might have used, but Stephens will have to give us an update on that." Stephens opens a folder with still shots from traffic cams in the area. "Based on the description given to Captain Erickson by base police, we did find a matching vehicle leaving the area around Mabella's. We pick it up in several locations headed North to an abandoned factory. It goes in but doesn't come out. Ten minutes later, this pulls out." He shows a photo of a black Tahoe.

"We don't get a shot of the driver, but we do get make, model, and the tag number. It's a late model Tahoe registered to a Penline Corporation."

Jim smacks his hand on the table, making Payne jump. "Hot damn! That's the corporation owned by the Battle family. We got him." He turns back to Stephens, "How far can you track this vehicle by camera?"

"We got him as far as the 80. After that, we need some help."

Jim shakes his head and smiles. "He's going home. That should be enough to get a warrant for OnStar GPS tracking."

He stands up and begins gathering his things, and I make my way over to him. "You still got room for me in this thing?"

He raises a brow, "Just you?"

"You know better than that. I've got two more."

"I shouldn't, but I realize we wouldn't have shit without you. We take off in thirty minutes."

I pull out my phone. "Hype, you and Shark get your go bags and be at the Columbus Air private hangers in thirty minutes."

"Got it."

"Stephens, can you check out the warehouse where Rogers dumped the car?"

Payne jumps in, "No, he cannot. He's not your damn flunky."

Stephens answers with a shit-eating grin, "I'd be happy to, sir."

Twenty-five minutes later, I'm parked outside the private hangers at Columbus Airport and reach behind the seat for my go-bag. Stepping out of the truck, I can hear her laughter in my head and feel her hands on my chest. The feeling is so real that it causes me to stumble and brace a hand against my truck.

I need to find her. I will find her. And I will snap this bastard's fucking neck.

Fueled by anger, I push off the truck and head toward the hangars with a renewed determination. Jim, Hyper, Shark, and I all seem to arrive at the same time. As we approach the plane, Jim moves to block the entrance and holds his hand out to stop me "Before we board, I need to make one thing clear. You want Erin back, and I want that too, but I need that house."

I take a step forward, "Excuse me?"

"You know how this works. We'll do everything we can to extract Ms. Westin safely, but our priority has to be taking these guys down permanently. Georgia and South Carolina state police have been contacted and instructed to observe and report only. They are not clear to approach."

I drop my bag on the asphalt and cross my arms across my chest. "You're just going to leave her with him."

"Yes... As long as he's en route, he can't hurt her. The second he stops and feels threatened, this all goes to shit. Now, I'm done talking here. You want to follow orders, you can get on the plane. If you can't handle this, keep your ass on the ground."

Hyper puts a hand on my shoulder, "He's right, man." I jerk out from under his hand, grab my bag, and shoulder past Jim.

Once we're all seated on the FBI's jet, Jim's team gets to work. "I want spotters at the I-95 and I-16 junction, on Highway 278, and at the Battles' yacht basin in Harbour Town."

Spotters? What the hell for? "Wait a minute, what about the GPS warrant?"

"Denied. Our only shot at this bastard is in person and red-handed. In order to do that, our job is to get in place before he gets there. Once we land on the island, we'll gear up and meet agents from the Savannah field office and a crew from the Cutter Hamilton. The Coast Guard is going to take us around the South of the island to avoid being seen at the Daufuskie dock. When we get word that they've left their marina, we'll beach and surround the house while another team covers the dock."

"Why aren't we setting up as soon as we get there?"

"No one knows what kind of security they have, and I don't want to risk tipping our hand to Spencer."

When the jet lands on Hilton Head Island, one of the Savannah agents approaches and leads the group to the cars waiting to take us to the dock. The agent gives Jim an update. "No one's reported any sightings on the 16, or the 95. It's possible he took the 80 all the way from Columbus."

"Dammit!... Keep state on the 278 and the marina then."

We climb in their vehicles and drive to the dock to board the Hamilton. Once aboard, the Captain greets us and introduces us to the crew we'll be working with. I can hear the engines engage as the teams discuss the planned strategy, but I'm focused on the map showing the location where I'll find Erin. "We'll anchor seven miles off Bloody Point to avoid being identified from shore. From there, we'll launch three longboats. Agent Krantz, you divide up your teams among the boats." Jim nods and the captain says, "We launch those boats in thirty minutes."

It feels like a lifetime has passed waiting in darkness off the beach at Bloody Point. It's been a little over an hour since the plane landed and a little over five hours since that asshole took Erin.

A part of me regrets climbing on that plane with Jim. My team could have driven ourselves and gotten here faster. Flying with the FBI got us to Hilton Head quicker, but the coordinating, communication, and the boats took way too long.

Jim must be thinking the same thing. Even in the dim light, he looks tense, but it's nothing compared to how I'm feeling. "Jim, we should have heard something by now."

"I know it. Even if he took the 80, we should have seen something."

The 80… I pull out my phone, covering the light, and pull up satellite images of the island. "Holy fuck!… Jim, he's already there."

"What the hell are you talking about?"

"He didn't go to Hilton Head. Look. The 80 goes straight to Tybee Island. There's a marina on the Northern side. That's not but five miles from here."

"No, we would have seen him."

I keep studying the dimly lit satellite images… Oh god. "Dammit! Look!" I point to a dock around the point near the Battles' beach.

"Son of a bitch." He picks up his radio. "Mark, there's a dock on the western part of the island. Take your boat and check it out."

Two tense minutes pass. "Jim, there's one boat here. The outboards are still warm."

"Dammit! This fucker's here. All teams move to the target now! Commander, get us to shore!"

Erin

Jack has a punishing grip on my neck as he marches me through the house. With the shape my feet are in, I trip and stumble as he forces me to keep his pace. He leads me down a long hallway to a dead end with a full-height, gilt mirror. Jack lets go of my neck and points his gun at me while he feels along the left side of the mirror. I hear a click and the mirror swings out, revealing a small lobby with an elevator.

After he pushes me through the hidden doorway, Jack secures the mirror door and presses the sole elevator button. The door opens, but I make no move to enter. That is, until I feel the barrel of his gun press between my shoulder blades.

When I do step in, I turn around and see the blood trail I've left on the otherwise pristine floor. Jack joins me in the elevator and presses the only button on the panel. I watch the doors close and feel the finality they represent. God, please let Sam be ok.

As we descend, I make a promise to myself. I will try to kill him. I will try to escape. If I can do neither, I will do the unthinkable. I will not allow this man to own me.

I remind myself of my training and force myself to focus on something other than the rising panic. Get him talking, distract him, look for vulnerabilities, watch for opportunities, and find a weapon.

Here goes step one, "What did you do to your brother?"

"Don't worry about him. He can't hurt you now."

So he killed his own brother over me. He's killed several people now. In my head, I'm berating myself. How did I not see any of this coming? Eight months we hung out; worked together on several project specs. Not once did I ever suspect he could be capable of this. Did I just not see it, or did something change along the way?

Stealing a glance at him, it's obvious that Jack has changed his appearance. He was handsome and muscular before; as if he worked hard on his physique. Now, he's thin and pale. Not sickly, but different. The darker hair color and styled beard make him look younger; hipster even. It's understandable how Mike didn't recognize him.

My attention is called back to the present when the elevator stops. The doors open to reveal a corridor that is reminiscent of an old hospital. Vinyl tile floors, hollow metal framing around the doors and windows, and even institutional wall guards.

Lost in my own thoughts, the sound of his voice breaking the silence startles me, "Now, a tour." Jack pushes me forward out of the elevator and stops me at the first door on the left. He presses a button beside the door, and the room beyond the window lights up.

It's a creepy-as-hell bedroom complete with a metal toilet and sink. What makes it so bad is that it's frilly as if made up for a young girl. The thought makes my skin crawl. He moves to a door directly across the hall and hits a similar button. This room is much different; rough concrete floor, block walls, prison type bunk. It's a nightmare.

"For now, you can have the comfortable room. Be good, and you can stay there. If not, you'll be moved to the cell."

I'm afraid I already know, but ask anyway, "What is this place."

"It's a training facility." I don't want to hear anymore. It's time to find a weapon. As god as my witness, one of us will be dead before sunrise.

Jack pulls me further down the hall showing me a total of five different "nice" rooms and five cells. Further still, reveals a medical room of sorts, a punishment room full of wicked implements, an office full of screens with views of every room in this dungeon, and finally, a room filled with cages on wheels. "This is our packaging room. From here, we can get the merchandise loaded onto a truck, then down to the dock where we deliver them to the customer via boat."

"So, I'm to be sold to some fat-ass sheik that can't get a woman to touch him willingly?"

"No. You belong to me. I would've had you a long time ago if your bitch sister hadn't shown up at your house that night." The look he gives makes me shudder. "I suppose it's my fault, though. The plan was to put you in the car as soon as the drugs did their job." He pauses to leer at me, "But, I just couldn't help myself."

He raises his hand to caress my cheek, and I pull away. Not to be defied, he jerks my arm up and spins me around, pinning me to the wall. "You're going to be fun to train."

I can feel his excitement as he presses his crotch against my backside. "I swear to god, I will never let you rape me again. You may as well kill me now because I will never stop fighting you."

"We'll see." He grabs my hair, twisting my head to the side, then puts his mouth on my neck. A shrill alarm sounds, and Jack looks around him. "Shit!" He opens the office door and shoves me inside. "Sit down and don't move."

I begin scouring the various screens just as he does. I don't see anything, but I hope against hope that somewhere in the darkness, someone is out there looking for me.

It's small at first, but eventually, I spot movement in most of the exterior camera views. As they begin to breach the house, additional alarms sound.

"NO NO, NO!" He stands and leans over to study one of the screens, blocking my view. Now's my chance, I start looking around the office for something I can use as a weapon and spot an intercom system. There are labels for kitchen, office, practically every room in the house. I keep looking for a weapon but don't find anything suitable.

Jack turns his attention back to me and appears deep in thought. As if he's come to some decision, he bends down to a drawer and picks up a small notebook, frantically looking through its pages.

Finding what he's looking for, he turns and opens a wall panel exposing a keypad. He punches in a code, and another door opens. I watch as he presses more buttons and see a timer start counting down from five minutes.

He's going to kill everyone in this house.

Jack picks up the book again and resumes searching its pages. While he's distracted, I take a step back and reach for the intercom panel. I hit as many switches as I can reach without turning around. Just as I'm lowering my arm, he turns his attention back to me and tosses the book on the floor.

"Let's go." He grabs my arm and jerks me into a standing position.

"What did you just do? Set a bomb? In case you haven't noticed, the house is surrounded. We'll just die in here with them." I glance beyond his head, and it's obvious by the reactions of the raid team that they can hear our exchange.

"Don't worry, we'll be long gone before this place goes up. These guys won't be so lucky." One of the men, seemingly the leader, is yelling into a radio.

"Well, with only five minutes and the upstairs full of police, how are we supposed to get out of this basement?"

"You let me worry…" His eyes grow wide, and he turns around to the screens. He looks confused, seeing the agents scrambling out of the house. That is until he looks behind me at the intercom panel. "YOU STUPID BITCH!"

I raise the only weapon I could find and strike. The pencil I wield burrows into his shoulder and breaks off becoming unusable. He howls in pain, and I deliver a knee strike to his stomach.

It seems like I'm gaining the upper hand until I fail to block his gun hand as it swings for my head.

Nate

Hyper, Shark, and I have taken positions around the back of the large home. Jim wouldn't allow us to be in the initial raid, so we decided that the most logical strategy would be for us to hang back and watch for concealed escape points.

The land elevation is steeper here than on other coastlines. That allows for the main floor of the house to be at ground level, but still out of danger of storm surge. I've identified one exposed part of the structure that's below grade and big enough to conceal an exit. This would be a prime location for a hidden access. It faces the back of the property and provides direct access to the path leading to the Bloody Point dock. My gut tells me this is it. I make myself invisible and put on my night vision optics.

I radio my position in to Shark and Hype, and they report their own findings. After several minutes, Shark keys in, "Something's happening here. They're all running out of the house as if their asses are on fire."

"Grab one. Find out what's going on."

Something's wrong. My body screams to get away, but my gut says to keep watching that wall.

"Squid. The place is wired. Somehow Erin turned on a communication system to warn the raiding team. She said five minutes."

"Shit!" I'm up and running for the house before I've figured out what I'm doing. "Shark, Hype, get to the boats."

"Right."

Halfway to the house, I hear the thunder of footsteps closing in on my left and right flank. "You two can't follow orders worth a shit."

"I don't recall voting you in charge. What do you see?"

"Seaming in the stucco. It's in a pattern. In Miami, you don't seam stucco. I think it was done intentionally to hide an opening."

Arriving at the base of the structure, I begin looking for a moving seam. Realizing what I'm looking for, Shark begins pressing on different points of the wall. Shark speculates, "It probably only opens from the inside."

Hyper opens his pack and starts pulling out primacord saying, "I can open it. I just need to know where."

Shark goes through his pack and pulls out a smoke bomb. "Stand back."

He tosses it, and we watch. After a second, he points, "There. Look." I spot it the same time Hyper does. The air inside the house is escaping and disrupting the rolling smoke.

Hyper yells, "Back up! I don't know if I'll hit latch or hinge, so this thing will either open or blow off." He attaches the cord to the seam and runs a fuse wire around the edge of the building. He hooks up the wires to a switch and begins his customary countdown, "One…"

After the blast, we rush back around and see the door hanging open. I peer inside and look back to my team. "Hype, find Jim. Shark, wait here in case Battle comes out."

They don't bother trying to stop me or even warn me. We've been here many times before, and each time, we rush in.

Once I've breached the busted door, the room I find myself in is filled with rolling cages barely big enough for an adult to sit upright in. It's sick as fuck, but I can't think about that now. Raising my weapon, I move through the room until I reach an interior door. I test it for sound, find it silent, and pull it open.

I'm in a corridor that is reminiscent of an asylum. It creeps me out, but that might just be because of what I know this place is used for. There is fresh blood on the floor in the pattern of footsteps. One set on the left side and a similar set on the other side. She's hurt.

I step forward and peer into the first room I come to. It's a surveillance office. In one wall is a panel showing a countdown with just over three and a half minutes remaining. I've got to move faster.

Moving back into the hallway, I work my way past a medical room, a torture room and arrive at the first of five sets of opposite facing doors. Each door is next to a large window. I test a button next to one of the doors, and the room lights up. Seeing that there's no place to hide in either room, I clear them quickly and move to the next set.

I get all the way to the end of the hallway when I find that one of the doors has been propped open. Taking a deep breath, I peer around the frame and see Battle.

He's holding Erin, cheek-to-cheek against his left side. On the other side of his head, he's holding a pistol to his temple.

"Take on more step, and you'll be the Savior of Nothing."

Chapter 16

Erin

My head snaps backward after the blow from Jack. It stuns me just long enough for him to get behind me and shove the gun into my side.

He drags me out of the office into the packaging room. At the loading door, he activates a panel on the left side. When a view screen loads, we can see outside the big door.

He swears as three dark figures appear to be searching the exterior wall for a hidden entrance.

He's trapped. Jack looks indecisive for a moment, then he gives me a hard look before pulling me back into the hallway. He doesn't stop until he's reached the last frilly room. He shoves me through the door and sticks a knife under the bottom to jam it open. The open door means that I still have a chance. I can't disarm him, but if I can get a good hit to his neck, I should have a couple seconds to make a run for it. It'd be worth the risk of getting shot to have a chance.

"I watched him kiss you." With the gun still pointed at my head, Jack stalks toward me. "You kept pushing me away, yet you let this man devour you in public… Tell me, Erin, did you open your legs for this man?"

I'm afraid of saying the wrong thing and losing what little chance I have of getting out of here. I open my mouth to answer but never get the chance. A blast sounds at the opposite end of the hall, and I close my eyes, thinking I've run out of time. My mind wanders to Sam and Nate. I say goodbye to them both and cover my ears.

When no additional explosions happen, I look around and see anger on Jack's features. He's realized before I did that the raid team must have blasted the door open.

Jack pulls my cheek against his and lifts the gun to the other side of his head. He's going to kill us both.

Several seconds pass when I see a reflection on the window across the hall. Oh my god, it's…it's Nate. Too many emotions to process swamp me at once. The prevailing thought is that I love him and can't let him die here with me.

"Take on more step, and you'll be the Savior of Nothing."

I've got to get him out of here. "Leave, Nate." My voice breaks as I say it, so I force myself to say it again. "Leave."

"Erin…"

"I said, go!" Please understand what I'm saying. "I don't want you here. Just leave Jack and me alone!"

"Fine! You can have him." He punches the wall outside the room, and he stomps angrily off down the hall. My heart feels like it's being ripped from my chest, but I can't think about that now. It's time to make my move.

My tongue darts out and swipes against Jack's bottom lip. He sucks in a breath, and I do it again, slower this time. Since my chest is pressed against his side, I lift my left hand to his thigh and inch my way up to fondle his crotch. I know I've gotten to him when I hear the feral groan in his throat. "If we're going to die here, touch me one last time."

He lets go of my head and presses his lips to mine. I fight the rising nausea and open my mouth to him. He either doesn't suspect anything or doesn't care and takes full advantage of the opportunity. I grab his left hand and place it on my breast, then his right hand goes to my back, pulling me closer.

From this position, I should be able to…

I thrust my right hand up against his chin and strike with my left. He makes a choking sound, and I only have a second to get out.

When I turn to the door, Nate is there. The shock of seeing him takes precious time that I might not have, but I do eventually move. As soon as I'm clear, Nate lifts his weapon to cover me.

Due to the close range, my knife hand strike must not have been very effective as I'm not out of the room before I hear three separate blasts of gunfire.

I'm not hit, but Nate drops to one knee. He's been hit in the thigh and in the arm. Sparing a glance back at Jack, I see a perfectly centered hole in his forehead.

My arms reach out to pull Nate up, but the wound on his leg is gushing, and he can't stand.

I grab the hand of his uninjured arm and start pulling. The smooth VCT helps, but he's heavy. He looks up at me, resignation evident on his face. It'll take forever to pull him down this long hallway, and I don't know how much time we've got left.

He apparently comes to the same conclusion and shouts, "Erin, run!"

My mind races back to that day in my house, him on the floor bleeding out. *Erin, run!*

Without hesitation, I take off.

Nate

"Erin, run!"

As soon as the words leave my mouth, she's gone.

Watching her hair swing as she runs away, a funny thought hits me. In the movies, the hero always demands that the woman run and save herself. Of course, in the movies, she never does. I never stopped to think about what would happen if she did. I've gotta say, it hurts a hell of a lot more than the bullets do.

Since being a Ranger means I can't give up, I toss my gun aside and work with my good arm and leg to make some headway to the exit. It's no good. There's no way I'll make it in time and, the more I move, the more I bleed. So much for being the Last Man Standing.

Closing my eyes, I think back to that day at the river and see Erin above me, eyes on fire as she takes her pleasure.

I could have loved her… Hell, I do love her.

From down the hall, I hear a crashing noise, then see her running toward me pushing one of those rolling cages.

She didn't leave. I've never felt so happy, but… damn her.

When she reaches me, she grabs me and starts pulling. "Get… up, soldier."

Together we manage to get me positioned over the top of the cage, and she moves behind it to push. She slips a time or two in the blood gushing from my leg but keeps going.

The slick floor paired with our momentum has us crashing into the dead-end which causes pain to shoot through my arm and leg.

She works to maneuver us into the packaging room and through the opening Hyper created. Shark's stunned face is there when we emerge. He quickly recovers and helps Erin push the cage as far away from the building as we can get.

We've made it about fifty feet before the night sky goes to hell. The blasts start at the front of the house and work their way to the back.

We're still moving when the downstairs goes off. The blast throws Shark and Erin and topples the cage. Debris rains down all around us, but we were far enough away to avoid being hurt by the pressure wave of the blast.

Erin and Shark jump up from where they fell and rush back to where I lie on the cold ground. Shark gets on the radio and is barking at someone as Erin checks me over.

Medics from the Hamilton got the message from Shark and rush over to our location. As soon as they spot me, they start cutting, pressing, and whatever else needs to be done. Through all the chaos, I see only Erin.

She's got a cut on her cheek and dirt on her face from when she fell. Her hair has leaves and other debris sticking out of it, and yet, she's the most beautiful thing I've ever seen.

"You didn't leave when I told you to." She looks at me like I've grown a second head.

"Of course not. I told you to leave first. You didn't, and you got shot, so I had to come back to save your ass."

"I love you."

"What?"

"You heard me."

"You… you can't tell me that here in front of all these people, laying on the ground with bullet holes in you."

"Why not?"

"You just… can't. Now, shut up."

One of the medics working on me clears his throat and addresses Erin. "Sorry to interrupt.

He'll live, but needs a little more work than I can do out here." As the medic calls for a litter, Shark, Hype, and Jim make their way over. Jim crouches down next to me and jokes, "Is this you fishing for sympathy, Squid?"

"Kiss... my ass," I bite out. He smiles and looks at Erin, "You must be Ms. Westin."

"Her name... is... Erin."

"Maybe to you, but I'm a gentleman. Are you even supposed to be talking?" For that, he gets the finger.

The litter arrives, and Hyper takes Erin's hand to help her up. She's shivering and winces in pain as she stands. Seeing her distress makes me worry, and I try to sit up. The medic pushes me back down and admonishes me, "Sir, I really wish you wouldn't do that."

Ignoring him, I look her over from head to toe and my gaze locks on her feet. She's not wearing any shoes, and it's freezing out here. I grab the medic's arm, "She's hurt and freezing. Check her feet."

"I'm fine," she insists. However, when I'm strapped down and the litter lifted, she takes a step and pain is evident on her face. "Hype." He acknowledges me with a nod and swings her up into his arms.

Of course, she protests, but Hyper takes it in stride. In fact, he teases her a little, "Do I need to break out my scary Hyper voice? Sam says it works wonders."

At the mention of Sam's name, Erin's voice goes quiet, "Hyper, how is my sister?" Jim jumps in to answer that question, "She'll be fine. Fortunately, that bastard wasn't much of a shot. The bullet missed all her organs, so their only concern is peritonitis. She's actually been pestering everyone about your status. Now that we can report good news to her, she'll give the nurses a break."

Once the group reaches the end of the small pier, Hyper sets Erin down in the boat, and the litter is secured onboard. Hyper and Shark climb in, and Jim speaks up, "This is where I leave you. You'll get fixed up on the cutter and be transported to the Savannah field office. As soon as I get my teams in place here, I'll be right behind you." Jim steps closer to Erin. "Ma'am, we all owe you a huge debt of gratitude. Your fast thinking saved the lives of twenty men and women in that house."

He reaches for her hand, and she obliges him. "Now, go get this jackass stitched up before he bleeds to death."

Erin

How the hell did I end up here?

I'm on a boat in the ocean, headed for a Coast Guard ship, surrounded by Army Rangers, Guardians, and FBI agents. In case the human cages and cells weren't clue enough, the presence of all these people certainly says something more is going on than the rescue of a woman kidnapped by a stalker.

I'm currently wrapped in a blanket, sitting on an equipment box while a medic tends to my abused feet. After he's cleaned off the dried blood, he whistles at what's underneath. "You've got several scratches and some puncture marks here. I'm sure they hurt like hell, but they're not too bad. It was my understanding that you were in the house. How did all this damage happen?"

"Before I was taken in the house, I ran. I wasn't wearing any shoes."

In his eyes, I see respect. "You must be one tough lady," he says before going back to his work. He applies an ointment and wraps my feet in gauze. "All finished."

"Thank you." He winks in answer and begins clearing away his equipment.

The first signs of sunrise are appearing as I look around me. I find Shark and Hyper talking with Nate as the medics continue putting pressure on his wounds. As I'm watching his face, he turns to me and smiles.

I hobble over to his right side and take his hand. He playfully asks me, "Can I say it yet?"

Looking up, I see smirks on the faces of anyone that heard him the first time. "No." If possible, his smile grows even wider.

We approach the Coast Guard ship from behind, and the boat is driven inside what I later learn is called a stern launch. Once everything is secured, we're met on deck by the captain and additional medical staff. I watch as the technicians take Nate away to fix him up and Hyper gives my shoulder a reassuring squeeze. "He'll be all right. Come on. Let's go find some coffee." An ensign leads the way, and Shark adds, "And some food. Not all of us went to Mabella's last night."

"All things considered, I wish I had just stayed on base and choked on my own cooking."

"I don't know. I've heard about your cooking. If I had to choose between that and being blown up… it's a tough choice."

"You are an overgrown child, just like the rest of them."

Shark shrugs off the comment, "Hey, you can't do this job if you aren't at least a little crazy."

When we arrive at the galley, my nose takes me straight to the coffee. I fix myself a big cup but nearly choke on the stuff. It's so strong you could walk on it; it's perfect. Shark and Hyper fix theirs, and we sit at the closest table.

After I've emptied the cup, I ask, "Is this what life is like for you guys on a daily basis?"

They both chime in, "Yep." Then, Shark adds, "That's why Rangers only deploy for three to six months at a time."

That's still unimaginable. I'm certain that I wouldn't survive if I had to do anything like this again. I have a new respect for them, but I never want to learn anything more about what they do.

In spite of the strong coffee, the nightmare of the night catches up to me, and I feel myself losing the battle with fatigue. I hear a chair sliding over the floor, and a hand guides my head to rest on a shoulder. As tired as I am, I don't even look to see whose it is.

Sometime later, I'm awakened when a man walks out of the kitchen and says, "I'm about to serve breakfast. You guys want some before the crowd gets here?"

I glance at my watch, "Breakfast at 5am? Who are you people?" When he laughs at me, Shark tells him, "Don't mind the civilian. We'll eat."

Hyper offers to bring me a tray in consideration of my feet, and I gladly take him up on his offer. The two men have fixed our trays and are about to be seated when the galley door swings open behind me. "I hope you saved some for me."

I jump out of my seat and turn to face him. Nate's standing there on crutches, wearing unfamiliar clothes. There's a bandage on his left arm and a larger bandage obvious under the borrowed pants.

My face breaks out into a huge grin, "Yep, and I cooked it."

"God help us."

Nate hobbles his way to the table and lowers himself into one of the chairs. I stand to go fix him some coffee but am met by the man that offered us breakfast. He's carrying a tray piled as high as Shark's and Hyper's and a large cup of coffee. "I got this ma'am."

He sets the tray down in front of Nate, and I sit back down. Once we all have our bellies full, we sit quietly, not quite ready to talk about what happened. Or, maybe they were quiet because I wasn't quite ready to talk about it.

When we start to hear voices in the corridor, Hyper says, "That will be the breakfast crowd. Let's split before it gets busy." He and Shark take away our trays as Nate, and I slowly make our way to the door. After a short discussion, the guys decide to wait on deck for Jim to return.

The early morning air is super cold, and I'm glad to still have the blanket the crew gave me. Despite the chill, it's a beautiful start to the morning if you look out to sea. On the other side of the boat, I can see the smoke rising from the explosion and subsequent fires around the house where I was held.

A commotion behind me draws my attention from the smoke and the waves. When I turn around, an older gentleman in a decorated uniform is standing there with several other men and women behind him. Even Nate, Hyper and Shark are standing with him sporting glowing smiles on their faces.

"Ms. Westin, I'm Gerald Richardson, Captain of the Cutter Hamilton." He reaches out his hand, and I do the same. "It was reported to me that several members of my crew only made it back to this boat because you risked your life to warn them about bombs planted in that house. Bombs that nearly took your life. The United States Coast Guard owes you a debt of gratitude and is bestowing on you the Civilian Service Commendation Medal for your selfless bravery in a dangerous situation."

I'm speechless. As much as I want to tell him thank you, I can't make a single word come out of my mouth. I stand up as straight as I can and fight back tears as I shake his hand. The captain then calls for attention, and as one, the Guardians and Rangers face me and salute.

I look around at everyone standing there. The sight is touching and humbling. The emotion of the moment is astounding, and the dam breaks. With tears streaming down my face, I offer the captain a whispered, "Thank you."

He reaches to shake my hand again and says, "No, Ms. Westin. Thank you."

Several crew members stick around to shake my hand after the captain leaves. Many of those were some of the people in the house that heard my warning. By the time the last one has gone, my knees are weak, and I sit back down. I look up at each of the Rangers, my new family, and they are all beaming. Hyper puffs out his chest,

"I don't know, Squid. You think baby sister will be proud?"

Nate stares straight into my eyes and all traces of humor leave his face, "She should be. I know I am."

I hear Shark say to Hyper, "Let's take a hike," and Nate joins me on the bench.

"How're you doing, Chief?"

"Sensory overload and running on fumes. To go from the worst situation imaginable to something so awe-inspiring is a lot to take in. I'm not sure I've caught up yet." Leaning forward to look at his arm, I ask, "How are you? You're the one that was shot twice."

"Like Jim said, the guy was a lousy shot. The arm was just a flesh wound, and the bullet went through the leg; fortunately missing the artery."

He opens his arm to me, and I gladly lean into him. "Now, just Close Your Eyes and rest for a while."

I haven't moved a muscle when Agent Krantz walks toward us. "We're heading in now. We'll catch a ride into Savannah and meet at the field office. I want to go over everything that happened..."

Nate interrupts, annoyance clear in his voice, "After what's she's been through, can we at least have a few hours to rest and clean up?"

"I'm not completely heartless you impatient dick. Before I was so rudely interrupted, I was going to tell you that you all have rooms at the

Bohemian with orders for a concierge to arrange fresh clothes for Ms. Westin. We'll meet at four. Happy?" The agent makes a face on that last word and Nate answers by blowing him a kiss. Those two must have history. "Yes, thank you, Agent Krantz."

Chapter 17

Nate

Around seven, we dock at the Savannah Coast Guard Base, and Jim herds us off the boat into a couple of agency SUVs. Just before he closes Erin's door, he hands her a phone, "Someone would like to speak with you."

Her eyes light up when she hears Sam's voice on the line. The conversation is mostly one-sided; Sam's side. Every once in a while, Erin gets a word in, "I'm exhausted but fine... Nate got himself shot up, but he'll live... I want to know how you are... We'll talk later when I've slept and had a stiff drink."

Sam must be getting tired as the conversation seems to wane. Erin hands me the phone, "Chase wants to talk to you."

"Omen, how's baby sister?"

"She'll be fine. She came through surgery without any complications. There could have been a lot more damage than there was, but regardless, they're bombarding her system with antibiotics. You know how belly wounds are."

I reach up to rub my own month-old scar. "Better than most... Omen, how pissed is the CO going to be with me being down again?"

"Well, considering the fact that you saved his wife's and sister-in-law's life all within twelve hours, he'll give you a pass."

"The hell you say. Is this what your secret

squirrel was about?"

"That and other things. Look, you don't worry about anything else right now other than resting and wrapping up this thing with the feds. We'll catch all this up when you get back."

"Yes sir, boss man."

"Suck it, Squid."

I pass the phone back to Jim and rest my head on the seatback. This has been a hell of a day already. Glancing at Erin, I watch as her head bobs in the way of someone that's losing the battle with sleep. My hand reaches out to slip around the back of her neck. She starts but calms realizing it's just me. Erin allows herself to be pulled against me and is instantly gone.

I must have dozed off on the trip to the hotel just as Erin did. The sound of Jim's voice startles me awake, "When we get to the hotel, we're going to go in through the staff entrance. Your injuries would attract attention, and I'm sure you'd like to avoid that for now. Erin, there's a female concierge waiting in your room to get some information from you. Once she has what she needs, she should return in a couple hours with clothes for you. Squid, I'm sure your go bag is the same one we were trained to carry so you and your men should be good."

After a few minutes of working through Savannah's traffic, the convoy pulls into the alley behind the hotel, and as everyone except the drivers pile out and head for the staff elevator. Jim's assistant grabs three black bags out of the back of one of the vehicles. "Here are your bags. We collected them from the plane."

"Thanks, Mark."

Jim steps forward to call the elevator. "I've booked all four suites on the top floor for your team and Ms. Westin." He proceeds to hand out numbered envelopes containing room keys.

My hope is that we won't need that many, but I'm certainly not going to say something in front of these men that might embarrass Erin.

The doors open, and the four of us enter the freight-sized elevator. Before the doors close, Jim says, "I'll be out front at half-past three."

I position myself against the back wall of the large box, Hyper and Shark are flanking me on the side walls, and Erin is standing blankly in the middle, a couple of steps in front of me. Movement on my left catches my eye as Hyper lifts his chin to get my attention. He gestures toward Erin with a nod and gives me a negative shake of his head.

He's worried about her. Fuck, we all are. We may be used to the adrenaline let-down after missions, but she's not. Every person reacts differently when their body sheds the excess epinephrine the body produces in stressful situations. And after the attack from Avery, I wasn't with her; I was on an operating table. It was Hyper and Sam that were with Erin at the hospital that night. He'd know better than I what to expect from her, but I'll be damned if I'll let anyone else around her right now. All I do know that I'm not liking how she's looking right now; blank. I'd much prefer the hellcat I know her to be.

As if reading our thoughts, she blurts out, "Knock it off. All of you." The elevator dings to let us know we've reached our floor, and the doors begin to open. As Erin moves toward the doors, she says, "All I need are ten showers and two gallons of mouthwash to get his…"

She stops mid-sentence and leans against the elevator's opening to steady herself. Hyper looks back to me, understanding in his eyes, and I call out to Erin, "Hey, Chief, you all right?"

"I'm…f-f-fine." She pushes herself upright again and takes a shaky step. I pick up my bag and place it cross-body at my back. Hyper picks his up and tosses it to Shark then moves to stand right behind Erin.

She takes one more shaky step, then buckles. Hyper scoops her up and takes off down the hall. "Damn. She's like ice," he says as he moves to the first suite door. "Who's is this?"

Propped up on the crutches, I pull out my key card even while he's asking. "It's me."

I pass the card to Shark who opens the door and holds it for the rest of us. Hyper moves through the suite, looking for the bedroom. He finds it but doesn't lay her on the bed. Instead, he moves into the bathroom, with Shark and me following behind him.

Erin has completely checked out and is still shaking. He sits down on the edge of the tub, holding her carefully. "Shark fill the tub while I get her undressed."

My rejection is fast and loud, "NO!"

Both men turn and look at me, shocked at my outburst. "You're the medic. You know we've got to get her warm, and you're in no shape to do it."

Without waiting for me to respond, Hyper turns back to Erin and grabs the hem of her shirt.

In a lethal, quiet voice, I say to them both, "I said no."

Shark asks, "What the hell, man? You know he's not going to hurt her."

"I know that, asshole. You both seem to have forgotten that the last time she was incapacitated, another man took off her clothes and did hurt her. Put her in the water like she is and get out."

Without another word, Hyper stands and lowers Erin in the tub, then turns to leave. When he reaches me, he stops, "You know that we would treat her with the same care and respect that we all showed Sam when we found her naked, hanging from that hook."

"Yeah, I do. But it's not worth that few moments of panic when she wakes up not knowing where she is, how she got there, or why she's naked."

The big man closes his eyes as if in pain. "Fuck, but you're right. I'm sorry."

"It's fine, you guys go get some rest. I'll call if I need help."

When I hear the door click shut, I leave the bathroom just long enough to roll the desk chair in so I can sit with Erin. After positioning the chair beside the island tub, I reach in the shower and get the shampoo and soap, then a towel and washcloth. Lastly, I grab one of the cups next to the coffee bar just in case.

Seated next to Erin, I reach out and stroke her hair and think just how close I came to losing her. The next thought to cross my mind is that when this is all over, she'll go back to Alabama an I'll be stuck in Georgia with deployments overseas.

I think back to all the talks about the domestic ops company Shark and Omen were planning to start. They wouldn't call it a security firm; it was more than that. It would have involved high-level security escorts, threat assessments, and hostage rescue; basically, the same thing we're doing now. I had always refused to entertain the idea of leaving the Rangers for something domestic, but the idea doesn't sound so ridiculous anymore. Of course, it's all moot now that Shark was reinstated and Omen was promoted.

I have no idea how anything would work out or even if it would work out for us. I just know that every part of me needs her and I'll do whatever is within my power to make her happy if she'll choose to be with me.

I lean over and kiss her on the forehead, then grab my crutches to help me into the other room. She'll need some food in her system to help her recover from the crash, so I decide to order a vast selection from the room service menu courtesy of the FBI.

Erin

A distant, yet familiar, voice pulls me out of a dream where I'm warm and safe. Keeping my eyes closed against the bright light, I listen for the voice to return. I don't know how long I have waited before I hear it again. "…can you open your eyes for me?"

I… I've… Someone's asked me this once before. It was when Jack… No, god, it happened again. I panic and reach out, only to confuse myself when I feel water. "Chief, Erin. You're all right. It's me, Nate."

Relieved and somewhat embarrassed, I open my eyes to see Nate sitting next to me in a desk chair. We're in a large and expensive-looking bathroom. I remember now… Jim, the hotel… the elevator… Looking down at myself and seeing me fully dressed in the water, I ask, "That bad, huh?"

"No. Hype carried you in here to get you in some warm water, but I wouldn't let him undress you. Since I couldn't undress you and get you in there myself, we went with the fully clothed option." Reaching down, Nate plucks a twig from my hair. "Now that you're warm, you think you could stand for a shower?" Looking at the twig in his hand, I answer, "I guess I better."

He stands and reaches his hand out to me. When he pulls me up, he laughs, "You look like a drowned rat. You peel those things off, and I'll get the shower going."

I bend down to drain the tub and work on removing the wet jeans, then the rest of my clothes. As I begin to lay them out to dry, I have a memory of Jack slipping his hand under my shirt. A shiver travels down my spine, and I gather the wet garments and shove them in the trash can. I'll never put them on again.

When I turn back to the shower, Nate has his back to me testing the water temperature. "It's ready for you. I'll just be outside."

I don't want him to leave. It's ridiculous, but I don't want to be alone. I whisper to him, "Please stay." As soon as the words leave my lips, I feel guilty. He's been sitting here with me for no telling how long. He must be exhausted and in pain. "I mean… unless you're… you need to lie down or…"

His answer is to set his crutches aside and pull off his shirt. I breathe a sigh of relief and step into the shower. Nate removes the rest of his clothes, then limps into the shower. After I wash all the dirt and debris out of my hair, I turn my focus to Nate.

I peel off the now-wet bandages and make him let me wash him. Remarkably, the more time I spend scrubbing Nate, the stronger I feel. It's as if caring for him this way gives me purpose; direction. I have something precious to me that all my focus goes into, leaving no room for thoughts of what I went through.

That feeling snowballs into another, and I realize that Jack doesn't matter anymore. Since waking up in that tub, all my thoughts have been of Nate. Needing him to be near me, wanting to take care of him, being… in love with him… The realization is sobering but also empowering.

With a renewed strength, I finish washing us both and dry us off. "Come on. Let's get you some dry bandages on and some clean clothes. Then I'm going to get us something to eat."

"I took care of that. Lunch should be delivered in about another ten minutes or so." With a towel around his waist, he grabs his crutches and heads out of the bathroom.

"Great. So, you go lie down, and I'll get you fixed up." He smiles a slow smile and does what I told him to do. Meanwhile, I find a fluffy robe hanging behind the door and slip it on, then lug his heavy bag to the bed. With his direction, I find bandages, a set of clothes for him, and a sealed pouch containing a hairbrush, new toothbrush, toothpaste, and mouthwash. "That's for you," he says. "It's not two gallons, but it should help."

"Yes, it will, but first, let's get you some fresh bandages on." He lies back, content to be fussed over, but does tell me that his arm will be fine without another bandage. Seeing my skeptical face, he defends himself. "I'm not being stubborn. It really is fine. I'm a combat medic, remember?"

I roll my eyes and put away the bandages as he reaches for his clothes. Just as he's pulling his shirt on, there's a knock at the door. "Room service."

Nate pulls a gun from his bag and makes his awkward way to the door. After checking through the peephole, he opens the door, and a very full tray is pushed in. The waiter unloads five plates, a basket of bread, and three large bottles of water on the dining table and quickly leaves. Considering my current state of bare feet, wet hair, and bathrobe, I look up at Nate. "Who's going to be joining us?"

He turns as he begins to speak, "Why do you? Oh." He notices the very full table and smiles sheepishly, "I wanted to make sure to have something that would appeal to you, so I went with variety."

"Good. I'm starved."

We put away an impressive amount of the food delivered before I put my fork down and lean back to stretch my tired muscles. Nate stands and stretches as well, but winces when his stitches pull. He moves toward the bed and pulls the covers back, then strips down to his boxers. "Since we're clean and fed, let's lie down for a while. Your clothes should be here in about four hours."

Through a yawn, I mumble, "Of course, you couldn't have arranged to have them here any earlier." He picks up his shirt and throws it at me. A laugh escapes me as I reach out to catch it. I drop the robe and pull on the shirt while Nate stretches out on the inviting bed. He pats the mattress beside him, and I crawl up to his side.

As I reach for the covers, I mumble, "Nate?"

"Yeah?"

"I'm glad you didn't bleed to death."

He chuckles and answers, "I'm glad you didn't get blown up."

I decide to make a bold move and once more, lift my head from his chest. "Nate?"

"Yeah?" he asks with a smile on his face.

"You can say it now."

Instantly, the smile leaves his face and is replaced by an intensity I've not seen before. He sits up, bringing me with him, and pulls me into his lap. "Erin Westin, I am in love with you. I think I started falling for you the moment you held a gun to my head."

I roll my eyes at him, but his face shows no humor. He shakes his head and says, "You were fiercely protecting your family. That day, you earned my respect and made me want to chase away the shadows and fear in your eyes. It was when you sacrificed yourself for Sam and me that I realized I loved you. Watching him drag you away… it felt like I was dying; like I couldn't breathe. And… when you came back for me in that house, knowing we could both be blown away at any moment, something changed for me. Nothing in my life will ever again mean a damn without you."

Before I have a chance to say anything, he pulls me to his chest and lays back down. I try hard to stay awake and digest everything he just said, but the trauma of the night proves to be too much. Wrapped up in him, I quickly fall asleep.

In what only feels like five minutes later, I wake to someone shaking my shoulder. "Hey, Chief, it's two-thirty. Your clothes just got here, and Jim will be here to pick us up in an hour." Groaning, I pull the covers over my head in protest. I'm not feeling enthusiastic about reliving the events of last night in front of an army of agents, police, lawyers, and god knows who else.

When I make no moves to get up, Nate cruelly pulls the covers off the bed. Not appreciating the rude awakening, I ready myself to release a vicious string of expletives. Opening my eyes, I immediately close my mouth when I see the warm smile on his face and the steaming cup of coffee he's holding out to me.

"Thanks," I offer as I reach for the cup. Nate sits down beside me, and I lean against his side. I sit still, soaking up his warmth and breathe in the scent that's so uniquely Nate. It's not a chemical, cologne smell, but a clean scent of soap and man.

He's must have gotten up earlier and let me sleep for a while longer. He's dressed and ready to go in sweats and a black Army tee. Me, on the other hand… I'm nervous and don't want to move from this spot.

As if he's read my mind, he says, "Don't worry, Chief. You're a hero to these people. Besides, I'll be right beside you the whole time." I let out a long sigh but otherwise, remain silent. I'm too touched by his words to respond, not trusting my voice to remain steady.

Nate reaches over and grabs four bags from the foot of the bed. "The lady said she picked out several types of outfits as she didn't know what you would prefer. Whatever you don't want, just leave in the bags on the desk, and she'll pick them up later."

He sets the bags down in front of me; I nod and hand him my coffee. Looking in the first bag, I find toothpaste, a toothbrush, deodorant, a few hair products, brush, and hair ties. This prompts me to reach up and test my braid. Yep, still wet. The next bag yields my favorite brand of skinny jeans, Asics, undies, a tank, and an

Alabama sweatshirt. Deciding this will work fine, I don't even bother looking through the other bags.

Gesturing with my coffee cup, Nate stands and picks up only one of his crutches. "I'll go refill this while you get dressed."

After he's closed the door, I coach myself up, "Come on, Erin. Get this over with so you can go see Sam." I sit there for a minute longer before I finally convince myself to get up and get dressed.

Chapter 18

Nate

"You can say it now."

I have been waiting my whole life to say these words to this woman. I have to make her understand what she means to me. All my plans, my career as a Ranger, everything now means fucking nothing if I can't have her by my side.

I sit up and pull her into my lap, and the words come spilling out.

"Nothing in my life will ever again mean a damn without you."

I watched Omen for ten years try to kill himself by taking on every shitty mission that no one else had the guts to. He did it just to try to end the pain of losing the only woman that ever mattered to him. And, if Erin walks away after all this is over, I'll be in that same hell.

The thought of a life without her terrifies me, and that puts me off-kilter. I'm the guy that handles shit. The guy that always has a plan. Never scared because I'm always prepared. Until now…

Despite the turmoil in my mind, I drift off to sleep.

Right around two, I wake up and decide to get myself dressed while leaving her to rest as long as I can. Remembering the concierge, I go to the bathroom and collect her discarded clothes. I write down the sizes shown on the tags and feel confident that this will do. Thinking back to the scene of the kidnap, I remember a number being embossed on the bottom of her shoe. It was an eight. I call the concierge and relay the information, then get back to my own state of affairs.

As I dress, I watch her sleeping form. Erin has come to mean as much to me as Sam means to Omen. In the six weeks I've known her, she's sacrificed herself to save someone else twice. She didn't do it for glory or because she was following orders, she did it for love. Love for her sister and… my god… love for me.

The realization hits me like a ton of bricks. She came back for me because she loves me.

I close my eyes and hope to god that it's not just my imagination.

Just after three, a knock at the door interrupts my thoughts. Grabbing my pistol off the nightstand, I go and check the door and see a middle-aged female on the other side. I open the door, and she introduces herself as the concierge with a delivery for Erin. She hands me a few bags and leaves.

I guess it's time to wake Erin. I'd better get some coffee ready.

A few minutes later, I'm armed with coffee and carry the bags into the bedroom. I wake her up, give her the coffee, and sit with her for a while before giving her some privacy to dress.

I don't know how much time has passed

when she emerges from the bedroom. I'm floored by the sight of her. She's just as beautiful as always. Her hair frames her face in soft waves; a face that's still beautiful without the makeup she hides behind. While I love seeing the made-up Erin in her power suits, this Erin seems softer, more real. Someone she doesn't share with the world; an Erin only I get to know.

She slowly walks over and leans into me. I kiss the top of her head and ask, "Feeling better, Chief?" As she opens her mouth to answer, there's another knock at the door. Frowning, I look down at my watch. "He's early."

Erin turns toward the door, but I stop her. Once again, I hobble over and draw my gun. Identifying the visitor through the peephole, I tuck the gun away and open the door. Jim is standing there in a fresh suit, looking better than he did this morning. Behind him, I see that he's already collected Shark and Hyper. Jim looks past me to Erin, "Ready to go?"

From behind me, she answers, "Let's get this over with."

I pick up my bag, and we file out of the room, following the rest of the group to the main elevators. As the doors close, Jim addresses the group, "As soon as we're done here, I'll have the jet fly you all back to Benning."

In no time, we're walking into the FBI Savannah field office. Shark and Hyper go with one group to pour over satellite images. Their job is to point out the location of the hidden access and help identify possible trafficking routes. Erin and I are escorted to a very large and very full conference room. Seeing the crowd, she tenses beside me.

I reach for her hand in an attempt to calm her frayed nerves. I'm so focused on her that I don't hear the announcement Jim makes to the crowd. After a short pause, the room begins to clear with people voicing their thanks as they exit the space.

"You've got quite a fan club, Ms. Westin." Jim gestures to a chair in the middle of the long table and takes a seat on the opposite side. Erin and I both sit and prepare for a long afternoon.

"Ms. Westin, Erin, I want to thank you again for the risk you took to save the FBI and the Coast Guard teams last night. I realize you have just been through a harrowing ordeal, but I want you to know that some great good has come from it. The Battle family has been under suspicion for human trafficking, but for the last four years, their activities have been so limited that no one has been able to get enough proof for a search warrant. I realize now that was due to Trey Battle being in prison for what he did to you. With him getting out, there's no doubt in my mind that their business would have resumed at full swing and you know what that means.

"While I would have never put you in this

situation, it was because of your abduction that we were able to gain access to the family properties, financials, and communications for the purpose of shutting them down. Currently, we have several teams at their businesses and sifting through the debris on Daufuskie Island for any usable data storage or records."

Watching Erin's face, it's clear to me that she's shell-shocked by all this information, but she keeps it together and nods for Jim to continue.

"I realize this won't make any of this easier to cope with, but I just want you to know that your actions helped to take down their trafficking operation and save the lives of countless young women and girls. Now, I'm sure you have questions, and I'll be glad to answer them. I would also like to get some information from you about the house, people you might have seen, and details about the basement. Can you start by telling me what happened after you arrived at the house?"

"It was dark. I had been drugged, so I had no idea what time it was. I was in the cargo area of a large SUV…."

She tells about the argument and fight between the two brothers, the escape, the return, and the attempt to take one of the vehicles to safety.

"It sounded like Jack, I mean Trey killed Spencer, but I didn't see anything."

"So far, we've only found one body in the debris from the explosion. It was in the basement, the farthest from the place you escaped from. We've already positively ID'd him as being Trey Battle, Jack Rogers."

Erin fidgets in her seat. "What about Spencer? Did you find his body?"

Jim looks apologetic when he answers, "No. We did find blood on the slab of the garage. It's not a match for Rogers, so we assume it's from Spencer, but there wasn't enough there to indicate he sustained a mortal wound. There's still a lot of ground to cover, though. Tell me about what happened when you went back to the house."

"After I'd watched for movement for over half an hour from the tree line, I went back into the garage to see if I could find keys to the car I was brought in. They weren't in the car, and I wasn't going to chance going into the house. When I turned to go back outside, Jack was waiting in the doorway."

She shivers and closes her eyes tightly. I think she needs a break. "Would you give us a minute, Jim?"

"Sure. I'll go arrange for some coffee."

After he leaves, I turn my chair and pull her into my lap. "I can still feel his hands on me."

"Hey, Chief, look at me." She turns red-rimmed eyes my way. "You beat the bastard. He's dead and can never lay a finger on you again."

A single tear falls and tracks down her cheek. Her eyes study my face for a long while, then she begins to speak, "When you were bleeding out and told me to run from Avery, I realized I had been wrong about you. I had tried so hard to keep you at arms-length to protect myself. When you tried to make me run from Jack's basement, I realized something important then too."

Erin reaches up and places a hand against my face. "I couldn't run. I had nothing to run to. Besides Sam, you're all that matters to me. I decided that I was either getting you out or I would die with you. I love you, Nate."

I weave my hand around the back of her neck and pull her to within a breath of me. "I love you, Erin."

She presses her lips to mine. It's not a gentle brush; her kiss is deep and claiming. When she pulls back, I get a brief glimpse of Boss Erin, "Yours are the only hands I want to feel on me ever again."

"I promise to wipe away the memory of his touch."

I kiss her again because I can, and there's a knock at the door. Erin moves back to her seat as the door opens and an assistant following Jim is carrying a tray of coffees. He sets it down in the middle of the table and takes his leave. Jim takes his seat again, and we all reach for the steaming cups. Erin mixes hers like she likes it while Jim and I drink it straight.

To his credit, Jim doesn't push Erin to begin again. He's been with me on hostage recovery missions before and knows how this works. You can't rush the victim. He doesn't have to wait long, though. After a break and some coffee, Erin's ready to begin again. "So, Jack is standing in the doorway with a gun pointed at me and forces me into the house…"

She describes the secret elevator entrance, the cells, hearing the alarm, and finally, the security room where he set the bomb, and she turned on the intercom system.

"Yes, Squid had described the layout and the packaging room to me on the cutter. I've got one team dedicated to searching through the office area. We hope that's where we'll find records of buyers we can use for victim rescue."

I know that there's a hell of a lot of information that no one knows yet, but I've got a couple of big concerns that I need him to be looking over. "Jim, Battle was able to find us in Springville and on base. He had to have had help." What I'm not saying in front of Erin is that I'm concerned about the missing body of the brother. If he's dead, I want him found so that threat isn't hanging over us.

"I agree. I suspect we'll find that it was Spencer. It's just going to take time to sort through all the evidence we're bound to find. I'll keep you updated as I learn anything. For now, let's just get you back to see your sister."

Erin

Well, that was and wasn't so bad. I made it through better than I thought I would. I'm glad it was just Jim in the room with us. I'm also glad that they found Jack's body and I won't have to spend the rest of my life looking over my shoulder. I'm nervous about Spencer though. He seemed to know who I was and was definitely angry that Jack had brought me there. I hope he's lying in a pile of rubble somewhere they just haven't looked yet.

Jim escorts us back to the lobby where Hyper and Shark are waiting. We load up in two unmarked SUVs and are taken to the airport. At the door of the plane, Jim tells us he's going to stay in Savannah to oversee the investigation to make sure every effort is spent to save other kidnapped girls. I reach out my hand to Jim. "Thank you for helping me." He smiles as bright as the sun and grips my hand. "Of course. You're family."

I guess I have a puzzled look on my face when I climb aboard the FBI jet. Hyper asks, "What's that look for?"

"Jim referred to me as family... but I don't even know the guy, really. You guys seem to throw that word around a lot." After the words left my mouth, I realize how rude that must have sounded, and I cut my eyes to Nate. He smiles and seems content to let Hyper handle the situation.

"We really don't. It just seems that way because we've all said it to you. This group of men, and now you and Sam, are the only family I have. Shark here was brought up in the foster care system, Omen was without his family for the last ten years, and I was an only child raised by absentee parents. Squid is the exception. He comes from a big family, and that's why he's such a big cut-up. My point is, this family we chose is the only family we've got. And I think you've seen the lengths we'll go to protect it."

He's right. I have seen it. Why else would these men put their lives on hold to come for me? "It's been a long time since I've had a family. Since our dad died, it's been only Sam and I. I think I understand what you mean. Anyway, I've always wanted a brother."

Shark takes his seat and adds, "You've got a bunch of them now."

"Yeah, it looks like I do."

"Well, I sure as hell ain't her brother." Nate tips me back and kisses me in front of the others. Just before he lets me back up, I hear the other two men groan and laugh, "About damn time," and "Here we go again."

The flight to Fort Benning is uneventful. Nate calls Chase to tell him what we learned from Jim. Chase, in turn, gives us good news about Sam's condition.

When we've landed at Benning and the craft is parked at its hangar, Hyper and Shark go their separate ways while Nate and I will be heading to the hospital. In a move that's uncharacteristic for me, I hug both of the large men and tell each of them, "Thank you, brother, for getting me out of there."

Hyper answers back, "Thank you for saving Squid. I know he would have tried to make you leave him." With that, they both get in their trucks and leave.

Nate puts his arm around me and leads me to his truck, "Sam is resting, so we're going to pick Chase up and get a bite to eat."

That doesn't sound great to me. My sister is madly in love with him, but he and I didn't exactly have a great start. Add to that, an obsessed man from my past nearly killed his wife of one week. I'm sure he's not thrilled with me about that.

I guess my nerves are obvious as Nate asks what's wrong.

"Are you sure Chase is ok being around me? My past nearly got Sam killed."

"Do you hold him responsible for what Avery did?"

"Actually, I did tell him that I blamed him for bringing that danger to Sam. I was wrong, but I couldn't take the words back."

"I'm sure he recognized your words for

what they truly were; concern for Sam's safety. Just as I'm sure, he doesn't blame you for Sam getting shot."

He rests his hand on my thigh and continues, "Besides, brother or no brother, if he gives you a hard time about it, I'll kick his ass."

"So much for family."

That elicits a hearty laugh, "Oh, like you and Sam never fought?"

"Touché."

A few minutes later, we're pulling up in front of the hospital. Chase jumps in the back seat, and I'm not sure what to say. Fortunately, he puts me out of my misery. "It's damn good to see you here and in one piece. Sam was afraid that she would never see you again." He puts his hand on my shoulder and gives it a gentle squeeze. "To give yourself up like that to save her life… Most people could never do what you did."

Touched by his words, I place my hand on his. I think he and I now have come to a place of mutual respect over our love for Sam. Chase then leans back and stretches his arms across the seatback. "I also heard how you had to save this guy's sorry ass. It sounds to me like you could've been a Ranger."

"Ugh. No thanks. I like wine, air conditioning, and working toilets too much for that." Both men laugh and just like that, our odd little family is whole again.

We share a simple dinner at their favorite pub and head straight back to the hospital. Walking the hall on the way to Sam's room, Chase runs us through the day she had. "She was a wreck. The doctors kept threatening to sedate her if she wouldn't lie still. She didn't sleep at all until we got the call that you were safely on the Coast Guard cutter. After that, she passed out and hasn't even woken up when the nurses come in to check her vitals."

We turn the last corner and Chase stops, "Here, this is it." The door to Sam's room opens, and a nurse walks out. "Oh, Mr. McDaniels. She's still asleep, thank god."

"Mildred, this is Erin. The sister Sam's been worried about."

The nurse turns her head skyward for a split second. "Honey, I'm sure glad you're here. Now maybe she'll settle down for good."

Nurse Mildred continues on to her next patient, and we walk into Sam's room. The men hang back to give me a moment with my sister and I step deeper into the room. She's so very pale. I'm grateful for Nate saving her life. I need to make sure he knows that.

As I near her bedside, she opens her eyes then smiles. "I knew you'd make it." Bending down, I kiss her on the forehead as tears begin to fall. "I had to come back to make sure Nate did a good job on you."

Sam ignores my attempt to keep things light,

"Are you… ok? Did he… did he hurt you again?"

"No. Nate didn't give him a chance to. He organized an army of Rangers, FBI agents, and even the Coast Guard to get me out."

"He's a good man, Erin. He would never hurt you. I think he loves you."

"I know he does. Just as he knows, I love him." We share tears and a hug as carefully as we can manage before she demands to speak to Nate. When he makes it to her side, she says, "Thank you for bringing me my sister back… You killed him, right?"

"He's dead."

"Good."

Nurse Mildred comes back in the room to shoo Nate and me out. I give Sam one last hug, and we make our way back to the truck. "Where to, Chief? Hotel? Base? Alabama?" I think about it for a moment. It's not even seven o'clock. We could make it back to Homewood tonight, but for the life of me, I can't think of one reason to go home. I don't want to go to a hotel either. All I know is that I don't want to be alone. "I want to be wherever you're going to be."

He smiles his megawatt smile and says, "Base it is," then turns his truck in that direction. When we pull into his driveway, I'm dead on my feet. It doesn't make sense considering I napped for four hours today.

Nate unlocks his door, and I march straight

to his bed. Not interested in pulling pj's out of my bag, I strip everything off and climb in between the covers. He's not far behind me and laughs at the trail of clothes between the door and the bed. "Any other time, I'd think you were tempting me."

He clomps his way to his side of the bed on his crutch and leans it against the wall. After stripping as I did, he lies down next to me and pulls me back till I'm spooned against him.

He sends shivers down my spine when he uses his hand to sweep the hair off my neck. Pressing his lips to my ear, he whispers, "You told me you love me today."

"I seem to recall you saying something similar." The shiver turns into full-on goosebumps as he plants little kisses all over the back of my neck and shoulder. "I did. Want to hear it again?"

"Yes, and then you can say it again without using words."

Chapter 19

Nate

"I love you, Erin."

Now to say it without words.

I continue to rain soft kisses on her neck and back before nipping my way up to her ear. I splay my fingers out across her middle and imagine what it would be like to feel a baby kicking inside her swollen belly. Not yet, but maybe one day.

I relish feeling all her warm curves pressing against me from ankle to chest. Holding her like this lets me feel all of her while giving me access to all my favorite parts. With that thought in mind, I trail my fingers north to explore her breasts. She sighs at the contact and presses harder into my hand.

My growing erection nestles itself between her ass cheeks. I know she can feel it when she starts to dance over it. I smile against her neck. "You need something?"

In answer, she places her hand over mine and presses it down. I know what she wants, but I have to tease her a little. I stop the downward momentum of my hand when it reaches her belly. Not giving in, she presses harder against my hand, lowering it to her soft curls. Part of me wants to tease her further, but I'm just as impatient as she is.

The instant I sink my fingers into her warm,

wet heat, her breath catches. Slowly, I circle the bundle of nerves at her center. I want to make sure she's ready for me without working her into a frenzy.

Erin apparently needs something to do with her hand as she lifts it to grip and massage my exposed hip.

I increase the pressure and speed of my fingers, and she tosses her head back, giving me better access to her neck. I flash a bit of teeth against the spot where her neck joins her shoulder and sooth the area with lips and tongue. Within moments, she begins whimpering. "Nate, I need you. Please."

I pull back and line up to her entrance, pushing in slowly. Not good enough. I reach down and lift her leg, pulling it back to rest on mine. That's it.

My hand returns to her center as I take her from behind. I can tell she's close, so I shift the angle of my hips to hit that secret spot inside her. This tips her over the edge. Her delicate inner muscles squeeze me tight as the orgasm shatters her. I move my hand up to the middle of her chest and hold her tightly against me. With my lips against her ear, I vow "My hands, Erin. The only touch you'll ever remember is mine." She adds her hand to mine, and I continue the slow and sweet love-making until I feel my release spilling into her.

Both of us sated, we fall asleep with our

hands secured between her breast and me still inside her.

I awake a couple hours later in the same exact position we fell asleep in. Carefully, I extract myself from the bed as to not disturb her. I pull on my boxers and stand, deciding to test walking without the crutch.

It hurts like a bitch, but I think I can manage. I limp my way into the darkened living room where I left my phone and laptop.

As I expected, I've got several messages. Most are from Jim, but there's one from Detective Peyton. Shit. She doesn't know about Erin or Sam. Or, maybe she does and is pissed at me for not telling her directly. Curious, I open her message first.

"Mike woke up today. Vision a little blurry. Time will tell if it's permanent. How's Erin? I can't get her."

Damn. She's going to chew my ass out for not calling. Not that she could have done anything; she had her hands full. Deciding it would be best to at least acknowledge her message, I send her a quick reply. "Something happened, but she's alright. Update tomorrow." I'm not the least bit surprised when my phone rings five seconds later. "No. Update now."

I give her the main points, and she stops me with questions along the way. "I saw a story about the Daufuskie Island explosion. It doesn't surprise me that it was some of your work… Tell me… The bastard's dead right?"

"He's dead."

"I hear a but in there." Damn, she's perceptive. Even for a cop. "There's a brother. Assumed dead, but they haven't found the body yet."

"And you don't think there's a body to find."

"I don't know."

"All you can do is keep your eyes open." I know she's right, but Erin's had to look over her shoulder for long enough. "I've got Erin. It's up to the FBI to find this prick."

"You're waiting on that Fucking Bunch of Idiots? I used to think you knew what you were doing."

Inter-agency rivalry at its best. "One of them used to be on my team. If it hadn't been for him and his resources, we never would have found her."

"Understood. I'll take care of Mike, you take care of Erin. She's been through enough. Oh, and… when's the wedding?"

Ok, so she's more than perceptive. She's clairvoyant. "You're scary, you know that?"

"Nah. I saw you coming a mile away. Mike and I both had you pegged at the hotel; even though she was leaving your ass to come with us. Keep her safe. This might not be over yet."

She's gone before I can reply. I open my emails and check the updates from Jim.

"Spencer's in the wind. He can't get far. All accounts frozen and all properties and assets seized. Regional hospitals put on alert as well as a nationwide APB. Still, watch your six."

I can smell Erin's shampoo before she walks in the room. I turn and see her standing there wearing my Go Army shirt and nothing else. "Everything ok?" she asks. I reach out my hand to her and pull her into my lap. "Yeah. Woke up and decided to check for any updates."

She lays her head on my shoulder. "What have you heard?" I tell her about the conversation with Eve and most of what Jim said about Spencer. Curious about her reaction, I open the last message. "Dude, when are you coming home for a visit? Mom went apeshit about you missing Thanksgiving again."

She turns to face me, straddling my hips. "Who is that? Brother or sister?"

"Brother two of three."

"Has it been a while since you went home?"

I think about it for a second while my hands sneak under the hem of her shirt. "Almost a year."

"You should go. You never know when it might be the last time."

"Maybe I'll get you to go down there with me." She shrugs a shoulder, "Maybe."

My hands slide up her thighs to grip her waist; my thumbs drawing circles on her skin. "Somebody's got to show them there are more three colors in the rainbow."

"I think you're right, Chief."

I grip her ass tightly and stand up. Her legs go around my waist and her arms around my neck. "Right now, I think it's time to put you back to bed."

"But I'm not sleepy."

"You will be when I'm done with you."

Erin

Morning light filters through the leaves and windows to land on my face. Keeping them closed, I smile, remembering all the things Nate did to make me sleepy again.

"What's with the Cheshire grin?"

His question encourages me to finally open my eyes. "I think I like your bedtime stories."

"Just wait till you see what I can do at Reveille." The look he is giving me right now gives me chills.

"So, what's on the agenda for today, Chief?"

"I'd like to spend the day with Sam."

"I think that can be arranged. Chase has some news and assignments to go over with the team. Let's knock out some breakfast, and I'll check in with him and get you to the hospital."

Two hours later, I'm sitting in a chair next to Sam's bed. She still looks tired and pale but is otherwise on the mend.

After checking on her progress, I make her tell me all about her honeymoon, minus the best parts.

She relays everything with a big grin, then starts in on me. "So, what about you? I imagine Lee is not happy with you missing so much work; something you never do."

"Well, actually, he kind of fired me."

"WHAT?" Her machines start beeping like crazy.

"Sam, calm down before they throw me out for giving you a stroke. He didn't fire me, technically, but forced me to take a leave of absence. Apparently, being around me is hazardous to one's health."

"That's just stupid."

"Says the one lying in the hospital bed."

Sam lets out an exasperated sigh. "So, what are you going to do now?"

I've thought plenty about what I'm going to do. Haven't formulated a plan yet, but I've thought about it plenty. Thankfully, it hasn't come up between Nate and me. Until now, I've been too afraid to say what I'm thinking out loud. This is Sam, though.

"I don't want to go home."

Sam reaches for my hand. "But he's dead. He can't hurt you anymore."

"That's not it. Home isn't home anymore. You're here now..."

A knowing smile blooms on my sister's face, "And Nate's here..."

I roll my eyes, look down at my hands, and

acknowledge what she says, "And Nate's here… I love Alabama; our house on the lake, and the people we grew up with, but my family is here. You and this batshit bunch of assholes are my family."

"Batshit?"

Oh damn.

My eyes fly open, and I look up at Sam. She's sporting a huge, shit-eating grin. "How long have they been standing there?" I hear laughter from the entire batshit bunch of assholes and Sam just stares back me unapologetically.

Nate walks up behind me and wraps his arms around my shoulders. Dropping his head, he leans in to whisper in my ear. "Long enough to hear that you're moving to Georgia."

His voice, once again, sends shivers down my spine and deepens my embarrassment. He lets go, and I stand to face the others gathered there in their fancy soldier suits. Chase is looking rather smug while Hyper and Shark are all puffed up. Hyper turns to Shark and says, "We can't call this one baby sister. What do we call her?"

I answer for him, "Ballbuster if you don't knock it off."

Sam's nurse, Mildred, picks that moment to walk into the room with a cup of broth. "Mmm-mmm. You guys make me want to fake a choking incident. Do all of you know CPR?"

Nate helpfully replies, "Well, two of us are taken..." He points to Hyper and Shark, "...but these two are free." The room gets quiet, and the smile that was on Chase's face disappears. I guess he just found out about Shark and Ava.

I stand and give Sam a hug before grabbing my bag, Nate's hand, and Hyper's lapel. It's time for a family discussion that we don't want to be a part of.

Both men begin protesting as soon as the door closes. "But, we're missing it," and, "I bought tickets to see this."

"Too bad. You both can help me find someplace to live."

We're nearly to the elevator, but Nate stops abruptly which jerks me and Hyper to a halt. "I kind of hoped that you might want to stay with me."

Now Hyper starts backpedaling, "Nope. Uh uh. I'm not hearing this. I'll just go clean my guns." He turns and heads for the stairs.

I lean forward and press the elevator call button. After a tense moment, Nate steps up behind me. "Erin?"

"Well, I had hoped you would want me to, but was taught to never make assumptions."

I feel him press his body against my back and do the wicked whispering thing in my ear again. "Please stay with me."

"If you insist." His arm snakes its way around my middle and holds me tight. "Oh, I insist."

When we get back to Nate's house on base, he proceeds to show me how much he's looking forward to having me move in with him.

Later in the afternoon, I wake up from a much-needed nap and tip-toe out of the bedroom to make some calls. First, I check in with Eve to see how she and Mike are doing. She drills me about how I'm doing, any news I've heard, and if I'm married yet…

My next call is to my landlord. It feels like I'm rushing things, but with Sam being here, I can see no path to regret in moving to Georgia.

Mr. Sanders answers on the first ring as he usually does. He has been hinting at retiring and selling a couple properties, mine being one of them. When I tell him that I won't be renewing in April and will be moving out immediately, he agrees to let me out of the lease and put the house on the market.

My last call will be the hardest; Lee. I know that he only did what he felt he had to. And, given what happened to Sam, he was right. Still, I can't help but feel betrayed.

I pull up his contact and hover over the call button for a long moment before dropping the phone on the table. I can't do this. He's way too important to me to have this conversation over the phone. I've got to go home to pack my stuff, and I'll meet with him then.

Feeling oddly at peace with the decision to

suddenly uproot my whole life, I walk back to the bedroom. As soon as I lie back down, I hear Nate ask, "Having second thoughts?"

"Nope. Just checking in with Eve... and getting out of my lease."

He rolls me on top of him. "Glad to hear it."

"I need to find a job here, go home to pack my stuff, and I have to meet with Lee. I need to tell him in person." He nods in understanding, then reaches up to tuck a lock of hair behind my ear. "When do you want to go back?"

"The sooner, the better, I suppose."

"We could head over first thing in the morning. I'd have to get a moving van first."

"No need. This was another furnished house. I'd only need a few suitcases and a couple boxes to gather my clothes, pictures, and coffee stuff."

"You don't get attached to anything, do you?"

"I never used to, but then I'd never had garlic hot dog bun toast before."

Now he rolls his eyes. "Oh, god." He rolls me over till he's on top.

"No, really. It changed my life."

Nate shoves his knee between my thighs, making room for himself there. "Is that all I am to you: toast?"

I call up my most serious of voices, "No. Not just toast..." I reach up and lovingly touch his cheek. "...garlic hot dog bun toast."

"Ohh. That's it, Chief. You're done." He jumps up and grabs me, throwing me over his shoulder.

As soon as I see that we're heading to the bathroom, I begin struggling. No way am I going to let this brute put me in a cold shower. He walks in, turns on the water, but then stops moving. After several seconds of nothing, I ask what he's doing.

"Just admiring the view." Admiring the… I look around and realize that he's standing in front of the sink with my bare ass staring back from the mirror. "You know, you really do have a nice ass."

I cover my face in embarrassment. He laughs and sets me down. "I thought you were going to throw me into a cold shower."

"I was, but got distracted by the scenery."

"You're such a guy." I reach in and turn the water off.

I get a smack on the ass. "Yep... Hey, now that we've got a plan that doesn't involve heavy lifting, do you want to drive back this evening? We could get an early start tomorrow."

"That's not a bad idea." We begin to move in the direction of the bedroom to get dressed.

"All right then. I'll run and pick up a couple of boxes while you get your stuff together and let Sam and Chase know. Oh, wait." Nate runs out of the bedroom and comes back with a package. "An agent delivered a package this afternoon. Jim said it was your bag recovered from the remains of the SUV in the garage. Because the bag is made from thick leather, the contents survived."

I rip open the package to find a charred purse. It has a bad chemical smell and has bits of melted materials all over it, but the insides are indeed fine.

Fully dressed, Nate picks up his keys. "Be right back, Chief."

Chapter 20

Erin

It's half-past seven when we get to Soho. We stopped first in Springville so I could get my garage door opener from my car. So we won't have to worry about clean-up, I suggest stopping for dinner at the Tower Bar. As soon as we get to the main bar room, Josh rushes out from behind the bar and wraps me up in a big bear hug. "It's funny. Chase shows up six weeks ago and then I don't see you or Sam again. What happened?"

Oh damn. I wasn't thinking when I suggested this place. "Um, well, Sam and Chase got married ten days ago." Knowing about the moves he put on Sam just recently, I'm not sure how he'll take the news.

I shouldn't have worried, he just shakes his head and says, "It's about damn time." Josh then gestures to Nate, "Who you got here?"

"Josh, this is Nate. He serves with Chase. Nate, this is Josh, he grew up with all of us." The men shake hands, and Josh says, "Any friend of theirs is a friend of mine."

Never one to be bashful, Josh then asks Nate. "So, Nate. You just a friend, or is there more to it than that?"

"A hell of a lot more."

Josh nods. "Good." He turns back to me, "You know where my table is. The first round's on me."

Josh returns to the bar, and I lead Nate to the table Sam and I usually occupy. As always, there's a reserved sign sitting on the edge. We sit, and our orders are quickly taken.

Since it's a weeknight, there isn't a band playing, and it's kind of quiet. TVs hung around the bar are showing football games, ESPN, and the local news.

Just as we're finishing our dinner, I catch Nate looking over my head toward one of the screens. His eyes go wide. "Son of a bitch!" He reaches for his wallet and throws some cash down. I turn to see what's got him so wound up, and the bottom of my stomach drops out.

The newscast is captioned Explosion on Daufuskie Island/Sex Slave Ring Uncovered by Local Interior Designer. "Homewood resident Erin Westin was a victim of this trafficking ring. She managed to escape and alert authorities…" My company's profile shot of me is plastered on their screen.

"Oh my god. Oh my god. Oh my god."

Nate grabs my hand, "Calm down. Let's just get out of here." As we're moving, people are beginning to point and stare. Noticing the newscast and the unwanted attention it's garnering for me, Josh steps out from behind the bar and reroutes us to the back. "Damn, Erin. I guess you left out a few small details."

"Yeah, well, don't believe everything you hear on TV."

"Still… Damn."

Nate turns me around and grips my shoulders. "I'm going to pull around back. Watch for me." Then, to calm my shattered nerves, he pulls me in and kisses me hard. Too soon, he releases me and rushes out the door.

Josh starts pushing me toward his office. From behind me, I hear, "So, you care to…"

"It was Jack. They let him out early."

"Mother…"

"Nate found me and put a bullet between his eyes. The rest is bullshit."

"Erin, god. I'm glad you're alright."

"Josh, I'm leaving. Sam's gone, and I can't live here anymore."

"I understand. Give Sam and Chase my best, and you take care of yourself."

I see headlights outside the office window. I hug Josh again and tell him, "Thanks for being there. For both of us." I kiss his cheek, then I'm out the door.

As soon as my door closes, Nate peels out of there. He's angry. I don't blame him; I'm angry too. He punches a button on the wheel. "Jim, what the fuck? Erin's name and picture are plastered all over the news."

"I don't know, man. It could have been leaked from any one of a hundred places. Where are you?"

"In her hometown to pack her up to move to Georgia."

"Move fast, my friend."

"Yeah. It's probably too late. There'll be press all over her place by now."

Nate disconnects the call with Jim and casts a glance my way. "I'm sorry this happened. If it's too bad at your place, I'll tuck you away somewhere and get one of the guys to come help pack up."

"Don't worry. The only place the press will go is to the empty lake house. As a safety precaution, all my official documents show the lake house as my residence. The lease on my house isn't even in my name. It'll take the press a couple of days to figure it out."

"Jack figured it out."

"That's different. He followed me from work."

"I still don't like it. We'll get as much packed up tonight as we can. We'll finish early and get the hell out of there."

"Solid plan."

When we get to my house, I'm relieved to see no news vans parked outside. Yes, I told Nate there wouldn't be, but I couldn't be absolutely sure. What I didn't expect to see was Lee's BMW parked next to my mailbox.

As we pull in the drive, I call him.... just to be sure. "What are you doing here, Lee?"

"I can't believe you're asking me that. First, I hear about this explosion on the news, then learn you nearly went up in it. The next thing I know, you're all over the news. So, I figure you're either some undercover agent or some shit, or you were kidnapped. Mind telling me which?"

"Come inside, and we'll talk, but we'll have to keep it short."

Thankfully, Lee walks down the drive instead of pulling in behind us. I know I'm paranoid, but I think Nate is relieved as well. He opens the garage and pulls in, leaving the door open for Lee.

Just as Lee makes it into the garage, Nate draws his gun. "Whoa, I'm not…"

I grab his arm and shush him. Nate instructs Lee and me to stay in the garage while he checks out the house.

As soon as he's out of sight, Lee starts in on me, "Erin, please, god, tell me what the hell is happening."

"Lee, what's on the news is only partially true. Yes, I was kidnapped, but Nate got me out and killed Jack. That's all I can tell you about that."

He sits down and puts his head in his hands. "When you left the office, I felt like a monster. I tried to check on you several times, but you had disappeared. I even tried to contact those detectives, but no one would tell me anything."

I kneel down in front of him. "I'm all right, but I need to tell you something."

He looks up at me, expecting the worst. "I can't come back. Not after all that's happened and with the news coverage."

"What are you going to do?"

"I'm leaving. Packing up tonight. By tomorrow, I'll be gone."

Nate walks back in and gives me a thumbs up. "Lee, I don't have a lot of time, so you need to go. I'm not going into witness protection or anything. You can call me, and I can call you. This is just a sudden move to another state and another job."

"I'm sorry. I feel like I let you down."

"Lee, no. You've always been like a…"

"Don't say it."

"Like a really cool uncle to me and I love you for it. I'm going to miss seeing you all the time."

He hugs me tightly and addresses Nate, "Thank you for having her back. Keep it up."

Lee kisses my forehead and is gone.

"I could use a drink after all that."

Nate echoes the sentiment, "You ain't kidding."

Given our updated timeline, we get to work with a sense of urgency. Nate picks up a box, and I direct him to the pictures and whatnots while I start in on the clothes. Once most of that is done, he moves the truck into the garage, and we get everything loaded. That only leaves cleaning out the fridge, bed linens, gathering towels, and other minor chores.

Finally done, we fall exhausted into bed.

My alarm wakes me at six the next morning, and I blindly reach for my phone to shut it off. When I lie back down, it occurs to me that this is the last time I'll wake up in this bed or in this town.

The thought crosses my mind that I've gone insane… that is, until a muscular arm works its way around my waist and pulls me up against a hard body. "Morning, Chief."

I snuggle into him. "Morning."

"Easy on the wiggling, or we'll never get out of here." He pinches me on the butt, and I squeal in surprise.

"Since everything is packed up, I'll run out and get some breakfast while you get started on the cleanup." I roll back over and stretch. "Look at you; already skipping out on chores." He stands and pulls on his jeans and t-shirt. "I'll make it up to you later. Keep the doors locked." I give him a mock salute and begin stripping the sheets off the bed.

The fridge is the next job. There's a bag of slime that used to contain salad in the crisper drawer. A block of cheese sitting on the shelf is no longer the color it should be. There are even a couple of take-out containers that I don't even dare open.

Nope. Not even trying. Everything goes in the trash.

Fortunately, there isn't much and doesn't take long to empty. Even less time to clear the freezer. Now that it's empty, I grab my disinfectant wipes to clean the inside.

Behind me, the door to the garage opens. "That was fast." I extend my hand for coffee, but none gets placed there. After a beat, I turn around, expecting to see Nate holding breakfast just out of my reach, but he's not there.

What is there is a rough-looking man aiming a gun at me. I've never seen him before. He looks a little like Jack but in need of a shower and a shave. There's a filthy bandage on his left forearm. So… Jack didn't kill him after all.

"You must be Spencer."

"And you're the bitch that destroyed everything and killed my brother."

Nate

I pull back into Erin's drive fifteen minutes after I left. The garage door opener is in her purse, so I grab the coffee and muffins and head for the front door. I've just rounded the corner when I hear the first shot.

I'm on the move and have my gun drawn before the coffee hits the sidewalk. When I hear the second and third shot, something inside me cracks. "ERIN!" I take off running, ignoring the burn in my thigh and all efforts at stealth. When I reach the front porch, I vault the railing and dive through one of the windows. I roll into a standing position and lift my gun, scanning the room. Seeing nothing, I walk carefully into the kitchen and see feet on the floor beyond the island.

With my back to the wall, I inch my way around to the other side and see my worst nightmare. Erin is lying in a pool of blood with Spencer Battle on top of her. Neither one of them is moving.

I tuck my gun into my pants and throw Spencer off her. She's breathing, but her chest is covered in blood. I pull out my knife and cut her shirt open so I can see her wounds. There's nothing immediately apparent, so I feel around for entrance or exit wounds. Still finding nothing, I turn to Spencer. When I check for a pulse, I don't find one. I cut his shirt open and quickly spot two holes in his chest. "You got off too easy."

I go back to Erin and notice the pistol on the floor next to her hand. I tap her on the cheek and call her name to try and rouse her, "Erin. Erin, wake up." Her eyelashes flutter, and she opens her eyes. "Nate?"

"Yeah, Chief. I'm here. Are you hurt?"

"I think I hit my head."

I help her sit up and find a lump where she made contact with the countertop. "Anything else?"

"I don't think so."

"Good. Let's get you off the floor and over to a chair, and I'll call Jim." She takes my hand, and I lift her off the floor. Once I've got her seated at the table, I kneel down in front of her to watch her face for signs of confusion or distress. Satisfied that she's not concussed or in shock, I pull out my phone and place the call, putting the phone on speaker. He sounds frustrated when he answers, "Krantz."

"You need to get a team to Erin's house in Homewood."

"Spencer?"

"Dead. He attacked Erin while I was gone. Apparently, there was a struggle, and she was able to disarm him, then put two rounds in him."

"Damn. I'm sorry he got that close. It'll be a few hours before I can get down there. I'll call Birmingham and have them take over from PD."

"Have your guy call Eve Peyton. I guarantee she'll be the first one here."

"Done."

The phone goes back in my pocket, and I drop my head. I take several deep breaths in an attempt to slow my racing heart. I have never experienced fear of the depth that I did when I heard those shots being fired. I just knew that I would walk in here and she would be gone and that I would never recover.

I need to touch her; to feel the steady beat of her heart against my chest, but I'm frozen.

Soft hands touch my shoulders as I begin to hear the coming wail of police sirens. I shake my head in disbelief. "I almost lost you today. I shouldn't have left you."

"Nate, don't do this to yourself. Nate… Squid look at me."

I lift my face, but sounds of running footsteps and shouting draw our attention to the front of the house.

"Police! Erin! Are you in here? Are you ok?"

"Eve. We're in the kitchen."

For the sake of the other police, I add, "The house is clear. The intruder is dead." Eve walks through the opening into the kitchen and looks down at Spencer's body. "The FBI is on the way. Is that the brother?"

I nod, "Eve meet Spencer. Spencer, Eve." She holsters her weapon and asks, "Erin, are you hurt?"

"Just a bump on the head." Eve looks to me and raises an eyebrow. "She's fine. No concussion." Realizing how Erin looks, I add, "The blood isn't hers."

The fading bruises around her eyes remind me of what Jack put her through. "You look like you're healing pretty well." She looks at the fresh scars on her wrists. "Yeah. I guess I'm pretty lucky."

An officer enters the kitchen, and his eyes widen at the scene that greets him. "Detective Peyton, the FBI agents are here."

"Show them in."

A few seconds later, a tall man the size of a linebacker and a woman, who looks as fragile as a ballerina figurine, step into the kitchen. "I'm Tim Williams. This is Natalie Miller. Which one of you is Erickson?"

I stand and face them. "I'm Erickson. Jim send you?"

"Yes. He said to take your statements and get you out of here." He then turns to Eve. "I assume you're Detective Peyton." He and the other agent reach out and shake her hand. "My ME is on the way. Our main priority is keeping the press out."

"Yeah. I know all about the leak."

"Then you know why we need to keep a lid on this. Can you put your people at both ends of the street?"

"I'm on it." Before she walks out, she goes over to Erin and places a hand on her back. "Call me when you're somewhere safe, Ok?"

"I will. Eve, hug Mike for me." Eve nods and her voice breaks when she says, "I will."

As soon as she's gone, Agent Miller takes out her phone. "Let's get this done so you guys can get out of here before the press finds out this is your house." She starts a recording and places her phone on the table.

"Let's start with where you both were. Nate?"

"I had gone out to get breakfast and was just getting out of the truck when I heard the first shot."

"Just to cover our bases and provide a

timeline, can you produce a receipt?"

"It's in the bag on the sidewalk." Williams nods to Miller who takes off to recover it.

"What about you, Ms. Westin?"

"I was sitting on the floor in front of the fridge, cleaning it out."

"All right, what happened next?"

"I heard the door to the garage open, but then nothing. When I turned around, he was standing there, pointing a gun at me. I said 'You must be Spencer,' and he said, 'And you're the bitch that destroyed everything and killed my brother.' I apologized to him and told him that Jack had kidnapped me. I said that I didn't want to be there any more than he wanted me to be there. That made him angry, and he yelled at me to stand up. He slapped me and said that thanks to me, he had nothing. That it was my fault for being a slut that his brother couldn't get out of his mind. Then he said we were leaving. He was going to make me clean out my accounts and hand over my car so he could leave the area."

Erin pauses in her account of what happened and rubs her cheek. "I told him that the FBI was watching for him, that cleaning out my accounts would have raised red flags, and they would be on the lookout for my car. He slapped me again and yelled at me to shut up. He was growing irate, and I was pushing him. I thought that if I could get him rattled enough, that I'd be able to get the better of him.

"It worked. He grabbed my arm and gestured to the door with his gun. I took the opportunity and attacked him. During the struggle, he pulled the trigger, but I had his arm pointing away from me. I managed to get the gun away from him, and he rushed me. I did the only thing I could and shot him twice.

"His momentum brought him down on me, and I hit my head on the countertop on the way down. Nate will have to tell you the rest."

"Thank you, Ms. Westin. Captain?"

I take them through the scene from the first shot I heard to Eve walking in. As soon as I finish, he turns off the recorder. "I think that takes care of that. Especially since we were already aware of the threat. The last thing I need is to confirm is that it was Ms. Westin that fired the shot. We'll swab for GSR on both of you then you can go… By the way…" He looks at Erin with respect in his eyes. "… where did you learn to disarm someone with a gun?"

"Oh, my self-defense instructor is a fifth-degree Tang Soo Do master."

He whistles. "That sure as hell beats taking free classes from the Y."

Agent Miller returns followed by the FBI medical examiner. "I found the receipt. Everything checks out. You made good time this morning."

"Not good enough, though, was it?" She gives a sympathetic nod but doesn't reply.

The ME starts his work and a technician swabs both mine and Erin's hands. "I'll get this recording to Jim. I'm sure he'll call if he has any questions."

Both agents shake my hand and just like that, we're released. I run out to the truck and get a change of clothes for Erin. There's no way she can leave the house in the shape she's in. Not to mention all the blood and the fact that her shirt was cut open when I was looking for injuries.

I remain in the bathroom while she showers although It's probably more for my benefit than hers. While she's washing, I gather all the destroyed clothes and put them in the trash bag I grabbed from the kitchen. In case the agents want them, they'll be gift-wrapped and ready to go.

Erin turns off the water and dries off, wrapping the towel around her before stepping out. As soon as she does, I give in to my need to hold her. Erin gladly steps into my open arms, and we stay locked in each other's embrace for a long while.

When I feel grounded enough to move again, I kiss the top of her head, and she looks up at me. "Nate, take me home."

"Yes, ma'am."

Epilogue

Erin

The next few days are a flurry of motion. Besides visiting Sam, getting settled in, and Nate's team getting back into their rhythm, I still had to find a job. I thought of a colleague of mine that does facilities management at Redstone Arsenal. Fort Benning is so much bigger; they are bound to have a similar team of architects, engineers, and designers.

On Wednesday, Sam gets to come home. She's tired of being a patient, and it shows. Being that Sam has always been the calm one of the two of us, I'm wickedly entertained by her whining and outbursts.

During one particularly contentious visit, Chase walks in carrying a steaming mug. She throws up her hand to stop him. "Chase, I swear to god if that's another cup of broth, I'm going to have to divorce you. It's been over a week since I've had real food or sex and I'm done."

I try really hard to mask my laughter. Chase takes it in stride and walks over to Sam and bends to say something in her ear. When he stands back up, he winks at me and holds out the cup to her. She takes it without another word. I'm pretty sure I can guess what he said.

I love my new job. During my search, I found that there was an opening in the on-base facility management team. After my interview, my new boss called me to say that he recognized Lee's name on my references list. When he called him, Lee told him to hire me on the spot or the man was an idiot. He offered me the job right then.

Agent Krantz came down to update us on the Battle investigation. As expected, it was ruled that I acted in self-defense when I shot Spencer. From the rubble on Daufuskie Island, The FBI was able to recover encrypted data they believe will show information on suppliers, transactions, and buyers. My hope is that the information will help to bring kidnapped girls home.

Eve has fully healed from her attack and is back on the job full time. Mike's vision has returned to normal, and he'll suffer no long-term effects from the head injury. He's not completely unchanged though. The attack on Eve, then nearly dying himself has made him question his priorities. He said he was tired of having to hide his and Eve's relationship, so he quit the force and asked her to marry him. She, of course, said yes. Since then, Mike started working as a PI and seems to be getting a lot of business.

I talk with Lee and Sherry at least once a week. I miss them both terribly, but I'm not alone anymore.

On to Nate. It's been three weeks since I moved to Georgia. I would have thought there would be an awkward transition period for us, but that's not the case. It's interesting to see how he can present himself as a light-hearted jokester when it suits him, but drop all traces of humor in an instant. For instance, he can crack jokes all evening and poke fun at my lack of cooking skills, but at the barest touch, this smiling man transforms into an intense lover that takes my breath away.

Being that he's a Ranger, I've been holding my breath waiting for the inevitable deployment. When the time finally comes, Chase and Nate sit down with Sam and me to discuss the near future. When Chase was promoted to Lt. Colonel, the brass already had in mind to use his team to form a new unit that does something they can't talk about.

Instead of the usual Ranger deployments, they would be involved in training, but be sent out on special missions to god-knows-where at a moment's notice. I'm extremely proud to be with a real hero, and I miss him when he's away. When they leave, Sam and I take turns staying with each other so we're not alone.

In early December, Chase and Sam decided to have a late Thanksgiving dinner for all of us since the team was out of the country for the holidays. We all went to their home in Springville for the occasion. To keep Sam from overdoing it so soon, he called in caterers to set everything up which had the mother hen pouting a little. He soothed her by whispering some magic words in her ear again. My sister; the little minx.

It turned out to be a full house that day. Besides Sam and Chase, Nate, me, Ava, Hyper, Shark, and even Cle was there.

Watching Ava and Shark breaks my heart. I don't understand what went on between the two of them, but it looks like they're very much in love. Several times during the evening, I would catch one or the other staring longingly at the other. Before we went off to college, Ava and I were close. Maybe it's time I had a talk with her.

I expected to see Chase to be put off by one or both of them because of the break-up. Instead, he kept maneuvering people so they would get stuck next to each other.

Cle was quiet. I don't know her as well as Sam does, but I've spent enough time with her over the years to know this isn't normal for her. The dark circles under her eyes say a lot too. Hyper doesn't seem to mind, though. He has glued himself to her side and is oblivious to her attempts to shake him; kinda reminds me of Nate…

Chase's team, named Ghost Team, was recently assigned a mission that came with a twelve-hour warning, which Nate used wisely. It was late in the evening when he walked in the door, in full dress uniform, holding a bouquet of flowers. I was just lounging on the sofa, reading a book… in the nude. He dropped the flowers on the floor and shrugged off his jacket before picking me up and carrying me to the bedroom. Walking down the hall, he asks, "Is it too soon to ask you to marry me?"

Surprised, but not frightened by the question, I respond with, "It's a little soon."

Undeterred, he jokes, "All right. I'll ask again in about thirty minutes."

I laugh with him but know in my heart that he's serious. And in thirty minutes when he asks again if it's too soon, I'll tell him no.

That ought to put an extra-large smile on his mom's face when we travel to Miami in two weeks.

Ava

I pull my Audi into Chase's driveway and park next to a large truck. That's Liam's truck. Damn… I can't do this.

I'm supposed to be here for a belated Thanksgiving dinner, but I can't make myself get out of the car. I sit there for a few minutes, and my menu screen indicates I've got a new message. I hit the button on the steering wheel, and the message from Chase reads out, "How long are you gonna sit outside?"

"Shit."

I love my brother. I'm more than thrilled that he's back after being gone for ten years. Happy as a clam that he and Sam found each other again and are now happily married.

The reason I'm loath to go in is *he's here.* Liam Callaghan, Shark, as Chase calls him. Chase's best friend and long-time teammate.

The man I might've spent the rest of my life with.

Wiping the tears that have fallen, I crank the car and throw it in reverse. Just as I let off the brakes, the front door opens. When I see Chase and Sam standing there, I put my foot back on the brake.

This is my family. The only family I've got left. I put the car back in park as I let out a deep sigh. "You can do this, Ava."

I turn off the ignition and step out of the car. Chase descends the steps as I walk around to the trunk to retrieve the wine and a batch of black cookies that our mom always used to make.

He greets me on the walkway with a hug and takes my cargo from me. I hug Sam gently, considering her still-healing body. "Your color is coming back."

"Yep. I'd say I'm almost back to full-operating capacity."

At her unusual description, I look to Chase. "You're a bad influence on her vocabulary."

"I do my best. Come on, let's go inside."

As I climb the three stairs, I take a deep, steadying breath. When I don't walk through the open door, Chase gently pushes me. I take an awkward step inside the foyer and feel Chase put a hand on my shoulder. He leans over and says, "Relax, Ava. Everything's going to be fine."

I don't know why that helps, but it does help a little. I straighten my shoulders and stride into the rotunda like I own the place.

Looking around the room, I first spot Erin and Squid. They make such a cute couple. Sam's friend Cle is here, and Hyper is hanging around her as he did at the wedding.

I don't see *him.*

I'm simultaneously relieved and saddened, but don't have time to process it. Erin jumps up from her seat and makes a beeline straight to me. She's a different woman from the last time I saw her. Her eyes are sparkling with happiness, and her effervescent manner makes me envious. "Erin, you look so... different. This smiling face becomes you."

She glances back at Nate before answering, "It's almost as bright as yours used to be." I drop my eyes to our joined hands, no longer able to look her in the eye. She bends down, forcing me to look at her. "Yours will be back. Believe me; if anyone knows that life can turn around for the better, it's me."

I turn away to hide the storm of emotion, sure to be visible on my face. Only... I wish I hadn't. Standing in the hallway entrance is Liam.

I feel as if the floor is falling away from beneath me.

I've always thought he was handsome; in a rugged, tough-guy sort of way, but I've never seen him like this. He's wearing black slacks and a silvery blue button-down that look like they were tailored for him. The sleeves of his shirt are rolled up, and he's leaning casually against the wall.

He's not smiling, but then he rarely ever is. However, his face shows none of the turmoil that I feel, and that pisses me off. It's not fair that I'm the only one hurting.

That assumption of injustice in the situation gives me the dose of steel that I need to get through today. I give myself a mental slap and determine to be unaffected by him.

Liam

I glance down at my watch for the fiftieth time. It doesn't look like she's coming. I'm disappointed, but not surprised.

Definitely not as surprised as that day in Sam's hospital room when Squid opened his mouth. I was certain that Omen would have my ass. Instead, he told me that he had expected Ava to run when I was offered the return commission. He wouldn't say why he felt that way, though.

Still, Chase shocked the hell out of me by asking me to come today knowing she would be here.

I guess it doesn't matter since she hasn't shown up. Seeing who is here makes it worse. Everyone here is partnered up. Even Hyper is hung up on that nerdy woman.

The only reason I don't blow out of here is because of Omen. Growing up as a system kid, I never had a family. I learned early on that I could only count on myself. It wasn't until I joined the Rangers that I learned what loyalty was. These three men, Omen, Hyper, and Squid; these men became my brothers, and I would give my life for any one of them if necessary.

Still… I need a break from all this lovey-dovey shit. It's time to see how well stocked the bar in his office is.

I leave the group lounging in the rotunda, not surprised in the least that no one notices my exit. Half-way to Omen's office, I stop myself. Getting hammered won't fix anything. And, there's no way I'd do anything that would hurt Sam.

The kitchen is to my left, and I decide to abandon that bad idea for a cold beer instead. The fridge is well-stocked with local craft beers. I pick an IPA and search in the drawers for a bottle opener. On my third try, I find one and head back to join the others.

I'm nearly to the end of the hallway when I hear her. I pause and stand with my back against the wall, out of sight of the others. When I hear what Erin says to Ava, my head tips back to look up at the ceiling.

I hate this. I didn't do anything wrong. Ava just can't live with the fact that I'm a Ranger. I shouldn't have to be the one feeling like shit. And yet, here I am, hiding in the hallway.

I've had enough of this. I'm proud to be an Army Ranger, and I'm a damn good one. It's her problem if she can't deal with it.

Pushing off the wall, I walk to the end of the hallway and lean against the corner. When my eyes land on Ava, my mouth dries up. Even with the shadows in her eyes, she's so beautiful that it hurts to look at her.

Everything I told myself in the hallway just went to hell.

###

Learn all about Ava and Liam in the next book *Lose Me*

Acknowledgements

Thanks to Perry and Mary for letting me borrow you for this book. You were fun to write about.

To my family of cheerleaders; once again, you've kept me sane through this process… even though I've driven you crazy.

Big thank you to my editor, Rose Lipscomb of Flawless Fiction. You continue to make this process easy with your coaching, provocation, and your commas.

About the Author

Jo Chambliss is an interior designer by trade, lover of good books by hobby, and writer by passion.

She lives a full life in Alabama with her husband and children where she's either teaching, designing, writing, or listening to her favorite hard rock bands.

She's such a fan that titles of her favorite songs are hidden in her books.

Think you could spot any?